ISBN 978-1-330-04568-8
PIBN 10012143

DESERT LOVE

BY

JOAN CONQUEST

Author of
"Leonie of the Jungle"
"The Hawk of Egypt"

NEW YORK
THE MACAULAY COMPANY

CONTENTS

PART I

PART II

PART III

PART I
THE SEED

PART I

THE END

DESERT LOVE

CHAPTER I

J<small>ILL</small> looked at the East!

At her feet sat huddled groups of women, just bundles
of black robes, some with discs about their necks, some
with chains or golden crescents upon the forehead, all
wearing the *burko* [1] covering the entire face with the exception of the eyes, and held in position between the eyebrows by the quaint tube-shaped *selva,* fastening it to the
tarhah, the flowing black veil which nearly touches the
ground behind, covers the head, and pulled down to the
eyebrows leaves just the beautiful dark eyes to be seen,
glancing up timidly — in this case — at the golden-
haired, blue-eyed girl above them.

Men of different classes stood around, or squatted on
their heels upon the ground, all in flowing robes of different colouring and various stages of cleanliness, some
with heads covered in turbans, some with the tarboosh,
others with the kahleelyah or head handkerchief, all
chattering with the exception of the higher classes and
the Bedouins, the latter clothed in white, with the distinctive thong of camel's hair wound about the head covering, arms folded and face passively serene, looking as
though they had stepped right out of the Old Testament

---

1 Yashmak or face veil.

on to the fly-ridden, sunbaked station of Ismailiah; whilst vendors of cakes, sticky, melting sweets, and small oranges, wandered in and out of the crowd screaming their wares. Shouts of laughter drew Jill's attention to the other side of the station, where, with terms of endearment mixed with blood-curdling threats, a detachment of British soldiers getting ready to start en route for Suez were urging, coaxing, striving to make that most obstinate of animals, the camel, get to its feet some time before midnight.

From them she looked at a group of native dwellings made of sunbaked clay. Small square buildings, looking in the distance like out-houses, with scarcely perceptible windows, and flat roofs given over to poultry. Near them the patient bullock did its monotonous round, drawing the precious water from the well with which to moisten the arid little patch of earth from which the fellah extracts the so very little necessary to him in his life.

A clump of slender palms, like forgotten scaffolding, stood out clear against the intense blue of the sky; the desert, that wonderful magnetic plain, stretched away in mile upon mile of yellow nothingness, until as minute as flies on a yellow floor, growing more distinct at every step, with solemn and exceeding great dignity stalked a string of camels, each animal fastened by a rope to the saddle of the one in front, each apparently unconscious of its seemingly overwhelming burden, as with heads swaying slightly from side to side with that air of disdain which the dame of Belgravia unsuccessfully tries to imitate when essaying to crush the inhabitant of Suburbia by means of long-handled lorgnettes resting on the shiny arch of her aristocratic nose, they responded without fail to the soft musical voice of the Arab seated cross-legged on the leader.

Then her eyes turned to the West.

To the mixed mob which had rushed from the *Norddeutscher Lloyd* at Suez, leaving the great liner to the wise few, while perspiring and querulous, and altogether unpleasant, they had filled the little train which chuffs its way along the edge of the canal to Ismailiah, and through the dust and fly-laden miles to Cairo, where it turns its burden out to clamour and argue vociferously with the wily dragoman who would take a herd of elephants to " do " the Pyramids in one hour if the backsheesh proved substantial enough.

With absolute loathing she gazed at those with whom she had passed so many weary days on the return journey from Australia.

There were of a certain type of English women not a few, sunburnt, loud of voice, lean of breast and narrow of hip.

Their sisters, wiser and better endowed by nature, had remained on the liner, taking advantage of the empty conditions of the boat to repair the ravage done to complexion and wardrobe by the sizzling, salt-laden wind which had tortured them since Colombo had been left behind.

Two daughters and a mother stood aloofly in the shade thrown by the indescribable waiting-room; the mother still labouring under the delusion that if you can't afford to send your girls properly wardrobed on a visit to relations in India, the next best method of annexing husbands for them is to take them hack-ing on a long sea voyage. For has it not been known that many a man driven to the verge of madness by the everlasting sight of flying fish, and the as enduring sound of the soft plop of the little bull-board sandbag, has become engaged to " a perfectly im-*poss*-ible person in the second class, you know," so as to break the deadly monotony of his surroundings.

They did not want to see Cairo or any other part of Egypt, for the East said nothing to them, even a rush view of the Pyramids failing to stir their shallow hearts; but they knew to a shade the effect on their less fortunate friends when in course of time they should murmur, " You remember, dear, the winter we were in Cairo."

Added to these there were raucous Australians, clumsily built guttural Germans, in fact the usual omnium gatherum unavoidable, alas! on a sea voyage, clothed in short skirts, shirt waists, squash hats, and thick boots as " they were going tramping about the sands," and each, of *course,* loaded with the inevitable camera which gives dire offence to many an eastern of higher rank, who hates being photographed willy-nilly along with all the other " only a native " habits of the westerner, who with the one word " nigger " describes the Rajah of India, the Sheik of Arabia, the Hottentot and the Christy Minstrel.

Free for one day from the restraining manners of those others who at that very moment were doubtless returning thanks on deck to Allah for his manifold blessings in the shape of some few hours of perfect peace, a few men of different nationalities were either boisterously chaffing the less plain of their companions,

or ogling the shrinking Eastern women crouching on
the edge of the platform. Mr. Billings in fact, in unclean canvas shoes and a frantic endeavour to find
favour in the bistre enlarged eyes of a certain slim
black figure, was executing the very double shuffle
which had "brought down" the second class dining
saloon honoured for the nonce by the presence of the
first class, on the occasion of one of the purgatorial
concerts habitual to sea life as known on board a liner.

CHAPTER II

JILL stood by herself!

Personally I consider as infinitely boring those descriptions written at length anent the past lives of the characters, male and female, which go to the building of a novel, so in as few words as possible will try to outline the years which had brought Jill Carden to the dreary task of waiting hand and foot upon the whimsies of a neurotic German woman of great wealth, and still greater disinclination to part with the smallest coin of any realm she might be travelling through.

Jill, an only child and motherless, had led a glorious care-free existence.

Adored by her father and her two friends, Moll, otherwise the Honourable Mary Bingham pronounced Beam, of the neighbouring estate, and Jack, otherwise Sir John Wetherbourne, Baronet, of the next county, big brother to Jill and worshipper at the shrine of Moll. Jill was also loved by all who waited on her, and sought after by not a few on account of her great wealth, and had laughed her way through seventeen years of life, to find herself suddenly minus father and money, with nothing left in fact but an estate mortgaged to the smallest pebble, and a heart-whole proposition from her chum Moll to "just come over the wall" and restart laughing her way as her adopted sister through the bit of life which might stretch from

the moment of disaster to such time that she should
find a life companion with whom she could settle down
and live happily ever after!

But although Jill's head was outwardly covered with
great plaits of auburn hair, through which broke riot-
ous, frivolous curls, the inside held a distinctly active
and developed brain, which had acquired the habit of
thinking deeply upon such subjects as woman, wife and
motherhood.

Added to this, which is already quite enough to put
out of gear the life of any girl brought up in convention
bound England, she had a heart as big as her out-
rageous longing for, and love of adventure, neither of
which bignesses she had so far been able to satisfy.

As I have said this was quite bad enough, but
through and above all, her whole rather exceptional
being was desirous of love. Not the shape which
clothes its diseased body in soiled robes of imitation
something at one and elevenpence three farthings per
yard, and under ferns in conservatories, in punts up
back-waters, in stifling tea-rooms, hotels, theatres and
night-clubs, exchanges sly look for sly look and soiled
mouth for soiled kisses, in its endeavours to pass itself
off as that wonder figure which, radiant of brow and
humorous of mouth, deep of breast and profound of
thought, stands motionless in high and by-ways with
hands outstretched to those futile figures, blindly hurry-
ing past the Love they fondly imagine is to be found
in the front row of the chorus, the last row of the
cinema, or the unrestrained licence of the country house.

Jill had never flirted and therefore had known no
kiss excepting her father's matutinal and nocturnal

peck. She looked upon her beautiful body as some
jewel to be placed in the hands of the man she loved
upon her wedding-night, so it was as unsoiled and as
untainted as her mind, although she knew that once
she loved she would go down before that mighty force
as a tree before a storm. Dull, you will say all this.
May be! but mighty refreshing in these days when
amourette follows amourette as surely as Monday follows Sunday, the only difference in the stock being
the trade mark, which stamps the one with the outline
of a perfect limousine, and the other with the front
seat on the top of an omnibus; though believe me the
Mondays and Sundays differ not at all.

Jill's ideas on franchise and suffrage, and a " good
time " as seen from the standpoint of the average society girl or woman were absolutely nil.

She wanted first of all a master, then a home, and
then children, many of them.

Her idea of love was utter submission to the man
she should love. Her ideal of happiness his happiness,
and although she had no fixed idea of her home, she
was positively certain she did not want lodge gates and
forelock-pulling peasantry, nor tame deer inside elab-
orate palings, nor the white-capped nurse stiff with
starch trundling a perambulator with a fat, ordinary,
rosy heir to the palings, deer, and pullers of locks.

So she sweetly but very definitely said no to a certain
millionaire, who had earned his banking account and
the thanks of many thousands by his invention of a
non-popping champagne cork, and who, adoring the
girl, had hastened the very day the news of the smash
had spread through the country, like fire on a windy

day, to lay his portly self and all that thereunto ad-
hered at her beautiful feet. The disgust of her relatives upon her want of common sense was outspoken;
for having overstocked their respective quivers with
commonplace female arrows, they quite naturally looked
with dismay upon an almost beautiful and *quite* penni-
less and homeless girl about whom, *after* having read
the will they referred to as "poor Jill, for whom I
suppose we *must* do *something* don't you know?" with
a quavering inflection at the end of the phrase.

But Jill did not stop on refusing the eligible owner
of an unmortgaged estate. No! she set out to look
for work off her own bat, and actually found it in that
occupation which, far less paid than more, opens up a
perfect vista of possible adventures under the guise of
a travelling companion.

She spoke French, German, and Italian like natives,
which was all to the good. She danced like a Vernon
Castle, knew almost as much about fencing as a Sa-
violo, shot like a George V., and rode like a cowboy,
all of which qualifications she erased from her list on
the termination of the freezing half-hour of her first
interview with her first would-be employer, who, until
the enumeration of the above sporting qualifications,
had seemed desirous of taking her along with a bron-
chitie pug to winter in Bath.

Since then she had done Europe and Africa pretty
well with never the suspicion of an adventure, and,
when you meet her on the station of Ismailiah, where
you change for Port Said, she was returning from
Australia, with a wardrobe at last beginning to fret
about the hem, and shine around the seams, a condition

accounted for by the emaciated condition of her purse; a memory of good things and hours worn thin by the constant nerve-wracking routine of capsules, hot drinks, hot water bottles, moods and shawls; and a fully developed rebellion in her whole being against the never-ending vista which stretched far into the future, of other such hours, days, months, yea! even years!

But everything was capped by a still more fully developed decision to brave it out, and out, and out, rather than return to ask the help of those whose hand-clasp had weakened in ratio to the dwindling of the gold in her coffers.

CHAPTER III

AND why did she stand by herself?

This is no riddle, the answer being too easy. Men would have answered, "Guessed in once, she was pretty!" And the women would guess in once too, but would keep silent, the pretty ones merely smiling, having sampled the Coventry-sending powers of plain women in the majority on board, and the plain ones from that unwillingness inborn or inherited in every woman to admit good looks, or good anything for that matter, in a member of her own sex.

And she *was* pretty, with the prettiness of youth allied to genuine red-gold hair, and the bluest of blue eyes, which looked at you in disconcertingly straight manner from between the longest black lashes you ever saw.

She sounds very much like a " Dainty Novel heroine," but I have met her and I know, and she also had a mouth turned up at the corners, and the loveliest teeth, a nose which also turned up, not unduly, and a skin on which lay the merest suspicion of powder like dust on a butterfly's wings, also two jet black *grains de beauté,* one at the corner of her mouth and the other on top of the left cheek, just under the outside corner of the eye.

Ravissante! Her beauty was nature's own, and she had the loveliest, longest, narrowest feet ever shod and silken hosed by Audet, and as lovely out of the silken hose as in.

But all that, though it pleased the eye, did not really constitute her real charm. It was more the idea of strength, and buoyancy, and the love of humanity she

19

gave out, that attracted young and old, rich and poor, dogs, children, and the sick of soul and body to her.

The type of woman who owns the husband of a roaming disposition and has not got accustomed to the disposition, or the woman eager to acquire a husband of any disposition whatever, liked her not at all, failing to see that she was genuinely uninterested in other people's male belongings.

Those who think to lure men by the mystery of a tobacco cloud permanently around the head, or to stimulate by the sight of a glass which looks like lemonade but isn't, nestling among the everlasting cards and cigarette débris, disliked her *intensely,* not so much because she did not ally herself *with* them, as for the fact that she did not range herself *against* them, having even been heard to remark that the world would be a deadly dull place if everyone enjoyed the same pleasure and the same wickedness. Just three more items to add to the long list against her on this particular voyage.

Firstly, had she not one sizzling Red Sea day appeared with her hair hanging in two great plaits reaching below her knees? Which escapade might have escaped uncensured if accompanied by the whitish eyelashes, forceful freckles, and pungent aroma usually allied to reddish hair, but as it was, the combination of the red-gold glory with blackest curling lashes, skin like satin, and the faintest trace of Devonshire lavender, created a perfect scandal among those whose locks were either limply curtaining their owner's cheeks or blinding the eye, or câchéd under some head covering were acquiring a wave which might with luck last out the dinner and bridge hours.

Secondly, although a penniless companion, she allowed no familiarity from the men and no condescension from the women; and thirdly, her shoes gave reason for envy, hatred, malice, and all uncharitableness, being on the day you met her exquisite champagne coloured things, her critics little guessing that the reason she. wore them was that she had none thicker, and no money wherewith to buy any.

This last point sounds almost absurd, but those who know will any day back the woman with dainty ankles, pretty feet, the glimpse of white lace and a plain face, against the really beautiful countenance up above the shapeless ankle-calf combine, and the foot that in two days gives a shoe the shape of the bows of a dinghey.

So because of all these reasons, also because all the nice, wise people who loved her having stayed behind, she stood alone, her heart clamouring for life and adventure, which comes to about the same thing, and which she sensed is to be found so much more easily in the East she was leaving behind in the space of a few hours. The rest of her rebelling against the West, the monotonous days on the boat racing her back to England in November, with nothing to do, too much to eat, and the trail of medicine glasses, cushions, gouty, dyspeptic, and neurotic employers lengthening into the drab future.

" Allah! help me! " she whispered, and really meaning it, as she turned to look again at the camels stalking on into the desert, and finding herself instead looking straight into the eyes of an Arab standing behind her.

And here, I hope, endeth the dullest part of the book.

CHAPTER IV

ARABS as a race are tall, most of them having a grave look of nobility, all without exception inheriting from their forefathers Ishmail or Johtan that air of studied calm, that seldom smiling, never restless attitude, which expresses the height of dignity and gravity. There were many of them in this motley station crowd, also Bedouins, smaller of stature, and the members of the many other tribes which go to populating the great Egyptian desert. But not one of all the men, magnificent though some of them were, could compare with Hahmed the Camel King, who, standing alone and motionless with folded arms, let his eyes rest upon this most fair woman from the West.

Jill was accustomed to being looked at, from the impudent stare of Frenchmen, the open look of admiration, both male and female, of the Italian, to the never-to-be-forgotten look of Berlin that had seemed to undress and leave her naked in the street.

But now under grave scrutiny she felt the colour, which made her even more lovely, rising from chin to brow, and longed to cover her face or to run away and hide, though there was nothing but a wondering respect in the Arab's eyes.

For one moment his eyes met hers, then she slowly lowered the heavy white lids with their fringe of curling lashes, and, turning, stood looking out over the desert, where she no longer saw the stretches of yellow sand, nor the string of camels stalking away into the distance, nor the mud houses and patient bullocks. No! nothing of all these, but instead, just one man's face, oval, lean-featured, eyes brilliantly black and deep-set under thick eyebrows, an aquiline nose, the lower part of the face covered in a sharp pointed beard, and the thick virile hair by a snow-white kahleelyah, bound by a band to the well-shaped head.

A man was he indeed with a width of shoulder rarely seen in an Arab, standing well over six foot, in spotless white robes sweeping to his feet, a cloak of finest black cloth falling over all in swinging folds, failing, however, to hide that look of tremendous strength which impresses one so in some of the long-limbed, lean, muscnlar inhabitants of the desert.

Jill walked over to the edge of the platform which as a rule is only raised a few inches above the rail, and after a few seconds beckoned her employer's special dragoman, who had annexed himself at Cairo and presumably would only be shaken off on deck.

He came immediately, all smiles.

All the so-called lower classes smiled upon Jill, from the coster in Whitechapel to the Kaffir at the Cape. And why? Why, because she smiled when she asked a service.

"Be more dignified!" she would indignantly reply when remonstrated with about the native. "They certainly show a varied degree of blackness in their skin, and have less brains than some of us, but they are human, so I shall continue to smile if I like," and smile she did, and they smiled too and ran to do her bidding.

Not that she indulged in the "our dear black brother" views of those people who, from utter lack of knowledge upon the subject, believe that with the exception of a certain difference in the pigment which embellishes the skin, the lowest type of Hottentot has the same ideals, desires, and outlook on life as the highest born, or, as I think to be more correct, I should say, the cleanest living individual in the Western Hemisphere.

She did not approve of the promiscuous mingling of the white and black as is so often and so unhappily seen in London, where a servant girl maybe, will ecstatically spend her evening out under the protection of some ebony hued product of Africa and, labouring under the delusion that the dusky swain is the direct descendant of Cetewayo, also totally lacking all knowledge of African history, will fondly imagine herself a queen in embryo, instead of which she is merely the means to feed the lustful longing for the white in some Cape boy, who believes he hides the roll of his native walk under an exaggerated skirt to his over-padded coat.

And she equally hated to see the social butterfly smile upon the high-born native of India, angling for his lakhs with the bait of a fair white skin upon which to fasten a string of priceless pearls, gathering her fastidious skirts about her at the sign of any feeling more human than that which she would allow from a respectable bank manager, recoiling disdainfully from a man whose ancestors were mighty in the land when hers were just beginning to break through the crust of serfdom, as a toad will crack and throw back the caked mud under which it has blissfully slept.

As a preventative to social and racial mishaps she thoroughly endorsed the theory that " East is East and West is West, etc." But in her heart, or rather in her somewhat searching brain, she had often wondered if there could be no exception to the ruling, if half of the East and half of West could never combine to make a perfect whole.

All smiles the dragoman ran forward, saluting her with hands to forehead, mouth, and breast.

" Do you know who that man is? " she asked, indicating with a scarcely perceptible movement of the head the Arab who had not moved a muscle since she had turned away from him to look at his homeland, the desert.

" 'Im! My lady! " replied the native, eyes and white teeth flashing as he essayed in his best Anglo-French to please the beautiful foreigner who so graciously spoke to him. " 'Im? Oh, 'im! is Hahmed the Camel King. 'Im provide the camels for Government ' Camels Corpse,' " pointing to the Camelry Corps, where perspiring Tommies and a seething mass of brown beasts were literally raising the dust on the other side of the railroad. " 'Im," he continued, " is ze great man, from far away over ze Canal from ze greates' and best part of South Arabia. Is rich, oh! rich! Oh! so very rich—*riche comme le diable, Madame*. Is master of many villages, many peoples, but is 'ow say, my lady — *est étrange* — and feared... 'Is word is ze law and 'is arm is ze iron and 'e can also shoot ze fly on ze top of Cheops! "

The man paused, literally from want of breath.

" He is evidently a very fine man," said Jill, it must be confessed a little disappointedly, having expected something a little less ordinary in the way of history, " but I can't say I see anything strange about it all! "

The dragoman, slightly downcast by the lack of enthusiasm on the part of his audience, took in a huge quantity of the absolutely stifling air and started afresh.

" Oh! *mais, Madame,* ze strange zing is zat wiz all 'is rich, all 'is camel, all 'is 'ouse — ah! I forgot zat is 'is Ismailiah 'ouse," pointing a long, brown finger to a huge pink edifice, standing like a huge pink birthday cake under the blazing sun on the edge of the town —" 'e 'as no woman — no not an one — not wife — not lady — zere is tales of one wife long ago over zere," pointing vaguely in the direction he imagined South Arabia might be, " but feared, we say and ask nozing — no! ze great Hahmed live alone — not zere ——" Once more pointing contemptuously to the pink abode. " Zat but a business 'ouse — ze most beautiful place in one oasis! Ze Flat Oasis! Ah Madame! *comme c'est bι lle* — I who 'ave been on camel business can tell, ze 'ouse, ze shade, ze water — but no lady, no children, no son, no one —'e go and sleep and live all by self alone — *triste,* Madame, because 'e is ze great, ze just, but go always alone in ze night to 'is oasis *bien aimée* and ——"

And here the uplifting of an angry guttural voice caused him to turn and run hurriedly towards a figure vehemently signalling with a huge fawn-coloured sunshade lined with green.

And as he ran the soul of the desert, born of the sun,

palms, ennui, flies, the sand, and Allah knows what
besides, suddenly sat up in Jill's eyes and laughed,
and as she laughed the words "Go always alone in
ze night to 'is oasis *bien aimée*" rang in the girl's
ears, as a strange and startling idea flashed across her
mind.

· For and against the idea ranged her thoughts; up-
held one moment by the insistent clamouring of her
whole soul for freedom; combated the next by the
inherited deference to convention planted by long dead
generations in the mind soil of almost every British
subject.

Why should she not break away and strike out on
her own, if only for a few hours? But would she not
be running into positive physical danger if she did so?
Still it would only be for a few hours — a swift ride
into the desert — a glimpse of a desert home — a break
anyhow in the deadly, soul-stifling monotony of her
daily round. Yes! but what did she know of the man
outside the eulogies of the dragoman, who for all she
knew might be leagued with him in nefarious schemes.

And yet, no one cared if she lived or died in soul or
body. Marry she would not for years, and years,
though of a truth that prospect would become more
and more remote as youth vanished and the waters
of her wealth remained at low tide. But the most
irresistible argument in favour of the mad idea was
that so far she had not had one single real adventure.

"Allah!" she whispered, clasping her hands involuntarily. "Where is my path? Show me the way
out!"

And even as she unclasped her hands, she heard a

faint tinkle of coins in the well-worn little bag hanging from her wrist.

"Allah has heard!" she murmured to herself, as she fished for a coin.

"Heads I speak — tails I go back to England," she continued, placing the silver coin on her thumb nail, flipping it into the air, and catching it on the back of her hand. "Heads. Oh!"

And giving herself no time to think, whilst the soul in her eyes first frowned and then laughed in glee, she turned and crossed the few yards covered by the sand which for centuries blown hither and hither had been waiting to make a carpet for her lovely feet to tread when Allah in his graciousness should show her the path, which would lead her to the way out.

CHAPTER V

JILL had an entrancing speaking voice. She spoke on a low note, and having trained the muscles of the throat to relax or tighten at will, she was able to throw all manner of inflection into the words, and all shades of tone and melody into the chords of the beautiful musical instrument which is so terribly neglected the world over.

So that when she spoke, her words sounded like the chiming of distant bells in the ears of the man, and his heart seemed likely to be engulfed in the golden stream of a voice through which continuously rippled a gentle laughter.

"Monsieur will forgive me for speaking in this abrupt way, but the moments are few in which to make my request. I hear that in the desert is a beautiful oasis, and many beautiful Arabian horses. I have never seen an oasis, for you see I know nothing of Egypt, but I once had an Arab mare. She was wonderful and white. Perhaps Monsieur has some of her brothers or sisters? And just for once I *should* like to see the desert stars at night, and the desert sun at dawn. Could Monsieur take me to see these things if ——" And then the golden voice stopped short, and the girl involuntarily took one step backward.

Those who know the race know that the Arab has a tremendous control over his emotions. He can love

and kill in one moment, but until the woman is literally swept off her feet, or the man or woman is dead
in a heap, neither by voice or gesture will he betray
the passion consuming him.

The voice, the greatest betrayer of mankind, is especially under control of these exceedingly strong men.
No matter what paroxysm of rage, revenge, or desire
may be shaking the man to the innermost depth of his
being, his voice flows on just as musically, just as
softly.

But Jill, being observant, had noticed that although
the hands lay folded on the crossed arms, the nails
were dug into the palms, and raising her eyes to the
sombre face for explanation, had encountered two eyes
blazing with a mighty anger.

There are many ways in which to incite the Arab to
wrath, but believe me, the way which will most surely
lead to sudden murder, or to long bloody feud drawn
out over many years, passing from generation to generation, is the way of *ridicule.*

Let him think that you are laughing at him, and I
should advise you to take the nearest camel, train, or
boat, or any other means of locomotion to hand, and
fly the country.

The *country* mind you, for hide you ever so craftily,
he will find you, even though your hair be white, and
your figure bent with the passage of years, and then,
only *then* will he be appeased, when the real or imagined jest at his expense has been lost in the deep
colour of your rich red blood.

So that when the Arab spoke a light of understanding dawned upon Jill, for, touching his forehead,

mouth, and a spot on his raiment just above his heart with his right hand, and murmuring the customary salutation, "May peace be upon you," he paused for a moment, and then continued, "But it pleases Madame to jest with me. She awaits the train to take her to the boat, how therefore could she come into the desert to-night?"

But Jill was absolutely unafraid! Having known no master, she cared not one *sou* for any son of man, or any untoward position she might find herself in, so opening wide her very beautiful eyes she simply smiled back into the angry ones which looked down upon her from some considerable height, and, with a little shrug of her shoulders, a habit acquired from one of a succession of foreign governesses, she made reply in her turn, and in words which though absolutely commonplace served as the golden key with which to unlock the bejewelled, golden casket of this man's love.

In any Western country the situation would have been *absurd!* An English girl, minus scenery and every accessory due to a book heroine, capable in five brief minutes of smiting the heart of one of Egypt's most renowned men!

Ridiculous!

Perhaps in the lands of fogs and fires, grey skies and east winds, but not in Egypt, where the sun, sky, winds, and memories serve rather to force the growth of the love-plant and hasten the budding of the passion-flower.

Studiously buttoning up the last button which she always left undone on her last pair of suède gloves, smooth as a newly born whippet puppy, and as yet

unruffled from the cleaner's manipulations, she spoke
with a ripple of laughter which made it impossible to
decide if she was speaking seriously or not.

"Madame permits herself to do just as she pleases.'
If by some unforeseen circumstances she were to miss
the train, would she be taken to see the oasis, and the
horses, and the stars?"

And let it be understood that, in her utter ignorance
of deserts, she imagined the oasis could be reached
after a journey of a few hours.

For one moment there was dead silence between
these two, the strings of whose lives Fate was inex-
tricably mixing in her fingers, palsied by age, and
fretted by the constant tugging and straining of those
other threads which, in moments of senile anger or
childishness, she gets into such hopeless tangles.

Then as the shriek of an engine whistle shrilled
faintly in the distance the man spoke, his voice sinking to that deep note which no other nation attains,
resembling in no way the Russian bass, and which in
the Arab upon rare occasions alone betrays some emo-
tional upheaval.

"Listen, woman of the West, who even at this moment stands in my shadow, between that faint engine whistle and the grinding of the brakes as the
train comes to a standstill, you must make your choice.
A few moments ago I saw you toss a silver coin and
decide quickly that which had been decided already for
you since the beginning of all time.

"Once more you shall cast your die. The table
is the sand of Egypt, the dice-cup is your hand, the

dice are your life and my life, the stakes our happiness. Decide again and quickly for I hear the rumbling of wheels. Make known your choice, for although we travellers through the desert of life lie down to sleep, and rise again to live, to fight, to hate, and above all to love, in obedience to the will which counteth and heapeth the particles of sand upon this station, yet are we allowed to voice our desires, being mouth- . pieces of Fate. Nay! wait one moment until I make clear the way, so that you may not put down your beautiful feet blindly upon a trackless waste of doubt and mistrust. If you come with me to-night, you come *alone*. I have no woman in my desert home, excepting one old hunchback slave, a withered bough but faithful. No woman has set foot within the belt of palms surrounding my house, and without the sand stretches! Mile upon mile of pathless sand!

"You will come into the desert alone with *me*, and the sand will close in upon you and keep you in the desert alone — with me!

"If you come, be at the gate of yonder pink house at nine to-night; if you are not there I shall know that your heart has failed."

But the soul of the desert glinted for one moment in the English girl's eyes.

"There may be no woman there, but there will be a man — a man indeed!" she whispered, as though communing with herself.

And the eyes so soft and blue looked up, and then down, down into the soul of Hahmed the Arab, so deeply indeed that a shiver ran from her brain to her

finger-ends, causing her to draw herself together sharply
and to turn and walk away.

.   .   .   .

So it came about as it was written that she had
decided when the brakes grinded, and that after re-
trieving her employer for the last time, and placing
her in a dusty corner of the stifling carriage, she
slipped away on the excuse of finding her dressing-
case, which she did, taking it with her into a corner of
the deserted waiting-room just as the engine announced
its immediate departure.

Without a qualm she watched "her crowd" jostle
and push their way into the small carriages, and the
train move out, leaving her alone — alone in the desert
town, alone with the dweller of that desert.

A wave of exultation rushed through her as she
thought of this her great adventure, of this her freedom for at least a short while, and of the unknown
quantity she was mixing into her portion of daily
bread which, up to this moment, had consisted of the
plainest, wholesomest, most uninteresting bun-loaf, not
even resembling that extremely dull and unappetising
cake named, I believe, Swiss roll, which hides its stale-
ness under the glass case of Life's shop window, lying fly-blown on the plate and heavily and unimagina-
tively on the digestive powers of those who consume
it for the thin layer of jam to be discovered between
its wedges of sullen dough. A soul-stifling mess to
be found in the drab sideboards of most English house-
holds along with its sister made of a pastry so flimsy
that it chokes, filled with a cream that is merely froth,
the whole hiding its cheapness under an application

of highly coloured paint essence, the consuming of which will prove as fatal as the Swiss roll.

So she raised her hands to the grimy ceiling of the dirty waiting-room and whispered to the dust, the buzzing flies, and vivid ray of sunlight.

" Verily, and indeed I have burned my boats behind, or perhaps I should say my liner before me ! "

CHAPTER VI

JILL, very fair indeed to look upon, and with seven-and-sixpence in odd money in her bag, stepped out bravely on to the road, scorched by the midday sun, with a curl at the corner of her mouth, a medley of disconnected thoughts in her madcap head, and a feeling of unromantic emptiness somewhere in the vicinity of her white leather waist belt.

A wisp of a boy, clad in very dirty garments, shrilled the equivalent of " Carry your bag, miss," in the Egyptian tongue, calling down the displeasure of Allah upon the foreign woman when she shook her head, and changed the heavy dressing-case to the other hand.

Ismailiah is no place for a beautiful English girl to wander in unchaperoned, especially when out of respect to the slenderness of her purse she gets off the beaten track in search of a cheap restaurant.

Indeed Jill was beginning to feel a little uncomfortable at the way the natives stared and even turned to look after her as she plodded on, so that it was with a feeling of relief that she espied " Cuisine Française " written across the window of a fairly clean-looking restaurant in a small street, into which place she turned, to be confronted by a fat, oily individual hailing from the Levant, who looked as though his business was anything but that of the kitchen.

Unsophisticated Jill, however, saw nothing wrong in

the person who bowed, and smiled, and rubbed the
palms of his hands in a rotary movement; and being
taken up in trying to amalgamate the scantiness of
her money, the prices on the carte, and the enormity
of her hunger, neither did she notice the burning eyes
in the handsome, sensual dark face of a middle-aged
native fixed upon her hungrily from behind a half-
open door, where he had been hurriedly summoned by
the man who advertised his skill in *" la cuisine Française."*

To pass away the time Jill lingered over her meal
until she was alone in the place save for the waiter,
who was aching to get away to smoke a cigarette,
and the native who had noiselessly entered and slipped
into a seat in the far corner.

Once Jill, inadvertently looking straight into his
eyes, and hurriedly looking away, had picked up a
paper lying on the chair beside her; glanced at the
first page, and dropped it like a hot plate, whilst a
wave of scorching red rushed over her neck and face.

" Allah! " she thought, " what an awful place, and
what on earth *am* I to do with two shillings in my
pocket, and not a cinema handy! " And feeling the
native's eyes still fixed on her, she beckoned to the
waiter, paid her bill, and once out in the street turned
sharply up the first on the right just as the native
and the Levantine came to the restaurant door in time
to see the last inch of her disappearing skirt. And yet
through all her haste and her annoyance the inner
membrane of Jill's mind, that delicate fabric woven of
intuition and divination, which gives women the pull
on so many occasions, and on certain courses get her

past the post lengths ahead of man, whispered to her that it had not failed her earlier in the day, and that if she could but stick out the next few hours she would find a sure reward for her present distress.

But she stopped short and clicked her teeth angrily when she met the native of the restaurant face to face in a narrow street, and turned and walked in the opposite direction as quickly as her dignity would allow.

But after the same thing had happened three times, and that it had suddenly struck her that she was being headed in the direction of a quarter where unveiled women peered from windows with great eyes made larger by the rims of kohl smeared on the lid, and the cheeks rendered dead white with the powder that proves so strangely attractive to the eastern prostitute, she suddenly made up her mind to get herself out of the danger and difficulty. She was utterly lost, and walking at a pace that was almost a run, turned into the street she found nearest.

Not one open door did she see; at least, not one that was not congested with women sitting smoking or eating sticky sweetmeats, or drying their heads plastered in the henna clay which would eventually dye their hair the red favoured of man.

She was wellnigh breathless and wondering for how long she could continue when the man suddenly appeared at the top of the street into which she had just turned, and seeing her salaamed deeply.

Back she twisted like a hunted hare and raced up the street through which she had just passed.

It was empty, but on her left standing ajar was a door painted bright blue.

CHAPTER VII

WITHOUT pausing to think she entered, closing **it** behind her just as the man relentlessly pursuing **her** passed in ignorance on the other side.

In the middle of the courtyard two Eastern women in the domestic act of disembowelling a kid looked up lazily, and one smiling, pointed to the upper storey of the house, through the small windows of which came the sound of stringed instruments, and seeing that the stranger did not understand, explained her gesture in broken French:

"*Au premiez étase — voz amieze — les anglaiseez.*"

No idea of any further possible danger entering her head, and at a complete loss to understand, but thankful for her present safety, Jill crossed the court, slipping unromantically on a piece of the animal's entrails which lay about, and entering a low door mounted the stairs.

Through a curtained archway the distinct twang of an American voice came to her as a message of peace, so pushing back the stuff she entered to find herself confronted by ten pairs of eyes of different nationality.

"Come right in," twanged the same voice, "guess you're from the same boat! Cute of you to find your way here all by your lonesome!"

The well-corseted wife of a Can-King, flanked on **one** side by her thin, leather-skinned, neat daughter, **and**

39

on the other by the inevitable Italian marquis, whose
tailor had evidently been a sartorial futurist, pointed
to a cushion on the nobleman's off side, on which perplexed Jill squatted in imitation of the others. The
party consisted of the aforementioned trio, two flash-
looking English women, who had in tow a certain type
of man who is only to be found on board ship, an obese
German, a French widow whose weeds grew more from
utility than necessity, and a dapper little Frenchman
who twinkled his over-manicured fingers for the benefit of a healthy, jolly looking Australian girl sitting
uncomfortably on the adjacent cushion. The party's
dragoman proffered a cup of coffee and a cigarette.
The former was excellent, the latter, after one puff, Jill
extinguished on the floor, for she knew tobacco when
she smoked it, and guessed at hasheesh without having
to look at the slightly brightened eyes of those who sat
smoking the same brand around her.

Then she glanced curiously round the room. Long,
low, with four tawdry glass and gilt chandeliers hanging from the not over-clean ceiling, cushions spreading
all over the floor excepting in the middle where lay
an exquisite Persian carpet, long mirrors on all sides,
little inlaid tables, and at the far end, built into the
wall with steps leading up to it, a bed behind gilt bars,
the door in which was fastened by a gilt padlock.

It seemed that their dragoman had brought them
to the house so as to add yet more perquisites to his
daily remuneration by regaling them with an exhibition
of Eastern dancing.

"What kind of dancing?" asked Jill with a slight
frown, as the twinkling music suddenly stopped.

" Guess we can't tell you! " replied the American mother, whose corsets were not in exact accord with the cushions upon which she sat, breathing heavily from her upper whaleboned register.

"*Nous espérons le mieux,*" said the Frenchman, winking at the dragoman.

And that moment they were enlightened.

The two English women emitted each a little screech, the American mother caught convulsively at her daughter, who coldly raised her long-handled lorgnettes the more fully to survey the picture before her. The Australian girl sat quiet, as did the Englishman who had been there before, the Italian ejaculated " *Per dio,*" and the Frenchman " *Mon Dieu,*" as the widow, pulling one side of her veil across her face, hid her over-crimson mouth, but in no way impeded her view, whilst Jill looked round hastily for a way of escape, but suddenly remembering the certain peril in the street decided, as she edged as far as possible from the marchese, to sit out the difficulties of the moment.

CHAPTER VIII

To natives, a dressed or undressed dancer is nothing more than a plaything, or something to help pass the hour; he will look at and criticise her with much less enthusiasm than he would a she-camel, and remunerate her or her owner according to the measure of pleasure he has found in her posturing.

But it is difficult, wellnigh impossible, to describe the feeling of the occidental women when three orientals of their own sex, without a vestige of clothing, suddenly one after the other, like ducks, sidled into the room.

They were none of them in their first youth, and the dragoman, after watching their movements, decided once and for all to withdraw his patronage from the house, and sat wondering how much he dared try to extract from his patron's pockets for such an exhibition, while Jill, who felt as though she had been suddenly struck between the eyes, sat hypnotised by the undulating forms before her, until she was overcome by a frantic desire to bury her face in a cushion and to give way to unrestrained hysterical laughter. This same feeling has been known to overcome one in Church when a hen, side-tracking through the open door, takes a constitutional up the aisle on a Sunday morning in the country; also it has been known to seize you in its grip at a levée, when your predecessor's shoe-buckles, not having been properly adjusted, flip up and down like shutters as their owner, in solitary state, stalks up the audience chamber; worse and stronger still is it when your revered bishop uncle, of whom you have great expectations, insists at morning prayers upon those things which have been left undone, when before your earthly eyes gapes the cotton dress of Eliza the cook, whose comfortable dorsal proportions have forbidden the matutinal union of a couple or so of buttons and buttonholes.

Try as she would she could not overcome it, neither could she remove her gaze from the three females who, poor things, were but doing their best to add to the family coffers. Up and down, and round and round they went, the string band twanging an accompaniment, until the gauze scarf of the middle lady catching in the hanging chandelier put an end to their rhythmical swayings, while like hens with a suspended cherry they hopped in turn off the ground in their effort to disentangle their one and only bit of covering.

Everyone sat still until the disentanglement had taken place, upon which event the dancers once more advanced in force, each selecting a special man victim, until Jill, absolutely helpless and afraid of raising native wrath by allowing even a glimmer of a smile to appear, buried her pretty head on the marchese's over-padded shoulder, which action he of course took for a sign of encouragement, responding to it by slipping his arm round the girl's waist, but circumspectly enough so that it should not be seen by the Can-King's relations, while Jill prayed for strength to resist until the end.

The end came in a positive Catherine-wheel exhibition of posturing, and a deathly silence on the part of the audience; the men not daring to make any comment, the women not daring to look at each other, until the widow, suddenly seizing upon the situation, clapped her little hands roguishly, and avowed in a babyish voice that " *C'était bien gentil et original, n'est ce pas,*" which she didn't think at all really.

Anyway her opinion served as a break, so that on the exit of the dancers in single file, which was tenfold more trying to the spectators than their entry, with stretching of cramped limbs and stereotyped utterances such as " how very Eastern," " so unexpected," the entire party rose to their feet, the dragoman holding a hurried whispered conversation with the men who each, and successively, and vehemently, shook their heads, leaving the women asking of themselves how on earth they were to continue existing relations with the men during the interminable weeks to Australia.

Jill, feeling almost faint from suppressed emotion and a revival of hunger, stood a little on one side watching them. An Eastern dancing house is a strange place in which to make the final decision of one's life, but in just such a spot she made hers. She knew that she had only to make up the tale of a lost boat, and something would be done for her; in fact she could probably go as lady's maid to the Americans on their *tour de monde,* having overheard them complaining bitterly of their own French maid who had not been retrieved at Algiers. But her whole soul suddenly rising in mutiny against the stultifying civilisation of the West, she finally made up her mind to stay with the strangers until the hour came when she could slip out of the hotel where they were staying the night, into oriental liberty, and glamour, and unknown possibilities. So she sat next the marchese at dinner, whose lovemaking was on exactly the same line as his clothes, and having found out from the maid in the ladies' room just how to get to the end of the town in which was situated the Camel King's house, she waited for a desirable opportunity, and slipped òut of the hotel on the pretence of looking at the stars, knowing that her unwitting hosts would think she had simply gone to bed.

CHAPTER IX

Jill's memory being of the kind which retains only the pleasant word and act, the disagreeable episode of the afternoon had completely evacuated that cell which in one second can raise us through the bluest ether to the heaven as understood by the prayer-book, or send us diving to the mud flats of the ocean bed to co-habit for a time with wingless and non-temperamental oddities.

Having stopped several times to discover by ear and eye if she was being followed from the hotel, and being satisfied that the sight of her dressing-case had in no wise aroused the hall porter's curiosity, she propped her luggage against the base of a palm tree growing casually in the middle of a small street and proceeded to take her bearings.

"Somehow it seemed quite easy to find when the maid was explaining," she communed to herself as she dug a hatpin afresh into her hat as is the way of woman when at a loss. "How stupid of me to try a short cut, because she distinctly said I was to stick to the main street until I came to two mosques side by side, and then to turn off sharply to the right. Oh! well, I turned off too soon and am lost — and I don't like these little streets — no! not one little bit, but that big red star hangs right over the house so I can but follow it — here goes!"

She picked up her case, and then drew back quickly behind the tree as a white-robed figure slowly crossed the street, turned up another and disappeared.

"Oh! Moll and Jack, what on earth would you think if you knew I was alone in Egypt. Alone! but free! Free! at last, quite, *quite* free!"

And stretching out her arms on each side and giving herself a little shake, Jill laughed ever so softly in pure exuberance of that feeling of freedom, which seems to make an air pocket all about you and in the middle of which you float contentedly, oblivious of the winds raging on the outside.

So glancing up at the red star, and once more picking up her bag, she too crossed the street and disappeared up a narrower one, halting for a moment at the sight of a man standing with bent head in the attitude of prayer and the beads of Allah hanging from the hands crossed upon the breast.

Jill's intuition was intense, and never once in all her life had it failed her, and though to her all Eastern men seemed exactly alike in the moonlight, yet her inner consciousness began to tap out a message of warning, and the bristles of her self-protection to rise at the threatenings of danger.

"Bother!" however, was her only comment as, keeping the star ahead, she walked steadily onward.

But she made a silent, strenuous, but unavailing struggle when something white and soft was slipped over her head and a hand placed firmly upon her mouth, as she felt herself lifted in a pair of strong arms and carried some considerable distance until she heard the click of a key, the opening and shutting of a door, and her captor's soft footfall through what seemed to be a deserted house.

She stood perfectly still when planted on her feet, and looked around her when the cloth had been removed from about her head.

White was her face indeed, but a little smile twisted the corner of her mouth as she noted the oriental luxury of the room in which she stood.

Ornate could hardly describe it so offensive was it in its multitudinous hangings, mirrors, lamps, and clutter of stools, tables, divans, and couches, inlaid or plastered with glittering sequins, bits of glass, and coloured imitation jewels.

But scorn simply blazed in the great blue eyes as she looked into those of a man standing in front of the one and only door to the whole apartment.

"You brute!" she said undiplomatically and in French as he moved a few steps nearer and salaamed deeply. "Why, you're the man who followed me from the restaurant to-day! What do you want? Backsheesh? I haven't any so you had better let me go at once unless you want the police after you! You can't treat English women in this off-hand way with impunity, I can assure you. Open the door immediately if you please!"

Poor little Jill, who by involuntarily harking back to the insular belief that the veriest heathen will quake in unison with the British culprit at the mere threat of British law, showed the absolute yarborough she held in this game, the stakes of which she guessed were something more precious than life itself, and in which she held not a single winning card.

"Let not Madame cause herself worry," answered the oriental also in French, as he approached nearer still, his eyes ablaze with passion of sorts as he looked the girl up and down from head to foot. "The police — the law — you are in Egypt, Madame, or I should say Mademoiselle I think. Money! when a man holds heaven itself within his grasp, does he open his hand to grasp a passing cloud?"

"I should advise you to let me go *at* once," repeated Jill, "if you don't want my friends to raise trouble!"

But her bluff was of no avail as she was soon aware when once more the man salaamed with a world of mockery in the action.

"But Mademoiselle has but now run away from her friends! No? — she has but little — oh! *very* little money! — yes? — and nowhere to go — it is for that that I have thrown my protection around her!"

Jill thought hard for a moment, wondering how much the man knew of her escapade.

"How do you know? *Who* told you I had no money? I *have* a friend as it happens ——!"

"Mademoiselle has no friend but me," interrupted the man; "she left them at the hotel when she went to take a walk."

And Jill retreated step by step before him as he came closer still, his voice sinking to a whisper, his hand within an inch of her wrist.

"I will not harm you because you are oh, *very* beautiful! You are a feast of loveliness and I — I am hungry!"

But still the little smile twisted the corner of Jill's red mouth as she looked unflinchingly into the brown eyes in the depths of which smouldered a something which was not good to look upon.

"I suppose you have stolen my dressing-case too," was her next, somewhat irrelevant remark. "Men of *your* type I dare say can find a use for everything from women to hair-pins. You black *dog,* who *are* you?"

Red murder flared in the room for one moment and then died down, leaving a little smoke cloud of uncertainty in the man's mind.

He was used — oh, *very* used to the breaking in of women, for was not his name notorious in Northern Egypt, and were there not whispers of many young and beautiful who had mysteriously disappeared.

Were not men and women in his pay in every corner of the big cities posing as honest individuals? And was he not in direct communication with them? And had he not a côterie of jackal friends who hunted with him, though of a truth not half so successfully or artistically as he?

And yet this slip of a girl, this pale white blossom, held him at bay, more by her seeming indifference to the fate before her than by any effort of will she made to combat the danger.

Blasé to tears of the exquisite women of his own country with their lustrous brown eyes, marvellous languorous figures, and well-trained, inherited ideas on love, the man was violently attracted by the whiteness of this girl allied to her indifferent manner and an intense virility which seemed to envelop her from head to foot.

True, there are natives of a white and surpassing beauty, but which whiteness when compared to the genuine colouring of a *very* fair Englishwoman has the same effect on the purchaser or temporary owner as would a white sapphire bought in mistake for a diamond.

Very, very beautiful, but somehow giving an impression of masquerade.

" Your so *valuable* dressing-case is behind those cushions, Mademoiselle, but you shall have things of gold to adorn your apartment, at least for a time. I tire easily even of the most perfect fruit, but I have friends, oh, many who are not so easily wearied! "

The man paused a moment as though awaiting some outburst, but none forthcoming continued the enlightening discourse.

" Who am I? — that will you know shortly. A merry chase you gave me this afternoon, and even baffled me for a time, but surely I have not enjoyed an hour so much for many a day. You are unique, therefore not to be run to earth by a *common* black dog, otherwise I could have secured you earlier in the day and by now ——"

The man's lips, of an almost negroid fullness, curved in a smile, the abomination of which sent a little shudder from Jill's high held head to her steady little feet.

" But I *have* you now, beautiful maiden, and if you will not bend to my will, I will break you to it, even if I spoil your satin skin and the soles of your small feet by the lash of the whip! "

" So! " said Jill after an interval in which the atmosphere, charged with the electricity of anger, lust, scorn, and all the kindred sisters of evilness, resembled what might be the result of a cross between a spitting eat and a wireless installation. "So! Am I to understand that you have vulgarly kidnapped me — and are holding me *not* for ransom, but for your evil pleasures and those of your friends?"

"Quite so, Mademoiselle! Your words are as clear as the stream running through a certain oasis which long I coveted, but which fell to my greatest enemy because he had a few more piastres than I — and maybe a little more diplomacy — a man who would kill me if he could but find the excuse, the moral breeder of camels, the fanatic son of Solomon, Hahmed the great, Hahmed the most noble — *pah!*"

For one brief second Jill's eyes scanned the sensual face in front, but seeing nothing more subtle than an intense hatred therein for the absent man, shrugged her shoulders and then flung up her hand sharply as the man's hand suddenly fastened on her wrist.

"Let go my hand at once," she said as indifferently as though she were asking for a glass of water, but she wrenched herself free and fled behind a divan almost hidden in a bower of growing tropical plants as the man let go at her command to suddenly grip her about the waist.

"I shall scream the place down, and bite, and kick, and scratch, if you touch me again."

For one moment they looked at each other across the pile of silken cushions, the dark shining leaves of the plants throwing up the girl's wonderful colouring, the white petals of a flower falling like snow about her as she stood waiting for the next move in the exceedingly dangerous game in which she was taking part.

The silence was absolutely deathly until the oriental

broke it, smiling the while as he might on a rebellious child.

"If you make a noise you will bring women and servants, and perhaps my friends, packing to the door from the most distant corners of the house. They do not know that you are here as I brought you in by a secret door and private way, also no one is allowed to place foot in my own quarter of the house without my permission, with the exception of the guardian of the big door itself; but their curiosity would outweigh their prudence if they heard cries, for their delight is unbounded when trouble reigns between their friend or master and a *woman*. If you bite and kick and scratch I shall have you overpowered and bound to *your* great sorrow, and *their* greater delight. It has been written that you shall be one of those whom I honour with my favour, why then try to fight against that which is ordained?"

Jill answered never a word, contenting herself with keeping a watch on the man's movements, though to the very innermost part of her she longed to fling herself upon him to mutilate or to kill.

"We will have coffee, O! very lovely daughter of the North, and consider this little matter settled even before we were born. Does my suggestion find favour in those eyes which are as the sky at night?"

But for all answer Jill moved round the couch and sat herself down upon the satin cushions, opened her hand-bag, and finding her cigarette case lit a cigarette.

"By Allah! but you are wonderful, you English girl. I do not understand you. I have had women here screaming, fighting, fainting, begging for mercy upon their knees. Pah! they sickened me, but you — well! I will go and order the coffee, not wishing to bring a slave into your presence, and give orders also, Mademoiselle, that no matter *what* noise may be heard I must on no account be disturbed! And death by knife, or whip, or water, is the *ordinary* punishment for those who disobey!"

Jill blew a smoke ring through another and smiled.

"It's no good ordering coffee because I shan't drink it!"

"You *will* drink it," was the sharp reply.

"Will you take a bet?" was the ready answer.

For a moment the man who was becoming more and more amazed stared in silence and then laughed softly as the absurdity of the situation struck him.

"Certainly I will, for do not we orientals love a seeming hazard? So although I take an unfair advantage of you I will lay this emerald ring engraven with my name against one kiss from your red mouth that within the half of one hour you will have drunk the coffee."

And taking the ring from his finger as he spoke he laid it upon a small table beside Jill.

CHAPTER X

SHE was sitting with her hands crossed on her lap when he returned, carrying a small tray bearing two cups filled with coffee.

"You have been a *very* long time," she remarked casually.

"An especially delicious coffee had to be prepared for Mademoiselle, and strict orders given that we were not to be disturbed until I give the signal. Also that this quarter of the house, which is mine, is to be cleared absolutely of all inhabitants. Therefore shall we be at peace even until this time to-morrow if I make no sign. Also to emphasise my orders, I ordered that a certain person be bastinadoed. She sickens me with her outpourings of love, and was loitering about this door seeking doubtlessly to enter. When she does she will most certainly not enter upon her feet if my orders have been strictly carried out."

And even as he spoke a distant piercing scream, followed by another, and yet another, rent the air, causing Jill's mouth to shut like a steel trap, and her eyes to blaze like fires.

"*That* is what happens when I am *disobeyed,* Mademoiselle! Here is your coffee, *drink it!*"

The tone was brutal, and Jill meekly put out her hand to take the little porcelain and silver trifle the man was bringing to her, laying it beside the emerald ring upon the table as he turned to fetch his own cup.

"Drop that!"

Jill had not raised her voice, but a certain unmistakable quality in it caused the man to wheel sharply.

He stared in blank amazement for a fleeting second, and then, still carefully holding the cup, backed hastily and sideways out of the direct range of a very small but very useful-looking revolver in Jill's right hand.

There was a curious lifelessness in the whole situation, and a quite distressing lack of drama until the oriental smiled contemptuously.

"Do not think to frighten me with that plaything, because I am totally unafraid. We hear of the Englishwomen who shoot and ride like men, but — well! we hear so many tales of Europe. Put up your little toy, Mademoiselle, and remember in future that no one with any respect for his life *ever* gives me an order!"

With an indifference that was not in the least assumed, he raised the cup he was still holding.

There was a crashing report in the luxurious room, a tinkling of broken china, and a wisp of smoke between a smiling girl and a *very* surprised man.

"Don't be a fool, and do as you're told if *you* have any respect for *your* life," said Jill tersely, as she moved her hand slightly so that her aim was on a dead level with a big button ornamenting an inch or so of satin on the middle-left of the man's undervest.

He stood like an image carved out of consternation, whilst streaks of rage seemed to flash across his livid face. Be it confessed, he was not in the least afraid, but no word in the Egyptian or any other tongue could be found to express the depths of humiliation in which he stood neck deep.

"Now, drink *this* coffee!" said Jill pleasantly, pointing with her left hand to the cup she had placed on the little table.

"*Never!*"

Jill smiled icily.

"I *thought* as much. You scoundrel! So it is drugged, and I, having drunk it, would have lain unconscious at your mercy. God! to think that such brutes as you are allowed to live."

The man was watching the girl's every movement, ready to spring like a cat from the area steps upon the unsuspecting sparrow in the road, but neither her eyes nor her hand moved as she continued speaking very gently.

"Listen! I should have killed you myself to-night, feeling myself justified, so that other wretched girls should escape the fate you had prepared for me — you, lower than the beasts of the field; but I am not going to do it, as happily I know of one more powerful than I who will enjoy it thoroughly. Think of what I say when you see his messenger with your ring upon his finger, to-morrow or next month or next year perhaps — and when your time comes, watch the procession of betrayed and tortured girls as they pass before you to catch your soul in their slim hands as it leaves your body. Now! drink that coffee!"

But the man stood stock still, and Jill frowned, for she was not a paragon of patience at any time, and the obstinacy of the man fretted her already jagged nerves.

"Very well," she said, "I give you one more chance.

If you refuse again I shall put a bullet straight through
your head just between the eyebrows, as I shall now
put one through that brooch kind of thing in your
turban."

There was another deafening report, and the turban
flew from the oriental's head just as a paper-bag will
fly before a March wind.

"Go and pick that turban up and put it on your
head. Hurry now, or we shall have the police or someone coming to inquire about the shooting gallery."

The eyes of the boa-constrictor in the Zoo were gems
of humanity in comparison with those of the negroid-
Egyptian's as he turned to obey, and then stopped
mulishly until a third little reminder chipped splinters
from the marble at his heel, whereupon he stooped and
recovered his headgear, minus the brooch, but plus a
neat little hole fore and aft.

"Now come and drink the coffee! It won't be very
nice as it is almost cold. And remember in future if
you are allowed to live, which I *very* much doubt, that
such supreme indifference as mine could only *possibly*
be the outcome of an absolute sense of perfect security."

Jill patted the silly-looking little ivory and silver
thing she held.

"You mongrel!" she continued sweetly, "I was
simply playing with you until the right moment — the
coffee moment which I knew must happen — should
arrive in which to give you a lesson. Why! when I
saw your eyes in the restaurant I took my little friend
from my pocket and made sure he was in order. I
may look a fool, and I may act in a manner still more
foolish, but I am *not* exactly what you would call a

born fool! Now drink that, I am late **already!** And don't spill a single drop or I'll shoot you on the spot!"

There was nothing for it but to obey, though the brute took the only revenge he could in pouring out a torrent of language beyond description, until Jill suddenly rose and levelled her revolver at his head, which seemed to send the sickly contents post-haste down his throat, after which Jill ordered him to stretch himself comfortably upon the flower-screened divan.

He did so smiling stupidly, the drug having begun to take effect; and the big eyes closed and opened and closed again, and the mouth relaxed as a gentle snore told Jill that as far as the present danger was concerned she was safe.

She stood for a second looking idly down upon one of the world's greatest criminals, and then at the thought of the dangers which might still be awaiting her on the other side of the door, unloaded her revolver and slipped a fully loaded clip into her little friend.

Then picking up the emerald ring from the table, and her dressing-case from behind the cushions, she crept gently across the room, and gently — oh! so very gently, opened the door which yielded noiselessly to her touch, and stepped into a deserted hall only to recoil violently from something at her feet.

Across the threshold lay a girl.

The agonised eyes in the beautiful dark face gazed up in terror at Jill, whilst a little hand searched weakly for a jewelled plaything of a dagger at her waist.

"Oh! Poverina!" said Jill, as she knelt to raise

the little head, and then stared in horror at the girl's
shoulders and the hem of her satin trousers.

Some expert hand had flicked the delicate flesh off
the back in a criss-cross pattern; what was left of the
feet lay in a pool of blood, the deep red of which
stretched across the hall far into the distance, showing
the path along which the child, left by her torturers
for dead, had dragged herself.

"Poor little, little thing!" whispered Jill, as she
made to raise the body in her arms. But the dusky
head shook feebly, and a dainty henna-tipped finger
pointed to a window across the hall, and Jill, feeling
herself pushed away ever so slightly, rose as three words
were whispered over and over again:

"*Vite — allez — mort — vite — allez — mort!*"

And understanding that there was nothing more to
be done she bent and kissed the child upon the cheek
and turned away, looking back as she opened the window which gave on to a balcony about ten feet above
the level of the deserted street, and even as she looked,
saw the door of the room she had just left being pushed
back inch by inch as the dying girl, strengthened by
love and agony, dragged herself slowly into the room
in which lay the man she worshipped asleep.

CHAPTER XI

TEN o'clock! — half-past! — eleven!

The usual noises of a night in an Egyptian town were at their height.

The distant and never-ceasing shuffling of slippered or naked feet on stone, or sand, made a dull accompaniment to the sharper notes of men's voices crying their wares of sticky sweetmeat or fruit, and the barking and growling of innumerable dogs.

Muffled ejaculations could be heard, little gurgles of laughter, which in Egypt, thanks be to Allah, do not degenerate into giggles, the swish of a whip in the shadow, followed by a woman's cry, and through all, above all, unfinished catches of music.

All kinds of humans, including tourists, writers, European officials and desert dilettanti, have affixed every kind of adjective to Egypt's music.

Ethereal, melancholy, wailing, plaintive, nebulous, and pathetic are but a few. Why — why try to tie a label to something which slips from the fingers even as they close about it? Why *try* to describe that which cannot be described? There is, or was, a certain line which in the heat of an Egyptian noon, or the stillness of an Egyptian night, when the first notes of a human voice, or stringed instrument, or rudely cut pipe-reed reach the ears, would creep out of some memory cell.

One loved the vagueness of those words:

"Out of the nowhere, into here!"

Loved the infinite space they opened up with their
aloofness and indefiniteness, until, alas! they took con-
crete shape when chosen as title to the picture of a
robust, Royal Academy, Fed-on-Virol looking babe,
which doubtless, when trying to grab some passing
Olympian butterfly, fell off the lap of the Gods into a
sitting position upon Mother Earth.

Also, one thinks of that mist wraith which on a
cloudless day stretched across some mountain's breast,
lies lightly upon the air, with diaphanous ends coming
out of and going into nothingness; for in just such
manner does the music fall across an Egyptian day or
night.

These catches of music have no end, and no beginning; they rise, linger a moment, and are gone, leaving
behind them an indescribable loneliness of soul, and a
longing to stretch one's hand back down the centuries
to pluck their meaning from the past.

Under the sand, the granite, the marble, buried deep
in the pyramids or merely covered by the earth of
shallow graves, there must surely be many instruments
of music wrought in gold or silver, studded in jewels,
or cut out of humble wood; many strings still unbroken, and near them many whitened bones of dusky
hands which, for all we know, at odd moments of day
or night set those strings a-thrumming, or lift the reed
pipes to ghostly lips.

Who knows but that the British Museum at night,
rid at last of those who gape at Egypt's dishonoured
dead, may not be filled with snatches of music from
throat or hand of those unfortunates, priest, priestess,
fair woman and honoured man, dug out and laid upon

a slab of grass for the education of the revellers of a wet Bank Holiday, or those others from Northern climes, who bid their snuffling, sticky progeny to " coom oop, lad, an' look at t' stuffed un ! "

And on this night of which I write, music was caught up, and carried hither and hither upon the breeze which clittered the leaves of the palms, and softly moved the flowing robes of Hahmed the Arab, who, perfectly motionless, stood in the ink-black shadow cast by the bougainvillæa, which trailed its purple masses over the walls of the house, shining faintly pink under the silver moon.

At the man's feet lay three camels, superb beasts. One red brown and one-humped, packed with a seemingly huge load which in reality it hardly felt, and two Bactrian or two-humped, pacing dromedaries of Dhalul, one of deepest black and therefore most rare, with black saddle cloth embroidered in silver, the third of a light golden colour, decked out in cloth of softest silk patterned with glistening jewels, and shimmering crystal specks, cushions padding the saddle-seat, to which hung stirrups of silver.

About this beast's neck, outstretched upon the sand, lay a garland of flowers, upon the ground by its side lay an Eastern rug of purple shade, covered inches deep in flowers of every kind.

There was no grumbling or snarling, they knew their master and lay still, until, with a slight grunt, one raised its head and looked towards the East, as the man with a muttered " Allah " slowly moved towards the gate.

Putting his hands to his lips and forehead and murmuring, " Peace be upon you! " he took Jill's dressing-case from her.

.   .   .   .

" I'm sorry to be so late," she said in a voice devoid of anything in the way of tone or inflection, " and I *had* to bring my dressing-case, it would be so tiresome to be stranded in the desert with no looking-glass or face cream, wouldn't it? "

" It would be terrible! " was the answer, as though a dearth in dates was in discussion.

And then Jill sat down upon a convenient block of marble, and searching in her cheap bag for one of those Russian cigarette cases of wood, which had the advantage of being inexpensive and distinctive compared to those of gold, silver, or silver gilt, which jingle so irritatingly against the universal gold, silver, or silver gilt bag, took out a cigarette, lit it, and began to make conversation.

It is very difficult to describe the girl's frame of mind at this moment when she stood upon the verge of great happenings, or in fact of any moment when danger, possible or certain, confronted her.

She was perfectly calm, in fact a little dull, with a heart which physically neither slowed nor hastened.

Yet it was not the fearlessness of blissful ignorance, or the aggravating recklessness of the foolhardy.

Three times she had been in actual danger of death: once when her horse bolted, making straight for the cliffs a short way ahead; another time when the receding tide had caught her, pulling her slowly out to sea, and never a boat in sight; and again when taking a pre-breakfast stroll on the Col di Tenda, she had encountered a fugitive of the law desperately making for the frontier, who, half crazed with fear, sleeplessness, and hunger, literally at the point of an exceedingly sharp knife had demanded money, or bracelet, in fact anything which could be transformed into a mattress, and coffee, polenta, cigarette or succulent frittata.

After each of the preceding incidents she had tried to analyse her utter want of feeling, her inability to recognise danger, her almost placid confidence in an ultimate happy ending.

"It doesn't seem to be me, Dads," she had once explained, or tried to explain, to her father, who, in the depths of an armchair and the *Sporting News,* had no more idea of what she was talking about than the man in the moon. "I seem to be standing outside myself looking at myself. A sort of something seems to come right down, shutting the danger right away from me. I know I'm in it and have to get out of it, but though I pulled Arabia for all I knew, and swam for all I was worth to reach Rock Point, and bluffed that poor devil out of taking Mumsie's bracelet, I kind of did it mechanically, not with any intention of putting things right, for I knew I was not going to die that time, because I'm sure that I shall *know* when I've got to die . . . understand, Dads?"

To which Dads had replied:

"Quite so, my dear, quite so! Personally I don't see how it could be otherwise. I agree with every word you say!" patting his red setter's head, which in the firelight he fondly believed to be his daughter's.

CHAPTER XII

AND so it was now as she sat under the African moon, whilst little rings and puffs of smoke helped to irritate the insects ensconced in the leaves of the creeper. She seemed to be standing on the other side of a wall, watching the outcome of the tossing of a silver coin.

"I've had a perfectly awful day," she announced with a ripple of genuine amusement in her voice as she proceeded quite unconcernedly to recount the doings of the last few hours.

"So naturally I was followed from the restaurant," she went on after a moment's pause, "and my bag was so heavy, and I was absolutely lost, and only just managed to give the man the slip by hiding behind a half-open door, painted bright blue of all colours."

"Allah!" murmered Hahmed. "An English girl hiding in a house with a blue door!"

"But," she went on, having for some unknown reason omitted the dance episode from her narrative, "that wasn't the worst part"— and continued, quite unconcernedly, to give a detailed account of the night's happenings. Whilst she was speaking the Arab moved nearer until he stood over her; there was neither shadow nor frown upon the fine face, or movement of lip or hand, but the air seemed to throb with the intensity of the white-hot rage within him.

"By Allah!" he said quite gently, as he took the

emerald ring Jill held out. " I do not need this, for behold for many years I have known of the doings of this thing of whom you speak. And yet so great has been his cunning, that until to-night I have never been able to lay hands upon him in his guilt. But to-morrow will dawn a brighter day for Egypt, in that she will be rid of one of her greatest evils. And were you not afraid ? "

Jill smiled up into the eyes fixed with love, plus worship, plus reverence, upon her. " I ? Oh ! no ! Why should I be when I am supposed to be one of the finest shots in Europe ? Are you going to kill him ? "

" He will be dead ere the sun rises, and I beg you to forgive me if I leave you for a while, for I must go to give orders as to his death."

Jill's thoughts can be most aptly described as tumultuous, but her smile was a festival of youth as she watched the Arab, in whom she had put her trust, walk up the long avenue, stop, and clap his hands.

She could hear no word of the orders given to the servant, who ran from out a clump of trees to kneel at his master's feet, but she guessed that it was the engraven emerald ring which passed from one to the other to be hidden in the servant's turban; and she felt a wave of absolute satisfaction sweep through her whole being at the thought of the man's death before the dawn.

At which sensation she mentally shook herself, feeling that the young tree of her experience, unrestrainedly shooting out in all directions within the space of a few hours, would require the sharp edge of the pruning knife if it was to be kept to the merest outline of the shape common to the ordinary life she had led up to now.

"It is well! He dies before the dawn!" announced the Arab prosaically, as he came towards this woman who, on the edge of a new life which might, for all she knew, bring ruin, despair, or even death in its wake, could so tranquilly talk of the risks she had already encountered in the course of the first few steps she had taken upon the path she had chosen to follow.

"And tell me, O! woman, whose courage causes me to marvel, how once happily escaped from the house of few windows and but one apparent door, did you find your way to these gates?"

"Oh! that!" said Jill, as she sat with her hands about her knee and her face upturned to the moon, which, throwing a deep shadow from the hat brim across the upper part of her face, made of the deep eyes a mystery, and a delirious invitation of the red mouth. "Amongst other till now useless accomplishments, I have learned to guide myself by the stars, though I'm positive they move over here. I had noticed that big one there, which we haven't got in England, that very big sparkling one, hung over the quarter in which the waiting-maid told me lay your house."

"Yes!" replied the man who, though he knew the West so well, was secretly wondering at the trait in a character which allowed a *woman,* on the edge of something unknown, fraught, perhaps, with every kind of danger, to talk unconcernedly of hotels, face creams, blue doors, and stars. "That is the Star of Happiness, it hangs also right in the middle of my oasis, right over my desert dwelling," and the string of beads hang-

ing from the waist slipped through the long fingers as
words of prayer fell softly on the perfumed air.

The girl got up and walked over to the camels.

" So I followed my star and suddenly found myself
at the gates! Is this my ship of the desert — and what
a beautiful coat, the dear thing," starting back as the
dear thing turned its head suddenly, bared its teeth
and snarled.

" Don't be afraid, she is always nervous with strangers, also is she a little spoilt, being the fastest and
most perfect Bactrian camel in the whole of Egypt
and Arabia. Her pedigree, on parchment embossed
with gold, goes back almost to Ismael, and is kept in
a Millwell safe in my oasis, which shows that East
does meet West occasionally. She has, up to to-night,
known no rider but me, and is used only for short
journeys of about seven days; you see these two-humped
beasts can only go three days with comfort without a
drink, but their pace is so smooth that it almost in-
duces one to sleep. Also Taffadaln, which means wel-
come, a name given to her after her mother had foaled
three he-camels, has a special guard both day and night,
for there are many who covet her, for she is the queen
of camels, with her blood and breeding enhanced by
many years of training and special treatment. But
alas! though her coat is as silk, the cushions of her feet
without fault, and her teeth unblemished ivory, her
manners are as ill-bred, and her indifference to those
who love her as great as that of the lowest of her species
which pollute the streets of Cairo." And leaning down
he patted the beast's head, speaking to her in the native tongue, whereupon she made juicy, gurgling sounds

in her long throat, and nuzzled the flowing sleeve, which
might have meant affection in any other animal but a
camel.

"More extremes," he added, as a long, soft blast
of a motor-horn sounded just outside the walls. "Will
you not sit down whilst I explain things for the last
time," unwinding, as he spoke, the soft black cloak
from about him, and folding it to make a cushion for
the stone, standing silhouetted against the shadow of
the walls, whilst the slight breeze blowing the snow-
white raiment outlined the tremendous width of shoulder, the slimness of the waist, and the muscular leanness
of the whole body.

And Jill sat down with a suddenness surprising in
so controlled a person, and to hide a sudden rush of
rosy colour which swept uncontrollably from chin to
brow, extracted another cigarette from the Russian
case.

"'Simon Artz,' I am sure! May I not offer you
one of mine? They are all made especially and only
for me. And do you prize the case? No!"

As the girl shook her head he took the wooden trifle
from her, closed his hand gently, and, crushing it to
matchwood, dropped it soundlessly on to the sand.

And when Hahmed, the Arab, had finished speaking,
Jill Carden, the English girl, understood that with her
only rested the decision, that even now, at the eleventh
hour, she was still absolutely free to go.

Outside the gates waited the man's car, ready to
take her wherever she listed on her way home! At
her feet lay the camels, ready to take her to all the
possibilities of the unknown!

There was absolute silence as she sat motionless, looking into the future. In the West she saw boats, trains, hotels, inner cabins, middle seats, back bed-rooms; felt women, mothers, and wives clutching their mankind so as to keep them from the pariah, the penni-less, pretty companion; heard the clink of the five or ten shillings a week paid monthly in silver, and all this to be repeated over and over again until she died, un-less she married a man she did not love and " settled down " for ever and ever and ever; though even this possibility seemed to have receded into the remote dis-tance with the receding of her fortune.

Then she looked up to the stars, and down to the sand, and out to the East, seeing her freedom if she dared grasp it, if she dared venture out on the many days' journey which, to her astonishment, she had learned stretched between Ismailiah and the oasis.

She scrutinised the man before her — this Arab with the impassive face, the camels at his feet, her life in his hands if she went with him.

His what? Wife! to settle down for ever and ever and ever.

His plaything? This was not the man to play or be played with, for had he not said:

" If you come with me, fear not that you will be a prisoner. The oasis, the house, my servants, houses, camels, all will be yours, and there will be nothing to prevent your leaving it all — nothing except the desert, the miles of pitiless sand, trackless, pathless, strewn with the white bones of those who have essayed to escape from Fate, the never-changing, ever-different ocean which beats about my dwelling."

Then once again she looked into the
were reading every passing emotion on
and putting out her hands made one s
camel, whilst the soul of the desert la
scarlet mouth.

CHAPTER XIII

A SHARP word of command and the pack-camel rose, moved a few paces on its noiseless feet, swaying from side to side as though to readjust its load, whisked its miserable tail, and stretching out its long neck began to nibble the leaves of a flowering shrub.

Jill followed the beast, stroked its silky coat, and prodded one of the water skins filled to bursting.

" Will that be enough to last us all the way? And what happens when we want to rest? And do we do all the cooking and washing-up ourselves, just like a picnic? What fun! " Which shows that Jill had no idea of what unlimited money can do to mitigate the discomfort of desert travelling by providing every possible comfort, even luxury.

" My servants have gone ahead with a caravan containing all that I think will be necessary for your comfort. The journey takes many nights of travelling when the cool wind has tempered the scorching sands. At sunrise we shall find our tents pitched; and you shall rest from then, an hour after dawn, until just before sunset, for it is unwise to be asleep at sunset in the desert. When we halt your bath will be ready, your meals as you desire, your bed as soft and spotless as your own."

" Really! " said Jill, who had imagined herself camping out under the stars with scorpions and spiders as bedfellows. "But if the men have to go on ahead of us, we shall have to get up early so as to let them pack and give them a start."

The Arab gravely shook his head, with never a glimmer of a smile rear the mouth or eyes.

"Ah! no! you need not worry, a caravan of many persons has preceded us."

"Many *people!*" ejaculated Jill. "What a lot of servants for two!"

"Let me explain! In Egypt, Arabia, or Persia, when we speak of sheep or horses we say so many 'head,' but not so of the camel. The camel is the most cherished possession of the Arab.

"There are three events which bring joy to us, and which are occasions of greatest festival, namely, the birth of a son, the birth of a she-camel, and the birth of a mare. The she-camel provides her master with food for both himself and his horses; for in an area, or season, where there is little water but an abundance of juicy grass in which the camel finds both food and drink, the camel's milk is given to the horses in lieu of water, the master's covering and tent are made of the hair, the waterless places are known to him through her. There are many other ways in which the animal is useful, and for which we daily return thanks to Allah, therefore we speak of them as persons, so many persons in a herd, because as the proverb says, 'God created the camel for the Arab, and the Arab for the camel.'

"Therefore for each resting-place there are two one-humped camels to carry all things necessary for your night's sojourn."

"Why one-humped?" asked the girl, who was of au

inquiring turn of mind, and was getting slightly mixed with her first endeavour to grasp something of Eastern life.

"The one-humped or, as we say, the Dyemal-mai, which means water-camel, although they cannot carry so heavy a load as the Bactrian, can go even up to eight or nine days without water.

"There is only one well between here and the water, and it is usually surrounded by caravans, with water as thick as the mud in a London street in November, and dirtier, being polluted by the filth of man and beast.

"This we will pass, contenting ourselves with the water we carry for ablutions and cooking, and with wine or coffee to drink. If there is water to spare the camels can have it, if not they can go without, with the exception of the two that carry us.

"But you will find the going irksome even on Taf fadaln, and so that you may rest, beautiful woman, whose name even I do not know, Howesha, which name, being translated, means that she is a past mistress in the art of grumbling, carries all that will give you repose if you should desire to stop before we reach our caravan."

And just as though she understood, Howesha the Grumbler, opening wide her mouth, proceeded to give a series of very fine imitations, including those of a nest of spitting snakes, a sobbing woman, and a choking dog — all of which she concluded by her masterpiece, of a child masticating sticky sweets, when her master, to stop her querulous upbraidings, thrust dates between her polished teeth.

And then he turned to Jill, who was laughing delightedly, and stroked her camel's coat.

"Later you shall have servants, many of them, who hand and foot, shall do your bidding, and carry out your slightest wish, but to-night and for ever I am your slave. Allah! to think that I, the worst feared man in Egypt, whose word is law, who condemns to death by the lifting of a finger, of a race who looks upon women as a useful plaything, at the most as a potential mother of sons, *I* crave to serve you from your lying down in the heat of the day to your rising up, when the sunset breeze shall blow the soft curls about your flower-face. Do you think I would allow a servant, some low-born son of a bazaar-dweller, to throw his shadow upon the ground over which your lovely feet must tread, or to touch a vessel which your white fingers might hold, to breathe the air which maybe has just passed from your sweet mouth, on this night when you make your journey into Egypt, *real* Egypt; for to us, Cairo and other such places are but tourist centres which we give to the foreigner readily, traversing many miles of sand and rock and hills ourselves, before we can lie down upon the soft breast of our own motherland.

"Come, woman! The moon tarries not, neither does the sun, and we have many miles to go."

. . . .

With the exception of a twopenny ride at the Zoo, few Europeans ever mount or ride a camel, thereby missing an art or a pastime or sport, which to the novice, until he has been thoroughly and literally broken in, is the most back, heart, and nerve-wearing means

of locomotion he could possibly choose in all the wide
world.

Jill stood ankle-deep in flowers looking down at her
mount, the prize of the desert.

"I do not know how you will fare, woman of the
West. I dare not put palanquin on Taffadaln for fear
that she might bolt from terror and take you far into
the desert, there to die. But arrived at our destina-
tion she shall be broken in at once, however, for in all
my stables there is no other camel with her sliding
step, not one who would not make you feel as though
your spine had snapped after one hour's journey upon
its back. We Arabs can sit a camel in more than one
way, but the easiest for you, and Allah knows it will
be hard enough after a time, is, if your skirt permits,
to sit astride and put both your feet round the pummel
in front. That, anyway, will prevent you from being twisted as you are with the shocking ladies' saddle
you use in England."

"Oh, but I ride astride," volunteered Jill, as she
raised her skirts, settled herself, and taking the gold-
studded rein, held firmly to the front and back peak
of the saddle as instructed, and awaited the word of
command.

A camel rises from its front or hind legs just as the
fancy seizes it, so that if you do not keep a fair balance,
also yourself in complete readiness to lean forward or
backward according to your mount's final decision, you
will assuredly find yourself ignominiously pitched in a
heap over the quadruped's nose, or just as ignominiously hanging head down in the vicinity of its tail,
either of which positions will cause her to chortle glee-

fully before the next lurch, which gets the rest of her feet into order.

A final touch is given by the imitation of an **infan**tile earthquake as she arranges you to her taste, and then you may consider yourself ready to start out on **a** journey which may make you more sea-sick than **any** rough channel-crossing in boat or aeroplane.

CHAPTER XIV

IT was with a feeling of exultation that Jill, from her elevated seat, looked down into the Arab's face, outlined in the scented dimness of the garden by the snow-white head-cloth, and her brilliant mouth widened in a low laugh of pleasure as she pulled down a bough of fluffy mimosa to sniff its perfume, and she also gave a little shriek of dismay as Taffadaln, taking matters into her own enormous feet, and utterly ignoring the frantic tugging of the silken reins, suddenly stalked off towards the gate.

There was a sharp word of command bringing the animal to a standstill, then a throaty exclamation from somewhere in the long neck as she pitted her hereditary obstinacy against the man's will.

Five times, with a blatant wink towards her sisters and a sneer in her hideous mouth, she journeyed towards the gate, and five times was she brought back to the starting-place, to be fastened at last by a strong lead to the bridle of her more submissive sister, who was making disgusting masticatory noises over a tough twig.

Then, upon the fastening of the lead, there arose a concerto of such growlings, fretting, sobbing, groaning, and roaring, as to make the inexperienced Jill beg to be allowed to dismount, for fear of having caused hurt to the hateful brute.

But it seemed that all the fuss came about through

the Queen of the Desert's objection to the unknown
lady on her back, an objection which was causing her
to twist her long neck backwards in the diabolical hope
that the loose-lipped mouth in the spite-contorted face
might reach something to bite, be it foot or saddle,
cloth or skirt.

"O! hateful, impatient descendant of a dissatisfied
mother!" suddenly ejaculated the man.   "More foolish than an ostrich, and as poisonous as a scorpion,
yet have I to put up with thy whims and fancies because of thy specially formed stomach.   I, who long
to strike thy repellent face again and again, and dare
not, for the fear that thy evil, dwarfed brain, twisted
with jealousy, might make thy beautiful rider the object of thy revenge, tearing her limb from limb, and
rolling upon her; [1] but behold! in as much as Allah
made thee, yet shalt thou, through thy disobedience
and ill-manners of to-day, be put to stud with thy
elder brother, who, for a camel, rejoiceth in seeming
good manners.   Then shalt thou be chastened, and thy
milk given to the feeding of horses."

This harangue might have been a pæan of praise for
all the change it made in the beautiful Eastern voice,
and the girl's low laughter rang out like bells on the
night air, as the man explained that the animal was
inordinately jealous of all and sundry who, in her sin-
laden brain, she feared might do her out of a handful
of sugar or bucket of water.

.   .   .   .

[1] To revenge the lash or whip camels have been known even
after a lapse of months to seize their victim, tearing and tram-
pling him to pieces, and then with infinite relish proceed to roll
time and again upon the remains

From all time women have revelled in a novel sensation, but never surely so much, or in such a one, as did Jill in hers, as, with peace restored, she passed through the gates with her companion, on her way to a life about which she had not allowed herself the slightest analysis.

And a great silence fell on the girl as they left the town, padding noiselessly through the outskirts where no one met them, and no sound was to be heard save for the barking of dogs, and the occasional wail of an infant; for the strangeness of everything had suddenly made her realise that of her own will she was standing on the threshold of a new life, laden — though this the usual narrow outlook and education of the West prevented her from understanding — with a love and passion and womanhood which cannot, and never will be, realised in countries where the dominant colour is grey.

Gone was her laughter, and vanished the merry exclamations and remarks, as she began to glean some idea of the width and breadth of the desert which was slowly engulfing her.

Once or twice she had looked behind at the ever-receding town, with the sheen of the fresh water canal becoming fainter and fainter at each step, until it at last vanished into nothingness. And the living silence of the desert seemed to close in upon her, and the canopy of heaven, weighty with stars, to press down upon her, and the snapping and breaking of generations-rooted conventions to deafen her, until like a lost child she suddenly sobbed, and dropping the rein, held out her hands to the man who, although she knew it not, had been watching and waiting for just such an outburst.

For he worshipped the sand and pebbles and rocks and dunes and hills of his adored desert, and knew the effect it sometimes made, even at the paltry distance of a mile or two from some teeming city, upon both male and female denizens of the West, who bloom palely in the heat of a coal-fire, and lift their faces thankfully to the red lozenge which, for eight months of an English year, represents the sun shining through fog or cloud.

Also must it be confessed that Jill's head was beginning already to swim a little with the sway of the camel, though of nausea she suffered not at all, and it was with a feeling of joy that she felt the animals come to a halt, saw the black one, upon a word of command, get docilely to its knees, heard Howesha grumbling fiercely to the moon as she went through the same gymnastic performance, and felt her own rocking and pitching until it came to the ground. Whereupon she dismounted lightly, and reeled against the man as the entire desert, herself and camels included, turned a complete somersault, after which she meekly sat down on Taffadaln's back and watched proceedings.

The pack-camel lay supinely as its master with strong deft fingers unbound and unknotted the various ropes until everything desired was found.

A rug of many colours was laid at Jill's feet, and cushions thrown thereon, upon which, with a great sigh of relief, she laid herself down, until something softly crawling round her neck brought her to her feet shaking with disgust.

" It is doubtlessly a sand-spider," explained the man. " They are perfectly harmless and to be found everywhere, and are even welcomed in some houses as they help to reduce the plague of flies from which we have suffered, with other things, since the time of Pharaoh. I am so sorry, but insects are a nuisance we have totally failed to conquer, though in your house, believe me, there will be none, not even the smallest."

Upon which assurance Jill sat down, took off her hat, arranged her hair in a pocket mirror, flicked a shadow of powder upon her nose, and settled down to watch and wait.

The man's agile fingers arranged some charcoal, which he lighted quickly in some desert fashion inside a square of four bricks, over which he placed a brass tripod.

There was a gurgling sound as water ran from a skin into a brass pot which hung from a hook on the tripod, and in a few minutes the water began to bubble furiously, as the fire, leaping and falling, cast giant shadows on the Arab's flowing robes.

Small boxes were opened, and the contents laid on plates: sandwiches, cakes, sweetmeats, fruit, and wine, red and white, in skins, poured into empty earthenware jugs in which to cool it. Small cups of Egyptian coffee, a " Cona Machine " for the Western idea of coffee, and a box of cigarettes.

" If I had known you would be a-hungered, I would have brought the wherewithal to make a repast of substance! "

" Oh, but it is all so topping! " cried the girl, and then stopped.

The slang words had suddenly struck her as foolish and silly, and out of place in a country where the syllables of words sound sonorously, and time **passes** like a slow moving river with its banks unchoked with "hustle weeds." And from that day, or rather night, Jill gave up slang, **and** one by one all the little **dreary habits which rub** the bloom **off the Western maid.**

CHAPTER XV

A STRIKING and unrealistic picture the two made as they lay on their cushions alone in the desert. The girl in her white dress, which in truth was somewhat crumpled, her white neck rising like a gleaming pillar from the low-cut blouse, the little curls rippling round the face which, under the moonlight and the stress of the past hours, showed white with shadow-encircled eyes, gazing at the man who rose and knelt with a towel of softest linen, and a basin of brass filled with water.

Jill happened to be one of those lucky individuals who can with impunity wash their face anywhere, and at any time of the day, and look the better for it. Neither had she to fear a futurist impression in vivid colours of Dorin rouge and blue pencillings mixed with liquid powder appearing on her face after a sudden rain storm.

So she put her face right into the basin, lifted it sparkling with laughter and rainbow drops to bury it in the snowy cloth. Her sleeves she turned back, and ran the water up and down her arms.

" And you must wash your feet, woman, for so small are they, they must assuredly be fatigued! "

And without hesitation the girl proffered her shoe to be unlaced, whilst without lifting her skirt, with a quick movement she undid the suspender which held her last pair of real silk stockings to the infinitesimal

girdle she wore instead of the usual figure-distorting
corset, peeled off the silken hose and put the prettiest
foot in the world in flesh, painting, or marble, into
another basin of brass laid upon the ground, and also
filled with water.

"Allah!" whispered the man, as he dried each little
foot, "so small, so slender, rivalling the arch of Ctes-
isphon, dimpled as the sky at dawn, never in the
most perfect Circassian have I seen feet so wonderful,
glory be to Allah, whose prophet is Mohammed."

And then the Arab, filling another basin, moved to
the far corner of the rug, where facing towards the
East he made ablutions of his mouth and hands and
feet, and raising his hands to heaven, gave praise to
his God for the wonder of the day, and bowed himself
in obeisance.

"I was returning thanks to Allah for you, O! Moon
Flower," he said simply, and led her to the cloth of
finest damask upon which the repast was spread, prais-
ing Allah anew as he poured the contents of the wine
jars upon the sands when Jill announced that she only
drank water.

Rested and cheered, the girl chatted merrily all
through the al fresco meal, in her turn inwardly giving
thanks for the Arab's perfect manners and knowledge
of table methods, for in her heart she, particular to
the point of becoming finicky about the usually so
unpleasant process of eating, had looked forward with
absolute horror to the moment when the man's fingers
should close upon some succulent portion of a mess of
pottage or chicken, and convey it to his mouth with
charitable distribution of rice grains upon the beard.

Reassured, her laughter 'rang out sweetly when the absence of methylated spirit for the " Cona Machine " was discovered.

"And I would really rather have yours," said she, " for am I not to become an Eastern ——" and suddenly stopped, for looking up she found the man gazing at her with eyes ablaze with love.

And once more a great silence fell between them, as they both sat staring wide-eyed over the desert, and up into the starry heavens.

Few, very few of those who live in the West have had the privilege of sitting alone under the stars in the desert.

This does not mean riding out on a tourist track with dragoman and camel-driver, and retiring a few yards from their perpetual chatter to gaze at the heavens in what *you* imagine to be the approved style, to the accompaniment of correct gasps, after which, finding you have left your cigarettes behind, you look at your wrist watch and wait another five minutes, until you can with decency saunter back to your cameldriver with the feeling of something quite well done, and the unuttered hope in your mind that everyone would not have gone to bed on your return.

No! it means, when wearied from long travel you call a halt, perhaps just before the dawn, when the very stars seem to commune with you.

Leaving your servants to pitch your tent, urge your camel to the distance when the clattering of pans, and the jar of inter-domestic feud shall not assail your hearing, then urge your camel to its knees, and set you down at a distance so that the pungent odour of the beast shall not assail your nostrils, and then removing little by little the outer covering of the worries and pin-pricks which have made the passing of the day unbearable, give way to your soul, or second self, or whatever you call that which causes you to joy in the coming of the spring, and to mourn when the fire refuses to heat but a portion of the room in winter.

For this is what happened to Jill, the English girl, as she sat on her cushions in the Egyptian desert, and has nothing to do with table-turning, or ten-and-six-penny visions in Maida Vale, or whisperings, or touchings in a conveniently darkened room; neither must you put it down to magnetism or hypnotism, or any of those " isms " which we, of a glacier-born country and a machine-made life, so irreverently tag on as terms descriptive to all that which we cannot label and place upon a museum shelf, or conveniently start by motor power.

A long dissertation on the Eastern's power of concentration, love of meditation, and utter detachment from self, would doubtlessly prove wearisome in the extreme, neither for a true explanation thereof can help be got from highly or lowly born native. Without movement for hours he will sit or squat, as becomes his station, staring, as we should say, vacantly into space, in reality seeing and hearing that which others, blinded by material enjoyment, can never hope to visualise or hear.

Jill afterwards tried to explain the outcome of this, her first step in the meadows of meditation, which she took without help and without intention, and in which she has become so versed, to the mystification of those

about her, who look upon woman as a bearer of children, a plaything for sunny hours, useful in time of
rain, endowed with the brain of a pea-hen, and as much
soul as the priests see fit to mete out to her.

"Something had left me," Jill explained later.
"My body seemed to be sitting on the cushions, and
I could minutely describe the way Hahmed was sitting,
and the exact shape of the shadow cast before him by
the moon, which was setting behind us. But inside
I was quite empty, whilst all sorts of little things I
had known so long, crept out and stole away into the
desert. I was just a husk, with no more impatience
or quick temper or restlessness, and I can remember
wondering if I were likely to break in two or crumble
into dust, I felt so thin. And then I heard all sorts
of whisperings, just as though thousands of people
were standing near me, trying to make me understand
something, and a violet shadow suddenly appeared between Hahmed and myself, seeming to get deeper and
deeper in colour, and then get less and less; and as
it lessened, so did my feeling of being a mere husk
leave me, until at last, when it had all gone, I felt —
well *full* is the only way to put it, and my heart was
thudding, and the blood pounding in my head, and well
— that's all!"

Very indefinite and very unsatisfactory, and of which
the whispering can easily be put down to the snuffling of
the camels, the passing of the faint breeze, or the intake
of the Arab's breath; and the purple shadows to the
folds of his black cloak. For the effect of fatigue, excitement, and strong Egyptian coffee upon the mind of
a Western maid is quite likely to turn the buzzing of a

fly into the flight of an aeroplane, or the dripping of a tap into the roar of a Niagara.

Be that as it may, the Arab made no sound or movement when with a low cry the girl sprung suddenly to her feet, and with both hands upraised, although she knew it not, turned towards the direction in which Mecca lay.

For a full minute she stood absolutely motionless, then gently moving towards the man, who had risen and was standing behind her, she put out her hand, saying softly, "Behold! I am ready to come with thee."

CHAPTER XVI

I<small>T</small> was close upon dawn when the two figures suddenly and silently emerged from the tree shadows in which they had been hiding for some considerable time.

Very simple and harmless they looked too, the taller one in spotless galabeah and red fez, his smallpox pitted face softened by the light of the dying moon; the other, a mere bundle of clothes with the yashmak covering all except the eyes, dragging back from the hand which pulled her ruthlessly up to the door of a house conspicuous by its length of wall unbroken by windows.

The faintest sound of music from somewhere about the immense building sounded as out of place at that hour as would a boy's shrill whistling in the middle of High Mass, but unperturbed thereby, the pitted-face man knocked gently three times upon the door, vehemently upbraiding the while his shrinking and protesting companion, who tugged still more forcibly at the restraining hand.

" Behold, art thou the daughter of ungrateful parents and not fit to be honoured by the great lord who awaits thee. Raise thy voice in protest, speak but one word, and thy back shall resemble the red pattern upon thy raiment, which has cost much hard toil to provide for thee."

The female figure suddenly sank back in all humility

at the feet of the upbraider, as unperceived — maybe —
by both, a small portion of the door above their heads
slipped noiselessly back to show a gleaming eye glued
to the little grille, taking in the scene beneath it.

Unperceived or not, the elder man, taking a deep
breath, continued in a slightly raised tone to adminis-
ter his admonition.

" Comely art thou, and young, and good is the price
paid for thee, and may he who has purchased thee be
not annoyed at the hour in which I bring thee, for in
truth was thy mother against thy flight from the nest,
being not awake to the advantages of the new bough
upon which thou wouldst come to rest — therefore was
I forced to bring thee by stealth.   Perchance —— ! "

The gentle voice stopped suddenly as the door was
thrown open by a much armed individual, who angrily
demanded the meaning of the disturbance.

" The peace of Allah be upon thee and upon this
house, into which, by the order of thy master, O!
brother, I bring a flower which he has deigned to pluck
from within the city.   Comely is she, and gifted in
music and the dance, but young, is affrighted at the
honour before her.   I ——"

Here the armed individual broke in ruthlessly upon
the pæan of praise, drawing a most gleaming and
curved weapon from somewhere about his huge person.

" Begone, disturbers of the peace," he ejaculated with
the difficulty natural to one who has had his tongue
split.   " My master awaits a flower in truth, being even
now o'ercome in sleep in the waiting, but the flower
will show a warrant the which will pass her through
this door of which I am the guardian.   By Allah ! it is

not opened at the tapping of every chance weed which the wind of poverty may cause to flutter, across this path!"

Things began to look somewhat awkward for the humble flower wilting on the marble step, until her friend, speaking suddenly and sharply, saved the situation by leaning down and quite violently snatching something from the little hand fumbling most awkwardly among the many feminine draperies.

"Behold the warrant, O! unbeliever. So desirous of this maiden is thy master, upon whom may the blessing of Allah rest, that he even gave unto her father the ring of emerald from off his right hand. Art satisfied, or is't best to risk the tempest by still further questioning and delay!"

The guardian of the door, not a little astounded, snatched in his turn at the jewel, and seeming perfectly satisfied after a prolonged scrutiny, stood aside and motioned the two to enter, and shutting the door behind them and ordering them to stand where they were until he returned from his dangerous mission of disobeying, by breaking in upon his master's privacy, stalked off with much dignity into the perfumed, half-lit, enormous hall.

Now if only he had been afflicted with one iota of the curiosity apportioned by time to Lot's wife, that man might have been alive even to this day. But he neither turned his head nor pricked his ears, thereby failing to note that with the lightning methods of the eel the comely flower had in some miraculous way slipped from her all enveloping sheath of draperies to stand revealed a wiry, glistening-with-oil youth, who, without a moment's pause, with knife in teeth, and as silently as a lizard, glided across the dividing yards of Persian carpet separating him from his quarry.

Across the hall and through endless deserted rooms they passed, the companion of the camouflage maiden bringing up the rear. Right to the far quarter of the house they went, one after the other, and the guardian of the house felt little more than a pin-prick when, just as his hand pulled aside the curtain screening a door, the youth behind him raising his right arm drove the knife clean under the left shoulder blade, catching the dead body as it fell backwards to lay it noiselessly upon the floor just as his friend appeared upon the scene.

"It was well done, O! brother — neatly, and with strength — leaving no trace of blood to speak of. But now must we proceed with cunning, else may we too be lying lifeless upon our backs. Take even thy knife. my brother, 'twere a pity to leave it in yon carcase!"

Indifferently turning the body over, the boy drew the knife, as indifferently wiping it on the dead man's raiment, and stood for a moment as still as any one of the exotic specimens of statuary which ornamented the whole house.

Truly and implicitly had the orders of the master been obeyed; there was no sound of any living thing in or near the place, so that after a few whispered words the curtain was gently pulled back and the door opened just as gently inch by inch.

For a long minute the two men peered in through the crack, their eyes searching swiftly for sign of him whom they searched.

Unavailing at first, until with a motion of the head the younger one pointed.

"Look! Yonder he sleeps!"

The room was still brilliantly lighted by the many lamps hanging from the ceilings and the walls, but the shadow of the great mass of growing plants fell upon the divan upon which Jill had sat some few hours ago.

Inch by inch the door was opened, until it was wide enough to allow the dusky slender body of the boy to slip in. Round the wall he slid, his eyes a-glisten, and the knife fast held between his teeth; then down upon his hands and knees he sank to crawl as quietly as a cat up to the back of the flowering plants. And then he quite suddenly sprang to his feet, beckoning to his companion, who sped straight across the room, knife in hand.

"Behold! O! brother!"

And a world of disappointment rang in the whispered words as the youth pointed disgustedly to the picture before him.

Very peacefully lay the man whose name had been a byword in the land of Egypt, and whose delight had been in the moral and physical terrors of women.

His eyes were closed and his mouth slightly open, showing the white teeth; the hands were gently clasped, but over the spot where should have been his heart, and on the silken coverings of the cushions, spread a great crimson patch of blood, whilst at his feet, lying prone across the couch, was the body of a girl. Her eyes were open, and a little smile widened the beautiful mouth, but from the spot above the heart which had so unwisely and so well loved, glittered the jewelled hilt of a dagger. One hand touched the hem of her master's coat, but what the bastinado had left of the little feet seemed to shriek aloud for vengeance, vengeance for the dead child, and vengeance for all those who had likewise suffered.

"Allah! Allah!" The cry cleft the stillness of the room as the boy's eyes fell upon the terrible sight; and the knife flashed twice and thrice, and yet again, until the evil beauty of the dead man's face had been entirely obliterated, and a strong hand gripped the supple wrist.

"Come, O! brother! Waste not thy strength upon the dead. Behold! Yon little maid has carried out our master's wish, may she rest in the delights of paradise with the beloved of Allah whose prophet is Mohammed, and may the spirit of him who is accursed enter into the body of a pig to live eternally in filth and dishonour!"

And the sun had risen upon a cleaner day when the twain departed from the house of shadows.

CHAPTER XVII

I⊤ was close upon dawn when to Jill's ears was borne a faint melodious sound.

Inexpressibly weary was she, exhausted to the point of fainting, for in spite of numerous haltings, the drinking of tea, coffee, and sherbet, and the eating of cakes and curious Egyptian sweetmeats, had in no way lessened the agony of her lower limbs, which she moved this way and that in the vain effort to relieve the terrible cramp that seemed to creep from her spine to her brain, and down again to her feet.

The stars danced before and around her, as she swayed to and fro to the deadly lurching rhythm of the camel's pace; one thing, and one thing only, having so far saved her from the utter dissolution of fatigue, and that being when, urged by their master's voice, the three animals had broken into a gentle trot, ending in a pace which literally took away the girl's breath; but even that relaxation had had to be abandoued as the nature of the ground changed.

Most people's conception of the desert is that of one huge expanse of smooth sand, with here and there a palm tree to break the monotony; an entirely wrong conception, bred partly, I think, from the highly coloured scriptural pictures of our youth.

There *are* tracts of sand extending for many miles, such as those around big cities into which you wander

on camel-back at so much an hour, and with the description of which you hold your less travelled neighbours enthralled, as you intersperse the munching of
muffins with the words " dragoman," " backsheesh,"
and " Cheops."

But even on a week or ten days of genuine travelling
you are likely to pass through and over a variety of
grounds, from hard gravel which is delightful for tent-
pitching, ground covered with a liberal supply of rocks,
under which lurks the festive scorpion, great mounds
of limestone which in the desert take on the proportions of mountains, marks of long-dried pools left by
long-dried torrents, defiles almost as narrow as the camel's scriptural needle, and in places, an earth, the curious marking of which will almost lead you to believe
that it is cloud-shadowed, if the heat of your head,
the state of your throat, and the lamentable leathery
appearance of your skin did not tell you that for months
no such thing as a cloud had been known to appear in
the blazing heavens.

At the first faint, flute-like note Jill thought that she
must have awakened from sleep or delirium, and, it
must be confessed, really did not care which was the
solution of the mystery; sinking back into a state of
apathy so exhausted was she, until the three camels
came to a standstill, and the Arab, with something that
looked like a dark cloak across his arm, drew his beast
alongside of hers.

"Behold, woman, the hour of Namaz is at hand,
when throughout the land the Muezzin is called, for
it is the hour of dawn. The hour when the curtains
of heaven are drawn about the stars, so that they may

not be blinded by the glory of their golden master,
as I shall draw this cloak about the fairness of your
sweet face, and the outline of your gracious figure,
which Allah in his bounty has placed within my unworthy hands, to hide them from the eyes of the high-
born, and the eyes of the low-born, such as yonder
slave who, though he be the sweetest maker of music
in all Egypt, is but my head camel tender, though
before Allah who is God, his worth as such could not
be purchased for the price of rubies.

"And now shall your weary form rest a while, while
I give praise to Allah, whose prophet is Mohammed."

Grumbling, the three animals subsided.

"Is all well with you?"

The girl nodded as she stumbled from her seat and
stretched herself full length upon the sands, the con-
vulsive twitching of her cramped limbs giving way at
last to the peace of oblivion.

"Will you forgive me if I leave you in your stress,
for behold, the hour of Namaz waits neither for weariness or joy, nay, nor even death."

But Jill heard nothing, neither his light footfall as
he moved some yards from the unclean Christian whom
he loved, and placing his prayer-rug upon the ground
turned towards Mecca, which in Islam is called Keblah,
which, being translated, means "centre"; nor the
splashing of water as he washed three times his nostrils, his mouth, and hands and arms to the elbow, the
right first as ordained, then head and neck, and ears
once and feet once, whilst murmuring a prescribed
form of words, these words being repeated in different
positions, standing erect or sitting, with inclinations

of the head and body, and prostrations in which the Arab in all humility touched the ground with his forehead.

For Hahmed was a true Mohammedan, carrying out the precepts of his religion as laid down by the Koran as fully and conscientiously as is within the power of man. But, you will say, he was voluntarily consorting with a Christian, who, by the edicts of the Koran, is considered unclean, inviting pollution by touching the bare skin of her hands and feet.

True! but the man was no evil liver, picking up to throw away, buying to regret the purchase within the hour, attracted by this pretty face or that lovely form. Nay. He loved the girl as it is unhappily given on this earth for but few women to be so loved, and with all the strength of his will he intended the outcome of this love to be one more triumph to the glory of Allah.

As for the pollution of her satin skin, did he not murmur the prayer of purification when in contact with it?

Neither did Jill notice that the man, his purification and his prayers ended, had come over to her, standing gazing down at the almost tragic picture she made outstretched on the sands.

Her death-white face was buried in the curve of one folded arm, the other, flung out, lay with the palm of the hand uppermost. The little feet were crossed under the crumpled skirt, from which peeped the folds of her last white silk petticoat.

"Poor little bird," he murmured, as the sense of mastership rose strong within him at the sight of the helpless child at his feet. "So weary, so beautiful, and so young. Behold, shall a nest be built for thee in which thou shalt rest, shaking off the plumage harmed in thy short passage through life, to appear at last more beautiful than the most glorious bird in Paradise," and bending he touched her gently.

But Jill, who had had no real sleep since she had left the boat, had passed at last into an almost comatose condition, from which it was doubtful she could have been awakened, even at the sound of Israfil's Trumpet.[1]

Crossing to the camels Hahmed considerably lengthened the lead, and attaching the camels Taffadaln and Howesha one on each side of his own, he bade the two former rise, which they did with alacrity, leading one to believe that they heard the flute-like music calling them to the cool of the palm tree's shade, the doubtful bucket of water, and the certain repast, terminating with a handful of luscious dates.

Stooping, the man raised the unconscious girl from the ground, holding her as lightly as a feather on one arm, and draping the dark cloak around her so as to cover the red-gold hair, drew a corner across the face.

Perhaps some may enjoy restraining the vagaries of a lead horse, which sees fit to proceed sideways at the encounter of anything in motion on the road, or execute a *pas seul* on the hind legs at the flutter of a leaf, without referring to what happens if a white paper-bag should attract the nervous eye.

But it is mere child's play compared with the leading,

[1] In Islamism there are four angels particularly favoured by Allah, who is God. Israfil is the name of one whose office will be to sound the trumpet at the Resurrection.

under certain circumstances, of one or more self-willed, obstinate, vain-glorious camels.

Seated across his black camel the Arab drew the girl's head against his shoulder, holding her gently but firmly in his left arm.

A word, and the camel pitching and tossing finally acquired an upright position. Things went well for a score or so of yards, the three animals proceeding at a stately demure pace, until verily the devil entered into Taffadaln.

Suddenly she rushed sideways, then with front legs wide apart came to a dead stop, jerking the black camel violently.

" Thou awkward descendant of clumsy parents, what aileth thee ? " exclaimed her master, as Jill's head bumped violently against his shoulder. " Take heed to my words. Enjoy this thy last ride through the glory of the desert, for verily at the end shalt thou, between the periods of bearing young, be put to the lowest tasks apportioned to the lowest of thy species."

Whereupon Taffadaln turned solemnly towards the speaker, and lifting her upper lip laughed, and with no more ado faced towards the palm trees, which to desert-trained eyes showed faintly some miles away, took two steps forward, humped herself together, collapsed on the ground, and stretching out her neck, half-closed her eyes.

Imagine the helplessness of her master, seated so high upon his camel as to render useless any chastisement with the *courbaash,* which whip applied deftly to certain less tough portions of the camel's body will usually bring the brute to reason, *if* he who wields the whip cares to risk the accumulation of revenge which the punishment will infallibly store up in the camel's brain. A veritable storm of anger raged in the man as he looked down upon the girl lying peacefully in his arms in a sleep which even the camel's uncóuth procedure could not disturb.

Once more groaning bitterly his camel and Howesha grounded, which latter word describes best, in condensed form, the camel's method of lying down.

Out of one corner of her half-shut, insolent eye, the beautiful Taffadaln watched proceedings, and just as her master, holding Jill gently in his arms, was slipping from the saddle, with a positively fiendish squeal of triumph, and one gigantic effort which beat any record for swiftness established in any camel's family history, she rose suddenly, and rushing forward once more to the end of her lead, caused the black camel to fall sideways and the dismounting man to stumble, and in order to save her, to place Jill with distinct vigour upon the sand.

Not one syllable did he utter, not one line appeared on the perfectly calm face, as he raised the girl and carried her further from the camels, where she lay as still as though the angel Azrael [1] had separated her soul from her body.

Walking to Taffadaln he stood for some minutes absolutely motionless in contemplation, whilst the object of his thoughts, blissfully ignorant of what was in store, and because it suited her mood of the moment, came meekly to ground on the word of command.

---

1 Azrael — Angel of Death.

CHAPTER XVIII

I AM sure that those who read the following and know the East will say that I exaggerate, that under no circumstances or stress of emotion would an Arab so treat a camel, especially the most perfect of her species.

But against this wish to hurt must be weighed the love that consumed the man, a love mighty and sudden, and for the advent of which, and the enjoyment thereof, he had trained himself from his youth, abstaining from aught which might cause his perfect body to deteriorate, and all that which by satisfying the senses might dull his mind. A love, in fact, which, stronger than the wind of the hurricane, swifter than the raging torrent, swept all before it.

The Arab's love for his camel is a love of gratitude, for does not the Koran say, " And hath also provided you with tents and the skin of cattle, which ye find light to be removed on the day of your departure, and easy to be pitched on the day of your sitting down therein, and of their wool, and their fur, and of their hair, hath he supplied you with furniture and household stuff for a season." His love for his horse is a love of delight in her beauty, and her endurance and her swiftness, causing the master even at the point of death in battle to pour forth the praises of his mare, and with his last breath call aloud her pedigree to the lucky person to whom she falls as booty.

104

. But once let an Arab love a woman with the love which has nothing to do with the arranged marriage of his early youth, or his attraction to some beautiful face which causes him to take the possessor thereof to wife, of which Allah in his bounty allows him four, or his desire for some one of his concubines, to the number of which there is no limit; *then* I say will the love of sons, love of beast, and thought for all save his religion, go down before it as a young tree before the storm.

Hahmed the Arab loved the English girl with just such a love, also had she been hurt through the brutish manners of the animal, who had been expressly chosen for the honour of carrying her, therefore his love for his camel had turned to seething hate, and when that happens in the East, it is time to remove thyself, and that hastily.

Unfastening the lead from the pack camel, the man knotted it firmly to the back of her flat saddle, which usually makes the foundation for the animal's burden, then urging her to her feet led her in front of Taffadaln, who, a little at sea as to the proceedings, was marking time with her head. The same thing happened to the black animal, and then with a swiftness which thoroughly befogged the small brain of all this trouble, the leathered thong across her soft muzzle was tightened to the verge of cruelty, and the reins twisted twice round the back of the head, and then knotted to the leading reins fastened to the saddlebacks of her two inferior sisters.

"Thus will I show thee who is master, O! shrew!" observed her master, as he surveyed his handiwork.

" Thou wilt not walk, then shall thy sisters force thee
to run; thou wilt lie down, then shall they drag thee
until thy mouth runs blood.

" Behold hast thou brought misery to thy fair mistress, O! curse of camels, and for each moment that
thou shalt have lost unto her the shade of the palm
tree, for each moment shalt thou shed a drop of blood."

Howseha of her own free will scrambled to her feet,
whilst the Arab raised the girl, who, sunk in a sleep
resembling unconsciousness, took no heed of these untoward events, and placing her so that her head lay
softly against his shoulder, mounted his camel and
brought the animal to her feet.

The forcing to their feet of three camels by voice
persuasion alone is no mean performance, but no voice,
not even the vocal chords of the Archangel Gabriel,
would have moved the cause of all this pother, for at
the word of command, in a tone which should have put
fear of death into her black heart, she slightly shifted
her hind-quarters and lay still.

" So thou wilt not move, thou daughter of a desert
snail! Verily then shalt thou so remain!"

A sharp word, and the two upstanding camels moved
forward, coming to a standstill as they felt the weight
of their recumbent sister. There was then heard a
sharp swish, as the *courbaash* delicately flicked each
astounded quadruped, astounded indeed, for never had
they felt the like before, and be it confessed, never had
their master been possessed of such a fury.

Simultaneously they bounded forward, if so one can
describe their action, bringing a snarl of rage from the
unrepentant Desert Pearl. Straining and tugging,

with the whip constantly flicking and stinging, they slowly dragged Taffadaln over the sand, until gradually the agony of the tightening muzzle-thong cut not only into the flesh, but into the very soul of the rebellious camel queen.

Foam began to gather round the bruised mouth, dripping from the teeth only half closed by the leather strap; a drop of blood showed red near the corner, cut by the cruel knot, sweat poured from the silky coat as again and again she vainly tried to scramble to her feet, whilst the eyes of her master, ablaze with hate, watched her futile efforts.

Suddenly he halted the animals, and sat contemplating the beautiful Taffandaln, panting and moaning upon the sand.

"Get up!" he suddenly cried, with a ring of steel in the usually soft voice, and obediently the brute scrambled to her feet, leaving red patches where had rested her mouth.

"Now that I have almost broken thy neck, will I essay to break thy heart." In which endeavour the Arab entirely failed.[1]

"Thou wouldst halt, therefore shalt thou run!"

But Taffadaln was no fool, no, not one bit. For the first few yards, as her sisters raced ahead, she hung back, pulling on the blood covered thong, and tearing her tongue between her vicious teeth. Faster, and faster, sped the forerunners, and how fast that can be may only be understood by one who has pressed this swift moving animal's pace. Resisting less and less,

[1] Having four times successfully foaled a she-camel, Taffadaln, the Glory of the Desert, was ultimately shot on account of her demoniacal temper.

Taffadaln raced after, until the agony and outrage of
the proceedings suddenly drove her mad, and also to
her fastest speed, until with a positive shriek of hate
she rushed upon the pack camel, regardless of the
slackened reins which were like to trip her at every
step, a scream of agony announcing the fact that the
bloody teeth had met in the camel's side. "Allah!"
ejaculated Hahmed as again and again he struck at the
animal's infuriated face, when she turned her attention
to her black sister, whom she had the full intention of
savaging, what time the three were tearing like the
wind towards those palms under which figures in white
could easily be discerned.

Finding she was unable to wreak her vengeance with
her teeth, her crafty brain conceived the idea of harass-
ing her fleeing companions, to whom she was ignominiously fastened.

What were they but snails in speed compared to her,
and if she could not pass them for the bonds which
held her captive, she could at least urge them on until
they dropped from exhaustion. So into first one and
then the other she bumped, with an occasional nip at
the tails, whilst the air was rent with agonising shrieks,
through which tumult Jill slept sweetly upon the man's
heart, until at last they raced up to the caravan.

Many camels and four men watched the arrival, the
former grunting and groaning as they scented the trouble, the men calling upon Allah to witness the madness
which had befallen their master.

At the sight of the tents and the men who had tended
them from birth, Howesha and the black camel stopped
dead, but too terrified to pay heed to the voice that

bade them get down, stood literally shaking with fear, or wheeling sharply to dodge the gleaming teeth which seldom failed to leave their mark, until Howesha, in a moment of absolute terror, twisted and met *her* teeth in the upper portion of the back part of Taffadaln's hind-leg, of which there is no tenderer part in the camel's anatomy, following which action ensued a pitched battle.

With a scream, the rage-filled Taffadaln flung herself upon the two camels and then upon her master and she who lay in his arms and who was the real cause of this unseemly fracas. The Arab, essaying to hold the cloak around the girl, so as to save her from the insult of a man's gaze, struck again and again at the mouth which tore great pieces from his flowing robes, the girl's covering, and chunks of hair from the shrieking camel's body.

Blood and foam covered the animal's chest, the girl's cloak, and the garments of the men, who, on account of the inextricable knotting of the leads which bound the animals one to another, and the three sets of teeth which were snapping and tearing at everything within their reach, found themselves helpless to calm the tumult.

But suddenly there was peace, just as Jill opening her eyes murmured, "What a dreadful noise the sea is making," and closed them again. For the maker of sweet music, and head-tender of camels, had grasped the danger to his beloved master, also the disaster impending among the seething herd, who were all upon their feet and straining at their tethers.

Swiftly divesting himself of his long, white, outer

garment, he waved it in front of the Glory of the Desert, whose price was above rubies, and temper a direct gift from Eblis.[1]

To her everlasting undoing, she paused for one moment to stretch her neck at length and eye the new menace. A fatal delay in which the offending object lighted upon and around her head, shutting her completely into outer darkness, whereupon she stood like a lamb whilst hobbles were placed about her feet; after which the shade was lifted slightly, leaving the eyes covered, whilst the blood-soaked thong was cut away from the torn flesh, and a kind of leather cage slipped over the muzzle, which would certainly prevent her from biting, or indulging in her usual wide yawn of indifference.

The covering being lifted from her eyes, her bonds were undone, and herself likened by the maker of sweet music, unto all that the Koran calls unclean, even unto the vilest of the vile, the pig, into the company of which she was relegated for all eternity. She was then ordered to ground in a manner reminiscent of the tones used to bazaar dogs, which order was emphasised with a flick of the *courbaash* upon a part which had known the meeting of Howesha's teeth.

But when at sunset Jill opened her eyes all sounds and signs of battle were stilled.

[1] The devil.

CHAPTER XIX

THE sun was sinking when Jill moved, stretched a little, half opened her eyes, and closing them turned over and went to sleep again for about two minutes.

Then she half opened her eyes again, stretched out her hand to pull uncomprehendingly at the white netting round her bed, through which she could see a blaze of red, gold, and purple; and laughing in the vacant manner of the delirious, or those but half-awake, tried to collect her thoughts sufficiently to explain the strangeness of her surroundings, sitting up with a jerk as the doings of the last twenty-four hours suddenly stirred in her awakened mind.

Wide-eyed she sat with her hands clasped round her knees, whilst the deadly stillness seemed to rise as a wall around her, cutting her off from laughter, love, and life, until wild unreasoning fear, seizing her very soul, caused her to tear and rend the mosquito nets, and force a way through them and out of the tent.

For a while she stood holding to the tent rope, looking this way and that for the sign of some living thing. Before her stretched one vast plain of gravel, miles upon miles of it receding into nothingness, on each side the same, behind her tent above, the palm trees waving gently in the evening breeze, and above again, a sky such as is to be seen only in this part of the world, for travel you ever so widely, you will find nothing to rival a desert sunset in its design and colour.

Above her head seemed to be stretched a canopy, made by some Eastern magic, of a mixture of colours woven by the hands of Love and Hate, Passion and Revenge, underneath which she stood disheartened, dishevelled, in crumpled clothes and shoeless feet, with fear-distended eyes in a fatigue-shadowed face, searching vainly for something alive and near, be it human, dog, horse or camel.

Owing to a sudden nervous reaction brought about by the cessation of all physical and mental effort, the girl's power of reasoning had gone, along with her will, her common sense, and her fearlessness.

That there was another tent beside her own made no more impression on her mind than the fact that a slight smoke haze softened the intense blue of the sky on her right.

She was absolutely terrified and ravenously hungry, also unwashed, therefore altogether unhappy, so with no more ado she flung out her arms, and with a great sob rushed headlong into that which frightened her most, the unlimited, uninhabited desert.

Her shoeless feet made hardly a sound as she sped like a deer from the desolation she imagined, to the certain desolation and death in front of her, but she had hardly cut her little feet over more than twenty yards when Hahmed, the swiftest runner in Egypt, was speeding after her.

"Allah! Be merciful to me! For behold, I fail to keep from harm that which Thou hast placed in my keeping," he murmured, as he ran abreast with the girl for a few yards, then putting his arm around her lifted her off her feet, holding her gently to him, and

speaking no word until the paroxysm of sobs had subsided.

"Where to fly you, O! woman, and whyfore are
you thus afraid?"

"I was simply terrified. I — I — thought you had
left me all alone to die, and I just ran and ran to find
someone or something else beside myself in the desert,"
answered a voice, muffled by the snowy garments of the
man who held her so gently against his heavily beating
heart.

"I will take you back to your tent, to the bath and
repast which awaits you. I dared not loosen your raiment without your permission, so having removed the
shoes from off your feet, laid you upon your bed, but
when you are bathed, I pray you wrap yourself in the
soft garments you will find, and clapping your hands
make known to your slave that you are ready to eat."

"Oh, there *is* a servant to wait on me. I thought
we were quite alone."

"I am your slave," simply replied the Arab, as he
placed Jill upon her feet in front of her tent, where
she stood with her hand on his arm, rooted to the spot
by the glory of the sky, whilst the man gazed down
upon her, as the dying sun struck the gold of her hair,
the blue of her eyes, and the cream of her neck.

"You, who are of those who are versed in music,
and of those who can make poetry, describe that glory
to me," imperiously demanded Jill, after a moment of
silence, with that suddenness and complete change of
mood which falls occasionally upon all women, causing the meek to scratch like cats, and the strong to give
in, often to their everlasting undoing.

"Bathe the white body of thy beloved in the blue-green of Egypt's river, so that the coolness and fairness may give delight to thee! Drape the satin veil of deepest blue about the red glory of thy love's hair; and bind a band of gold, set deep in sapphires, above the twin pools of heaven, which are her eyes. Set turquoise, threaded with finest gold, a-swing in the rose-leaf of her ears, to fall and wind about the snow of her white neck.

"Fasten the blue flower which spies upon thee from the shelter of the golden corn, within the glory of her hair.

"Perfume her hair and her breasts, anoint her hands and her feet, and wrap they delight in a garment of passion, sparing not the shades therein, for in them shalt thou find thy delight.

"Let the garment be heavy with the gold of love, rich with the purples of passion, aflame with the crimson of thy desire, forgetting not the caress of the rose, nor the light mingling of opal and saffron, and the faint touch of amethyst and topaz, in which shall *she* find *her* delight.

"Bind thy love with the broad bands of the setting sun so that she cleaves unto thee, and carry her unto the twilight of thy tent, which shall slowly darken until the roof thereof is swathed in purple gloom, through which shall shine the stars of thy beloved.

"And there lie down in thy delight, until the hour of dawn calleth thee to prayer."

The voice was stilled, whereupon Jill lifted her face bathed in rosy colour, which might or might not have been the reflection from the sky, whilst her red mouth quivered ever so slightly, and her great blue eyes looked for a moment into those of the man, and as quickly looked away.

So seductive was she in her youth and utter helplessness that the man stepped back two paces, and saluting her for whom his whole being craved, gathered his cloak about him and departed to his tent.

And Jill also entered her tent, and having earlier and under the lash of terror departed therefrom in blind haste, stood amazed.

She had imagined a mattress, a rug, an earthenware basin on the ground, and sand over everything, and on the top of the sand scorpions, spiders, and all that creepeth and flieth both by day and by night. Not at all.

A carpet of many colours stretching to the corners of the desert tent, which is not peaked like the European affair, into which you crawl fearing to bring the whole concern about your ears, when if you should be over tall you hit the top with your head. It was as big as a fair-sized room, high enough for a man of over six feet to stand erect, not so broad as long, with sides which lifted according to the direction of the sun, and through the uplifted portion of which the faint delicious evening breeze blew refreshingly. A white enamelled bedstead covered in finest, whitest linen stood in the centre of the carpet, surrounded by a white net curtain hanging from the tent ceiling, each foot in a broad tin of water. In the corners were a canvas folding dressing-table, a full length mirror, a long chair and a smaller one, over which hung diaphanous garments of finest muslin, and a shimmering wrap of pearl white satin, and through a half-drawn curtain which hung across the narrower end of the tent, the vision of a big canvas bath filled with water, big white towels, and another canvas table upon which stood all the things necessary to a woman's toilet.

So that it was a very refreshed Jill who, wrapped in a loose Turkish bath-gown, with little feet thrust into heelless slippers, went in search of raiment. And wonderfully soft, simple things she found into which she slipped, and out of which she slipped again, holding them out at arm's length for inspection, then burying her face in the soft perfumed folds in very thankfulness.

And she laughed a delicious little laugh of pure glee as she replaced the garments on the chair, and slithering hither and thither in her unaccustomed footgear, tidied the tent and made her bed, regarding ruthfully the torn mosquito curtain.

"Oh, for a maid," she sighed, as she wrestled with the mattress, and "Oh, for dear Babette," she sighed again, as she wrestled with the masses of her hair.

And the tent was filled with a blaze of light, as, wrapped in her bath-gown, she stood in front of the steel mirror, plaiting and unplaiting, twisting and pinning her hair, until with an exclamation of impatience she let it all down, holding great strands out at arm's length, through which she passed the comb again and again, until the red-gold mass shone, and curled, and rippled about her like a cloak of satin.

It is hopeless to try and describe the shining, waving masses which curled round her knees, and fluttered in tendrils round her face, and it would have been hard to find anything anywhere so beautiful as Jill when, clad in the loose silk garment and soft satin wrapper, with her perfumed hair swirling about her, she stood entranced at the opening of her tent, until the sun suddenly disappearing left her in darkness, whereupon she clapped her hands quickly.

CHAPTER XX

JILL had finished the first of many evening meals she
was to partake of in the desert, and was lying on a
heap of cushions listening to the clink of brass coffee
utensils and porcelain cups, whilst sniffing apprecia-
tively the aroma of Eastern coffee Easternly made,
which is totally different to that which permeates the
dim recesses draped with tinselled dusty hangings, and
cluttered with Eastern stools and tables inlaid with
mother o' pearl made in Birmingham, in the ubiquitous
Oriental Café at which we meet the rest of us at eleven
o'clock on Saturday morning at the seaside; nor does
it resemble in the slightest that which is oilily poured
forth in London town by the fat, oily, so-called "Son
of the Crescent" who, wearing fez and baggy trousers,
in some caravanserai West, Sou'-west or Nor'-west, has
unfailingly been chief coffee-maker to the late Sultan,
vide anyway the hotel advertisements.

She was smiling as she lay stretched full length
with her chin in her palms, thinking of the meal just
eaten. Whilst waiting for it she had imagined a mess
of pottage perhaps, or stewed kid as *pièce de résistance,*
with honey or manna as sweets, and a savoury of fried
locusts, which she, with many others, imagined to be
the all-devouring insect. She knew by now, and returned thanks, that the man neither ate with his mouth
open nor gave precedence to his fingers and teeth over

knives and forks, but in her wildest dreams she had never imagined that such exquisite things, served in such an exquisite way, could be laid before her in a desert.

When the light had suddenly closed down upon the two adventurers on the Road of Life, she had been led to the tent adjoining hers, a sudden shyness preventing her from asking where the Arab slept, which she found alight with the soft glow of many candles, and spread with a carpet upon which were many cushions. The table had certainly been the ground, but everything upon it had been of the daintiest, and all that she had eaten, although she had had no notion of what it had consisted, might have been the outcome of some *cordon bleu's* genius.

"Our life is one long picnic," had replied the Arab to her question anent the cooking facilities in waste places. "So why should we not all, high and low born, learn to make the picnic pleasant, for behold, we know not what a day may bring forth, nor in what place the night shall find us."

And Jill came quite suddenly out of her reverie when asked if she would like to go outside for coffee and cigarettes. "For though the moon in her youth has gone early to bed, the stars are shining like your eyes."

"Oh," said she, as she got into a half-sitting position, "I thought we should have to pack up; it's late already, isn't it?"

"You are tired from unaccustomed travelling, and your limbs must ache, therefore if it pleases you we will wait until to-morrow night, so that with many baths and much refreshing sleep you will feel glad to mount your camel, who is not the begotten daughter of sin, Taffadaln, and come still further into the desert."

So Jill went outside the tent and looked up to the blazing stars, and the soft wind blew her hair so that a burnished red-gold perfumed strand fell across the man's mouth, and behold he trembled, for great was his desire, but greater still his love for this woman.

And when she sat down upon the cushions he stood apart and watched her, until a little hand, like a white moth fluttering in the dark, beckoned him, and he moved towards her and sat at her feet; and the wind whispered to the palms and the hours fled as the English girl lay on the cushions and listened, and she had learnt of many things before she rose and passed into her tent to sleep again.

Hahmed was of Southern Arabia, and therefore with truth could claim direct descent from Kahtan. He was the first-born of the great Sheik el Has'ad, his father, and his favourite wife who, on her marriage, besides much wealth, had brought a dowry of purest blood, and wonderful beauty, to her lord and master, so that the man who sat at the English girl's feet under the stars, and who trembled at her nearness was *pur sang,* and further than that you cannot go.

Worshipped by his father, idolised by his mother, at the age of ten he had been betrothed to the daughter, aged seven, of the Sheik el Baujad. She was also *pur sang,* and already of looks promising great beauty.

And so he had grown in the warmth of his parents' love, trained in what we call outdoor sports, but which are life itself to the Arab, until at fourteen no one could surpasse him in running or horsemanship or spear-throwing, whilst with rifle or revolver he could clip the hair off the top of a man's head, the which strenuous accomplishments he balanced in passing his leisure moments in the gentle arts of verse-making and even music, in spite of the latter being condemned by religion; also did he learn to converse in foreign tongues. Do not think that these qualifications were enumerated with the zest and glorification which usually precede the distribution of dull books at a prize-giving, for the man might have been talking of the sunshine or the sand or the flies or any other part of that which goes to the making up of Egypt, rather than that which had helped to make him the finest man in the country.

And yet another trait which he touched upon lightly, and which had served to make him the subject of comment in the bazaars, and of gossip in the harems.

In regard to his womenfolk there is no man sterner the world over than the Mohammedan, shielding them from harm, and insisting on the absolute privacy of their lives and their bodies. Upon just this subject, from the first day of his understanding, Hahmed the Arab was stern to fanaticism, intolerant even to injustice. He disapproved of licence in all things, but especially in speech, food, and religion. When forced by circumstances, he went to the feasts to which he was invited, eating sparingly as was his wont, taking no more interest in the more or less clothed dancing women than in a set of performing dogs, departing thankfully when the hour came.

Let me recount, in his own words, the happenings of his youth, which served to change the whole tenor of

his life, and was to culminate in the high adventure
of an English girl.

"At the age of fourteen I was to marry and was
content, for the desires of my own woman had come
upon me, and I longed to possess the beauty of which
my mother told me, and which, save for her father,
had been seen by no man.

"My own woman I desired, I say, for bought women
were not for me, and I had refrained therefrom, therefore was I unsoiled at the time of my wedding.

"True my marriage had naught to do with my horoscope cast at birth, for it had been read that water
would bring me joy, and water would bring me grief,
and that water again would bring me everlasting happiness, so I thought with others that it had lied, and
was amazed.

"But behold, when after great festival and feasting
my bride was in the care of her handmaidens who
prepared her for my coming, one came, and casting
herself at my feet, covered her head in dust, begging
a word with me.

"It seemed she was a master in the art of tinting
the fingers the pink which we Arabs love.

"I thought she had a boon to crave so listened to
her, but when she told her news I took her by the
throat to strangle her, but in choking breath she vowed
the great vow, therefore I listened again, and though
I were like to die of shame I took counsel with her,
asking her the price of her information, whereupon she
merely muttered ' revenge,' and showed her breast which
was a festering sore caused by the boiling water which

her mistress had flung upon her when the scissors had proved over sharp.

"Whereupon I withdrew the handmaidens from the beautiful Zuleikha with the exception of one, cross-bred of French and Tunisian, who, though of passing beauty, scorned all men, it seemed, and passed her days in waiting upon the whims of her mistress, and tending to the beauties of her body.

"I know not how far the women of the West are versed in the knowledge of evil, therefore will I speak in words that are veiled. Be it that I — I, Hahmed, the son of my great father, demeaned myself to spy between the perfumed curtains of my bride's chamber, to witness the passionate farewells of the two beautiful women. Allah! That such things should be. Tears streamed down the cheeks of she who was to share my couch, as the slave, the unclean half-caste, beat her breast in her despair, and letting loose the strands of thick black hair which covered her to the knees, knotted it around until it covered, as a mantle, the body of she who had been anointed for my pleasure.

"And then I tore down the curtains and strode in upon them, bound one to another in their disgrace, and clapping my hands brought eight women as witnesses to my shame. And still bound with the thongs of hair I threw the sinners naked across my horse, and made my way to the woman's house, and before a great assembly, for behold, the guests had not yet departed, I flung them at the feet of the woman's father, and calling my witnesses spake my tale. And when I had finished, the wailing of grief was heard in the land. And then they were unbound and brought before me, and the half-caste mocked me. Me! Until I took her hair within my hands and twisting it about her neck, stopped her speech for ever, and when she fell dead, Zuleika my wife, Allah! hear me, my wife! screamed in terror, for I ordered my slaves to seize her. And then the Sheik el Baujad, her father, pronounced judgment, quoting from the Koran as is written in the second verse of the 24th Sura.

" ' Shall you scourge with a hundred stripes, and let not compassion towards them prevent you from executing the judgment of God, if ye believe in God, and the last day.'

" And to the scourging was added the punishment' of death, for behold, the Moslem law is less lenient than the Holy Book, also of such a case is it not written in the Koran. And Zuleika, my wife, was bound naked to a pillar and scourged with a hundred stripes. And the city in which had taken place the marriage, and in which both her father and my father had great property being built upon flat ground, there was, therefore, no height from which to throw her, neither well in which to fling her without fear of polluting the water, for time, alas, is making us softer towards misdeeds, so that such places of punishment are disappearing quickly."

Hahmed the Arab stopped short as with a little rustling sound Jill raised herself to her knees, her hair sweeping to the satin cushion, her hands stretched before her face as though to blind her eyes to the word-picture which the man was painting in a perfectly indifferent voice.

"How awful! How awful!" she whispered. "Surely, surely you never let them *kill* her!"

For a moment the Arab sat silent, as he forced his mind to an understanding of the Western outlook upon what to him was so simple a matter.

"But she was unchaste, woman, therefore there was nothing else to do!"

And at the tone of finality in the gentle voice, Jill sat back on her heels and said, "And then?" and listened without interrupting until the tale was done.

"So," continued Hahmed, "she was taken screaming to a public spot and there buried to her waist, and after that her mother had thrown the first stone, was put to death by men and women who, following the edicts of the Moslem law, meted out death by stoning to the unchaste. And from that day I fled my country and my home. East and West I travelled, passing many moons in England, hence it is that I can converse with you in your own language.

"There are many good things in your country and there are some bad, the greatest of the latter, to an Eastern mind, being the freedom of the women, who, even in their youth, go half-naked to the festival, so that all men, yea, even to the slaves who serve at table, may cast their eye of desire upon wife, or wife to be, taking from the husband the privilege of possessing all the beauty of the woman for himself. Also did I see the women of the West go down to the salt waters to bathe. Naked were they save for a covering which

clung as closely as the skin to a peach, so that if I
had had a mind I could have discoursed upon the
comeliness of the wife of el Jones, or the poor land
belonging to el Smith.   Allah! I remember well a
bride-to-be of seventeen summers, comely in her outer
raiment, displaying to her future husband, without hesitation, the poor harvest of which he would shortly be
the reaper, for I think that the majority of the women
of the West strive not to render themselves beautiful,
develop not the portion of the body which maybe lacks
contour from birth, bathes not her body in perfumed
waters, feeds not her skin with delicious unguents,
cares not if her hair reaches in wisps to her shoulders,
or falls below her waist as a natural covering under
which she may hide at the approach of her master,
neither does she daily perfume it, nor her hands, nor
her feet, nor any part of her."

Once again Jill snapped the story thread, but this
time with laughter, for her mind's eye, aided by her
companion's scathing comments, had called up picture
after picture of friends and acquaintances who, at
balls, theatres, or by the sea, had draped themselves
or not according to what they imagined to be their
menfolk's outlook upon life.

"How funny!" she laughed, "how too funny!"
And added: "And then?" as she lit another cigarette which she did not smoke.

"For many years," continued Hahmed, "I wandered, even unto Asia and to America. In truth whilst
there the desert suddenly called me. My body craved
for the sun, my eyes for the great distances of the
sand, my ears for the familiar sounds of the East.

"But I could not return to the place of my shame, likewise were my parents dead, leaving me an equal part of their great wealth.

"So I went to other parts and bought 'the flat oasis' as it is called, on account of the many miles of perfectly flat sand surrounding it, absolutely unbroken by rock or bush or sand-dune. And perforce because I needed it not I acquired wealth, and yet more wealth, buying villages and great tracts of ground, breeding and selling camels and horses, diverting myself with my hawks, hunting with my cheetahs, or greyhounds, to occupy my time, heaping up the jewels in my bank at Cairo, keeping the best of everything for my wife, the woman predicted in my horoscope, for there can be no real happiness without a perfect helpmate, and real happiness has been promised me.

"And all these things I have done for her, yet am I looked upon as mad by many in that at twenty-eight years I have not begotten me a son, for they could not understand the disgust which had taken root in my whole being, so that in love or passion or desire I laid not hands upon women.

"You cannot understand, woman of the West, what it means when I say this to you, for in the East a man's greatest desire is to propagate his race, to have sons, many sons, with a daughter or two, or more as Allah wills, and to satisfy this longing in the shadow of the law, Allah, who is God, in His all-powerful goodness and bounty has allowed us as many as four wives, and as many women slaves or concubines as a man can properly and with decency provide for, the children of the latter, if recognised by the father,

sharing equally with the offspring of the former.
Though why a man who has found his love should
wish to cumber his house with other women, seething
with jealousy and peevish from want of occupation,
is beyond my power of comprehension.

"So I have none, because it is within me to love
one woman only, and to find the light of my life in
her and the children of her loins, and if Allah in his
wisdom sees not good to grant me this woman, who
must come to me of her own free-will and love, then
will I go to my grave in Allah's time without wife,
without child, although the Koran sayeth that he who
fails in his duty towards his race is accursed among
men."

And behold, a great trembling fell upon the English girl, as rising to her feet she stood to look out upon
the desert, and drawing the glory of her hair about
her so that she was covered from the gaze of the man
who stood apart, passed into her tent.

And the hour of prayer being at hand the man puri-
fied himself, and turning towards Mecca praised his
God, and divesting himself of his outer raiment laid
himself across the entrance of the woman's tent so
as to guard her through her sleep, until such time that
Allah, who is God, should open the entrance of her
chamber unto him, and place the delights thereof into
his hands for ever.

CHAPTER XXI

AND the first day was like unto the second and the third, for these two desert farers went but slowly.

Each dawn, if they had travelled in the night, they found their tents pitched; each night they moved on, or not, as pleased the girl's mood, each hour of the day strengthening the love in the man's soul, each minute of the night passing over him, as he lay outside the entrance to her tent, so that, at the slightest sound from the dim, sweet, scented interior, he might spring to his feet, awaiting the little call for help which never came. Jill slept as peacefully as a babe, stirring only at a dreamed of, or imagined, swaying of the bed, as does the seafarer sometimes who sleeps for the first time after many months upon a bed, the four feet of which stand firmly on the ground.

During the waking moments after her first night's rest, uninitiated Jill had in imagination gone through and ardently disliked the frightful hour in which she would help collect, and clean, and pack a litter of soiled pots and pans, and other such abominations, which collecting, etc., seems to constitute one of the chief charms of a Western picnic; so great had been her relief on hearing that there was absolutely nothing to do but to see that the cushions and coffee were safely strapped upon Howesha's back, the only patient part of the animal. They were standing in front of the tents with the animals at their feet, the man watching the girl's every movement. Jill herself, being vastly rested, was absolutely radiant as to looks; strange dishes and hot winds and cold causing no havoc to the skin, nor the lack of Marcel methods unsightliness to her hair.

The dusk hid the dilapidation of her tailor-made, which looked the fresher for being pressed under the mattress; she always travelled boot-trees, so her shoes were all right, and the two Jacob's ladders, falling on the outside of her stockings, looked just like clocks neatly mended; her lovely hair rioted under her blue hat, and her high spirits rioted in her blue eyes, as she fed the camels with dates and wiped her sticky fingers on the silken coats.

"What!" she had exclaimed. "You don't mean to say that you are going to leave all this for the first thief to collect," withdrawing as she spoke her basket of dates from the vicinity of her new camel's mouth.

Verily, a beast of great beauty and worth was she, but shining as a mere rushlight, in comparison to the Blériot head-light radiance of the fallen Taffadaln.

"The Arab does not steal!"

"Oh! but ——" said Jill, putting a date into her own mouth by mistake, and therefore speaking with difficulty, "but they do steal, and murder, and do all kinds of *dreadful* things like that — I learnt it all in school!"

"No," reiterated the man calmly, "the Arab does *not* steal, he merely carries out the order of Allah, who, when Abraham turned his son Ishmael from his door, gave unto the boy the open plains and deserts as a heritage, permitting him to take and make use of whatever he could find therein.

"And as it is written that every hand was turned against Ishmael, so his descendants turn their hand against the descendants of those who persecuted the son of Abraham; but amongst their own tribe, or to those who ask of their hospitality, you will find the greatest honesty.

"In a camp everything is left unguarded, and nothing goes astray. If you, clothed in fine linen and arrayed in jewels, were to enter the tent of some half-starving Arab, and ask of him hospitality, he would share his last few coffee beans with you, and give you his couch, if by chance he was possessed of such a luxury, and speed you on your way the morrow, and believe me, you would not find a ribbon missing from your attire, even though you had left him without the wherewith to make his beloved coffee."

The girl laughed, for she really cared not a rap either way, and was only arguing for the sake of drawing the man out, having found argument the best and simplest method of breaking through the Eastern reserve, up against which she had more than once found herself during the last few days.

"Well! I call that splitting hairs. I really can't say I see that the persecution of Ishmael makes stealing different from stealing; to my mind, taking sugar from a bowl that is not yours, and diamonds that are not yours from a safe, are one and the same thing, as both ornamental and necessary booty belong to some one else."

"And yet," replied the Eastern, "in the West a man who cheats at cards is damned everlastingly, but a nation is acclaimed who takes the land with all its

wealth from some wretched, half-educated native; takes
it by force of arms or diplomacy, which, nine times out
of ten, means trickery. Yes! Acclaimed with such
adjectives as valiant, strong, beneficent, applauded to
the skies, whilst reams are written anent the glorious,
victorious campaign. Victorious! Allah! When the
nation goes out with artillery and unlimited forces to
meet a handful of men, whose strength lies in a spear,
and pride in some dozen flintlocks, which have been
sold to the benighted heathen for solid gold or shining
lengths of purest ivory.

"Besides, the Arab requires 'what he gains,' as is
his way of expressing himself. No people on earth
endure such hardships as this my people; never enough
to eat, burnt in the summer, frozen in the winter, buried
in sand, tortured with thirst, fleeing from place to place,
never at peace, yet always happy in his miserable tent.

"For the *gazu* or raid on caravan or camp, which
will yield booty of horse, or camel, or women — well!
that is in the blood, and both sides are prepared. If
you or they should have the better horses, or the better
cunning, both of which we of the East so dearly love,
one can hardly be expected to sympathise with those
who lose from want of forethought."

And as he spoke, he raised a light spear, which he
held in his hand, and drove it through one edge of the
tent flap which covered the entrance, deep into the sand.

"That is a sign that I am coming back, and believe
me, the worst of Arabs would pass this way and seeing
the sign would leave my belongings unmolested. Yes!
even if many moons passed, until the skins had rotted,
and the sands had covered the rotted remains."

After which explanation, Jill remained silent for a
space, and then approached her camel, feeling that the
rapping of her knuckles, however slight, had been quite
unwarranted, for her sympathy in human beings and
their feelings was great, and the understanding which
kept her from wounding the sensibilities of those humans even greater.

Her wish to draw out the man had caused her figura-
tive feet to make a *faux pas,* in fact she felt that her
pedestal had tilted ever so slightly, causing the drapery
of decency, and courtesy, to swing aside for one moment, exposing a particle of clay upon the ivory of
her beautiful feet to the eyes of the man whose outlook
on life was so broad, whose principles were so stern,
and whose people she had so rudely criticised. Therefore she was dissatisfied with herself. Though, if she
had known it, the man looked upon her with the same
solicitude and tenderness, as you or I would look upon
the babe, who, in its first efforts to get from table to
chair, pulls the table-cloth about its unsteady little feet.

Also sensing that the woman he loved was troubled,
there was no gladness in the heart of the Arab, so that,
in his anxiety to remove the pebble from the path, he
approached her, as she stood with skirt lifted in readiness to mount her recumbent camel, whereupon she
looked up at the grave face and apologised truly and
sweetly, and by her sweet and humble act, causing the
man of the East to marvel at her strength, and to salaam
deeply before her as he accounted himself as the sand
beneath her little feet.

" Now wait a moment! " laughed Jill, whose worries
disappeared beneath the warmth of her happy nature

with the vanishing celerity of the dew beneath the sun. "I am going to try my hand with the camels. I really have a good deal of influence over animals — domesticated ones, I mean —— Oh! Yes! I suppose they are, but of course in England we don't have them hanging around as we do horses and dogs, you know. I don't like cats, however — I simply can't stand the way they look past and through you, at the spirits I always think, which we humans cannot see standing beside us.

"I had one once, I found her in the picture gallery one night, who positively made me creep. She would get up suddenly from the fire and go sidling and wriggling across the room in the most absurd fashion, purring and simply confused with delight, to rub herself up and down the empty air, and by the way her tail was flattened down and then shot up again, I was positive she was being stroked. She almost lived in the picture gallery, sitting staring at the pictures of an ancestor of mine, who had the most *frightful* reputation.

"The worst of it all was that the whole village began to suffer from catalepsy as Dads said, and then it all got into the newspapers, and occult societies camped at the gates, water diviners drilled on the lawns, the *Merry Harvester* was filled with 'ologists hailing from this country, and some genuine catamaniacs, until I had the bright idea of fastening a placard on the gates to say that the cat was dead, though she had suddenly disappeared the night the picture of the ancestress fell, owing *honestly* to a faulty plug in the wall. Now! let me try and see if my knowledge of the Arabian tongue is good enough to be understood by the camel."

Lowering her voice a tone, she suddenly cried "Get up!"

Whereupon the animal rose clumsily to its feet, as the girl, laughing aloud, clung to the man's arm.

"Oh," she cried, "did you ever know anything so funny, though why, I am sure I can't say — fancy a *camel* obeying me."

"Get down!" she suddenly ordered in her sweet, broken Arabic, at which the camel knelt, leaving the Arab astounded, for the beautiful, lazy woman of the East troubles not her soul in the training of beasts, nor has she any command over them.

Having mounted and got the three animals to their feet, Jill laughed delightedly, announcing her intention of starting the trio and leading them for a short space, to which the man, craving to satisfy the slightest wish, consented, fastening the pack camel to the off-side of Jill's beast, so that she should be in the middle, upon which they started off triumphantly, leaving the tent to the stars and moon.

For an hour they travelled over the sand, covered in patches with low shrubs, and broken here and there by sand dunes, until Jill suddenly stopped her chattering and pointed.

"There's a caravan or something over there, and we seem to be heading straight for it — it's — yes — it's a tent under some palms — why! Yes — no! yes it is — oh, it's our tent — how *can* it be our tent when we have been going straight ahead all the time, haven't we?"

Without the glimmer of a smile, the Arab shook his head.

"We have been describing a circle ever since we started."

"But no!" argued the girl, who was half mortified, half ready to laugh, "there is no left rein, and I left the right one hanging ——"

"Yes, but quite unconsciously you kicked your camel with your left foot when we were some way from the tent — you didn't notice, but she immediatly began to turn to the left; after that, you patted her continually on the left side, and camels, who, from pure stupidity or hereditary instinct, will go straight on to eternity untouched, are trained to turn in the direction of the side touched by hand, foot, or whip; the single rein is of very little use, and hardly ever used by a native, for once a camel bolts, nothing will stop him, excepting a cloth flung over his head, or the birth of some passing fancy in his head, which serves to divert the evil tenor of his benighted brain. And I defy any-one unused to the desert and its markings to know if they are really going straight or in a circle, and you were too taken up to notice the stars. Try again! Keep that red star straight ahead, those two close together, just behind your right shoulder, and you will unfailingly reach the so-called mountain, in the shadow of which we shall find our tent."

And the maker of sweet music bowed low from afar, and salaamed with fervour, when, just before the hour of dawn, three camels came to a halt, and knelt on the word of command of this veiled woman, who spoke his language sweetly, but as a stranger.

CHAPTER XXII

FEW have or ever will make use of the route which the Arab was explaining by means of a sharp stick and a flat stretch of sand. And in truth 'twere wise to leave it to those who are born of the desert, for even if ignoring the danger signals of her cumbersome covering, the body, the soul should urge the would-be traveller to tread the unknown path, he will, if he sets foot thereon, find the discomforts out of all proportion to the interesting dangers.

'Twere best to eschew it, keeping to the normal route of boat or rail; even if the soul of the desert, wrapt in mystic garments, stands with plump, henna-tipped, beckoning forefinger; for she is but a lying jade, outcome of some digestive upheaval; the spirit of the sand, the scorpions and the stars, beckoning to but the very few, and baring herself to none; though the wind may lift her robes of saffron, brown and purple, revealing for one sharp second the figure slim to gauntness, and blow the thick, coarse black hair from before her face, exposing those eyes of different colouring, and flaming mouth, luring to kisses, which will steep the mind in intoxication, and rasp the lips with stinging particles of burning sand. No! take rather the boat from the round ring, which the Arab drew in the sand, christening it Ismailiah; whereupon Jill got up from her place in the moon, and crossing over to the man, crouched down beside him, the better to view the map, taking it for an offering of prayer, when the sweetness of her breath, and the savour of her perfume, assailing the man's nostrils, he suddenly raised his hands to the starry heavens, praying to Allah to give him strength.

The stick starting from the ring christened Ismailiah turned slightly to the West and continued in a line which curved at every inch.

" I haven't the vaguest idea where we are," remarked Jill, as she took a proffered cigarette, and proceeded to blow smoke rings in the still night, from a mouth contracted until it looked like one of those little leather jug purses, whilst her head, thrown back, showed the beauty of her bare throat. "Are we going towards Cairo ? "

" Nay, woman! Having crossed the fertile land, outcome of the fresh water canal at Ismailiah, we continned to the West for a space, and then came South, winding in and out so as to miss the higher hills and sand dunes.

" To-morrow we pass through the mountains of the Jebel Aweibid range, and find the Haj road, which, glory to Allah, will be free of pilgrims until next moon. That road we will follow as far as the fertility of Airud, passing that spot afar off, as even in this month caravans will congregate there; then crossing the canal a space higher than Suez, where crowds embark and disembark, we will pick up the Haj road on the far side, making use of it to pass through the Jebel Rabah range, leaving it, once through, to strike to the East, and find our way at last to the peace of my own habitation."

Upon which explanation Jill sat back on her heels, and wrinkled her brow.

"But surely the *easiest* way would have been by *boat* to Suez!"

"True, O! woman, whose eyes ringed with the shadows of fatigue are as blue flowers growing in the mountain's purple shade. I pondered long before I made decision in my choice of roads. Upon the one we traverse, you could but meet fatigue, and in this month, but few travellers upon the way that leads to Mecca.

"Upon the boat you would have met many of your land, friends maybe, who perchance would have turned upon you the eyes of suspicion, the shoulder cold with disdainful convention, whilst their tongue, more poisonous even than the forked tip of the *cerastes cornutus*,[1] might, nay, *would,* have striven to corrupt your mind with a festering mass of doubt and suspicion and misgiving. Therefore have I brought you on this journey, which is so much longer, and is likely to kill you with fatigue. Verily, for behold the half is not yet accomplished."

Jill, who had unconsciously taken the sharp stick from the Arab, and had also, unconsciously, been drawing monstrous beasts in the sand, lifted her head and made a slight grimace.

"Oh! but you will kill me, you will really! And to think that I thought you lived quite near Cairo! Where *are* we going *really?*"

And Hahmed, overcome by an almost irresistible longing to take the girl in his arms and hold her close against all dangers and discomforts, suddenly rose to his feet, standing towering over her, and when she held out both her hands, asking to be helped up, leant down

[1] The most poisonous snake in Egypt.

and raised her as lightly as though she were of thistle's down.

Then there came about one of those pauses which sometimes do come to pass between man and woman, a pause in which, as there is no midway, either much is won or lost.

As still as a mouse, Jill lay in his arms, until he very gently set her upon her feet; and though a little ripple akin to disappointment disturbed the smooth surface of her content, she said " Thank you," and smiled sweetly into the grave face which showed no sign of a pulse disturbed by a thudding heart. And then Jill sat down again upon her cushions, drawing her knees up under her chin and clasping them with her hands, and the shadow of the man falling upon her, left her well content, and still more content did she feel when he stretched himself full length beside her and continued speaking.

" Where are we going? Oh woman, who has placed her hand in mine, we journey to my own country, unto the desert of Arabia, until we shall come to the place which was mine, but now is yours. Although, verily, it is unworthy of your eyes, you will bear with it for a few moons, until a habitation worthy of your beauty is erected. Nay, as oasis, it is not over large, but it is fertile beyond thought. Many have essayed to steal it by force of arms, or buy it, but I prevailed through the magic of much wealth and the virtue of patience. I bought it bit by bit from those who owned it, and now they rent it from me — I did not want their money, but I desired to make the ground productive and the people happy.

" The grain plains require good workmen, also my date groves, my paddocks, and stables for camels and horses. The fruit and vegetables and other produce, which were once mine and now are yours, are cultivated and tended by some hundreds of especially trained men, who, with their wives and numerous offspring, live in the shadow of the acacia, loving, quarrelling, hating, dying, but always happy. My own habitation is in the shade of the palms, removed from the unseemly wailing of children and barking of dogs, and as I have told you, no woman has placed foot therein, save for the hunchback. Verily the flat oasis is unique in the desert annals, and to bring unto perfection requires but a son to take on the work, when these mine hands are clasped in the handshake of death."

But those very hands showed no sign of their master's desire to close them upon those clasped whitely round the girl's knees, neither did his voice portray the desire of possession raging within him as he continued speaking.

" If later you should desire to travel, then shall the boats, the cars which were mine, but are now yours, be at your disposal, so that in comfort shall your journey be made, wiping out the bitter memory of this your first."

But there was no doubt about it that Jill was suffering acutely from a cumulative fatigue, engendered by the unaccustomed mode of travelling, the intense heat through which she essayed to sleep during the day, the biting cold at night, when the temperature fell many degrees, as is its agonising wont in that part of the world, the strain of the mind as it valiantly essayed to accustom itself to the new way of everything; but above all, the inability to change her under raiment, which, strive against it as she would, managed to conceal particles of sand and insects, which, though they did not bite, crawled most successfully and irritatingly.

So that as in a dream she passed down the Haj road to the water, with a vague recollection of a few wayfarers and beggars squatting on the roadside, many men who salaamed with fervour at the water's edge; a boat, a quick passage, and more of those who salaamed, and a three days' rest, when the tents were pitched on' the near side of the mountains. Three days in which she slept, and slept, and slept, rising to bathe and eat, grateful to the man who spoke only when she asked a question, and who, though sign of servant there was none, forestalled her every unuttered wish. Then followed they the Haj road through the mountains and left it to take a line in the Eastern direction, which they also followed until the hour when the Arab called his camels to a halt, and pointing straight ahead, exclaimed:

"Behold, woman, your land!"

Upon which Jill strained her eyes in vain, for her untrained sight revealed nothing but sand, and yet more sand.

"Yonder lies the oasis, O! woman of the West, and beneath the star of happiness the dwelling which will serve to throw a shadow upon your path in the heat of the day, and from the roof of which you may watch the changing of the moon, and learn the way of the Eastern stars, whilst listening to the million voices of the desert night."

The girl made no reply, neither did she turn to look at the man.

There was no sound save for an occasional grunt of satisfaction from one or other of the beasts, who sensed their home and the termination of their labour.

There was nothing to break the silence, and nothing to break the never-ending stretches of sand, as the two, caught in the inevitable fingers of Fate, sat motionless, looking ahead beyond the oasis, beyond the stars, to the moment when the first wind blew a particle of sand to find its mate, with which to multiply and form the desert, the birthplace and burial ground of so many; whilst gnarled hands playing with Life's shuttlecock drew a golden thread to a brown, proceeding to weave them in and out with the blood-red silk of the pomegranate, the orange of the setting sun, the silver of the rising moon, and the purples of the bougainvillæa, until upon the background of dull greys and saffrons appeared an amazing pattern of that which is called Love.

And suddenly the girl looked up into the man's face, and stretching out her hand spake softly, calling upon him by name, so that his heart quaked within him, and his being was suffused with love.

"Hahmed! O! Hahmed! Is it happiness?"

And Hahmed the Arab, raising his right hand, called heaven to witness.

"As Allah is above us, O woman, it is happiness. Glory be to Him Whose prophet is Mohammed."

CHAPTER XXIII

LITTLE by little the face of the desert began to change, just as changes the face of a fainted woman, which, drawn and grey and pinched about the mouth, starts to relax and fill out and to colour faintly, when life begins to return to the limp form. Rough shrubs grew in patches, giving way to rough grass growing about the roots of short trees. A clump of palms and then another, a mimosa tree scenting the air from its diminutive yellow lanterns, and then great stretches of land, some light with the grain silvered by the waning moon, some dark from the plough's drastic hand, undivided by hedge or wall, yet as evenly marked out as a chess-board, reminding Jill of a very great patchwork quilt held together by some invisible featherstitching.

Her questions fell like rain, and in them the man seemed to find great joy. That was an artesian well, and this a grove of Tailik dates. Yes! the rivulet which would sing her to sleep on its way through the sand was a very bounteous spring, more precious than gold or jewels, holding only a second place to Allah, Whose prophet is Mohammed, in the esteem of the fellaheen, but being a playful spring, almost disappearing at one moment to gush out the next, artesian wells had been made so that the oasis should not depend solely upon her caprices, though, be it confessed, she had bubbled and laughed her way contentedly

144

through many years, and had even deigned to widen into a diminutive lake, which lay between the principal dwelling-place, which contained the sleeping apartments and living rooms of the master, and the house which had been built on the same principle for the innumerable guests, and the quarters, hidden from view by a belt of palms, in which such servants as were necessary to the well-being of the house cooked and worked and entertained such wayfarers as were of their own station.

Many figures had seemingly sprung from nowhere at the sound of the padded feet, which were only prevented from breaking into a swift trot by the voice of the man who guided them.

These figures had salaamed deeply, and lifted up their hands to the starry heavens as though to call down a blessing upon the heads of those who passed, but they had not approached until the Arab suddenly cried aloud a name, whereupon a figure, standing apart, had sped quickly forward, salaamed, listened to his master's words, and had sped away as silently as a panther, as swiftly as a deer.

"Your runner, O! woman, who, after your slave, is the swiftest in all Asia and Africa. If ever you would speak with me, and I were perchance afar off, bid that man to your presence, give him your message in script or word of mouth, and say but, ' Thy master — Cairo,' or wherever I might sojourn, and he will find me, over desert sands or mountain range; he would die for me, and therefore he would die for you.

"We approach the grounds around your dwelling, may it find favour in your eyes."

Gradually the grass had deepened and softened, until like a velvet carpet it lay spread. Great groves of dates threw ink-black shadows, slender palms with feathery heads swayed slightly in the dawn-coming wind, when suddenly of their own accord the camels stopped.

To right and left as far as the dim light allowed, Jill saw what looked to her like an impenetrable wall.

" This is the dividing line, a high wall with its nakedness covered in creepers, which separates your dwelling from the land upon which common feet may tread. No one can pass without the permission of Mustapha, the blackest of all black negroes; no one can leave, not even my guests, unless they are accompanied by some one of the servants of my house. Thus will you be safe in the care of black Mustapha, even if I should be called to a distance from which I cannot guard you from harm. Enter, O! woman, and may the blessing of Allah fall upon you, even as the petals of the purple flower will fall upon your head."

And they fell in showers from the purple bougainvillæa which trailed its length over the wrought arch above the gate, of which one half swung back by the hand of the biggest, blackest man ever dreamed of in nightmarious slumber.

"Master! Master!" cried the product of Africa, and, prostrating himself, flung the desert sand upon his woolly pate; then rising, ran towards the man who owned him, lifting the black cloak to his huge mouth through which scintillated white, unblemished ivories.

The Arab stretched out his hand, and laying it upon the girl's cloak spake but one word, upon which the negro once more prostrated himself before Jill's camel.

covering his already sandy hair with yet more glistening particles, murmuring something unintelligible, until a sharp word brought him to his feet, whereupon
he backed towards the gates, flinging them wide apart,
falling upon his knees as the camels stalked disdainfully through the opening.

Through a long avenue of trees they passed, the
trunks twisted into uncouth shapes, the heads of long
spear-shaped leaves glistening as though drenched in
dew, the roots buried in masses of flowering shrubs,
behind all of which showed an occasional glint of distant water.

The camels made their sedate way across a great
plain of grass, stretching without a break from the
avenue up to a belt of palms, before which they stopped,
swayed a moment, grunting disapprovingly in chorus,
and knelt.

"Your journey's end is here, and even though it
should prove the last effort of your will to combat
the fatigue which surely crushes your slight form, yet
will I ask you to give me your hand so that I may lead
you to your dwelling, as by the will of Allah I will
lead you slowly or quickly to that which we call happiness."

And as he spoke the Arab slipped from his camel,
to stand tall and straight beside the little figure en-
veloped from head to foot in a long dark veil, from out
of the folds of which stretched a little hand, pulling the
flimsy covering from the lower part of the face.

"Nay, that you must not do, for behold! although
you see them not the tenders of my camels hover
around, waiting till we have passed on to fall upon

those three beasts and lead them to their stables.
Come!"

The silence was intense between the two as Jill, with
her hand in that of the Arab, passed slowly over the
grass up to a long, low, two-storeyed house which, with
two wings, made a quadrangle round a great court, in
the middle of which splashed a fountain. A multitude
of figures stood absolutely motionless under the palms
surrounding the house, who, even as the two passed,
with one accord, called aloud as they raised their right
hands to heaven:

"Allah — Jal-Jelalah!" which, being translated,
means: "Praise to God the Almighty!" disappearing on a sign from their master as he turned to explain to Jill that this being his first visit in six months,
his servants, with twenty-four weeks of grievances and
domestic feud upon their minds, and a near prospect
of being able to unburden themselves, were doubtlessly
delighted to see their master.

Jill passed into the house too dazed to notice much
of her surroundings, heard the swish of silk curtains
closing behind her, and stood alone in a most exquisite
room.

Six lamps, hung from the ceiling by bronze chains,
threw a shaded light upon the soft-toned Persian rugs
covering the floor; a divan piled high with silken cushions of every shade of mauve, covered with silken
sheets, and smothered in the white folds of a mosquito
net, stood against the far wall; there were small inlaid
tables, piles of cushions, and a dressing-table glittering with crystal and silver in the light of the lamps,
and a small fire which flung out sweet resinous odours

from the burning logs; stretching right across one
wall, a low cupboard showed gleaming satins and soft
silks behind its open doors, and through an archway
of fretted cedar-wood she saw a Roman bath of tiles,
into which you enter by descending shallow steps, and
over which hung a lamp with glass shade of many
colours. Little white tables smothered in towels and
bottles and little pots stood about, and across a low
seat was thrown a garment of shimmering gold and
silver cobwebby tissue. Dusty, tired Jill stretched out
her arms, opened the cupboard doors wider, and in-
spected the garments therein one by one.

And she frowned.

A net had been spun in which she had been caught,
her silly ears had listened to an absurd tale, she had
stretched out a greedy hand to . pluck an unknown
fruit to find it bitter; in one brief word she had been
fooled. Whereupon she pulled back the silken curtain
of the door with a vicious rasp, which seemed to have
spread to her voice when she called aloud. The curtain swung back as the Arab entered, murmuring the
Eastern prayer of greeting, and though furious, and
therefore ripe to cut and hurt with woman's weapon,
the tongue, the girl stood still and silent for a moment,
instinctively feeling that tale or no tale, net or no,
the great man before her was master here, though
no one would have guessed at her momentary weakness as she flung open the cupboard doors to their
widest, and taking an armful of soft feminine attire,
held them out for the inspection of the grave Arab,
whilst her voice rang through the room, giving exactly
the same impression of trouble as does the wind which,

springing from nowhere, usually precedes the storm.

"You said no woman save an old peasant had ever placed foot within this house. If so, what do these Eastern things mean?" holding out as she spoke a feminine something which seemed to be composed of sea-form and pearls.

"For myself I only see a few bedroom wraps, and — and a garment in — in the bathroom."

And her heart suddenly stopped a beat, and then made the blank up by multiplying the next, for she had seen the man's face as he had taken the offending garment, and tearing it across and again across, dropped it at his feet, before he moved slowly towards her across the dividing space to take her two hands in his, holding them against his breast in a clasp that hurt.

"Listen," he said. "I shall speak this once and never again! Listen!" For a moment the quiet voice stopped, so that the gentle cracking of the burning logs could alone be heard above the heavy thud of the girl's heart, which to her ears sounded like thunder of the surf at dawn. "You are *mine, mine,* do you understand? You are no silly child, you knew what you were doing when you came with me, neither am I a man, for man or woman to play with. And now I have you, as Allah is above us, I will never let you go, for although the oasis and the camels and horses are yours, you will find no soul to lead the beast across the sands so covered with the bleaching bones of those who have gone astray. Oh! be not afraid," for the little face beneath his was white. "You are mistress here. You need but draw the curtain and no one will enter, no one until you clap your hands and *call them*

by name. You will forgive the lowly room which en-
tours you, and the unseemly garments which in haste
I ordered, guessing at what you might require. To-
morrow you shall order what you will, and your slaves
shall bring all from the great cities at the greatest
speed, for as I have said, a dwelling worthy of your
bèauty shall be erected before many moons have sped.
I will leave you, for doubtless you would remove your
dust-laden raiment. I will send your slave, who even
now is returning thanks to Allah in that I have found
her worthy to wait upon you, and who also prepares
some dishes for your refreshment. You are not hungry, and you do not wish her presence! Then shall
she not disturb you."

And Jill found herself alone, upon which she took
stock of herself in a long mirror which stretched from
floor to ceiling, and hurriedly removed her outer garments.

CHAPTER XXIV

IT was a very beautiful girl who stood by the fire listening to the intense silence which precedes the dawn. The golden shimmering garment fell from her shoulders in soft folds, clinging here and there as though it loved the beautiful form it covered; her feet slipped in and out of the golden *mules,* in which, try as she would, she could not walk; her hair fell in two great plaits far below her knees; she was perfumed with the perfumes of Egypt, than which there is no more to say.

And she was afraid.

There was absolutely no sound, save for the fall of a charred log which sounded like a pistol shot, the rustle of her raiment, which sounded like the incoming tide of some invisible sea, and the quick intake of her breath, which might have meant unadulterated terror, and — did.

She shivered slightly, for of a sudden she saw a woman's face in a corner unreached by the light of the lamp. A long brown hand drew back the coarse hair, which curled and tangled under a veil, black brows frowned down on great eyes, which looked at her steadily, but the mouth, crimson as blood, parted in a smile wonderful to behold in its understanding, as Jill called softly:

" Speak, woman! who are you ? "

But when the silence remained unbroken, and the girl, rushing swiftly across the room, touched just ordinary wood, she looked quickly round for escape; then hesitating, raised her hands and clapped them softly; raised them again when the silence remained unbroken, dropped them and once more shook with terror, which was really fatigue, when a something rustled behind, being in truth the catching of her garment on the fretted edge of a table; then once more she clapped her hands as she whispered, so low that the words hardly seemed to carry beyond the firelight:

" Hahmed !   Hahmed ! "

Whereupon there was a faint rustle, the swinging to and fro of the curtain door, and the man stood before her. Not a sound broke the stillness, not a movement caused a flicker to the flame of the shaded hanging lamp, which, just above the girl's head, threw down the light on the radiance of her hair, and the wonder of her body which the diaphanous garment half concealed and half revealed.

Not a sign on the Arab's face, this dweller of the desert, whose forefathers in wonderment had watched the ways of wisdom with which Solomon in all his glory had ruled more than one fair and obstreperous woman among the scented Eastern sands.

Face to face they stood, whilst the racing blood fled from the girl's face down to the finger-tips of her contradictory hands. The hands she knew so well, the square back, the square finger-tips, the long, square, high-mooned, deeply laid nail. Hands which, coming to her down the centuries through Quaker and through Puritan, were calling to her to stand firm and hold the scales well-balanced, whilst the soft, rounded palm, hidden in the golden fringe of her garment, and the over-sensitive finger-tips, with little nerve-filled cushions at the end of each, clamoured aloud for beauty and sweetness, tenderness and mastery, as the great man, with the beads of Allah slipping noiselessly through his fingers, reading the girl's thoughts as though they were written on the wall, marked and watched with sombre eyes in the breathless silence of the coming dawn.

Slowly the girl raised her eyes and scanned the man, from the snow-white turban on the dark head, the softness of the silken shirt, showing through the long, open, orange satin front of the voluminous coat, which reached almost to the ankles, leaving exposed the trousers of softest white linen, fastened close above the leather shoes, whilst quite subconsciously she wondered what he would look like in European evening dress.

Slowly she stretched out her long thin arms, until they almost touched the golden embroidery on the coat, as slowly she turned her hands, and looked at the glittering nails, the hands she knew and feared so much, and turning them back again, with a little smile drew a finger-tip over the hills and valleys of the palms. Higher still, until the pink and scented palms were on a line with the man's stern mouth, whilst a sigh, faint as the passing of a fly's wing, left his lips, as taking the little hands in his, he drew the girl closer yet.

"Behold,' you are beautiful, O! woman, whom I would take to wife. You start! Why! For what manner of man have you taken me? Did you think

that being an Arab means being without honour? Nay!
When my eyes fell upon you standing in the sun, I
knew that my heart had found its desire, that the
woman who for all these years had, invisible to others,
walked beside me in my waking hours, and hovered
near me in my dreams, had come to life; that before
me, if Allah willed, stood my wife and the mother of
my children. I know that the English race, from lack
of sun perchance, love not in a moment with a love
that can outlast eternity. I do not ask you if you love
me, only that you will be my wife, honouring me above
all men, delighting me with such moments as you can
give me.

"Listen, O! woman. I ask of you nothing until you
shall love me. You shall draw the curtains of your
apartment, and until you call me, you shall go undisturbed. *When* you shall call me — then — ah!" and
his voice sank to infinite depths of tenderness as he
drew her to him —" then you will be all mine — all —
lily of the night you are now — rose of the morning you
will be then, and I — I will wear that rose upon my
heart. You are even as a necklace of rich jewels, O!
my beloved. Your eyes are the turquoise, your teeth
are the white pearls, even as the ravishing marks upon
your face,[1] and may be upon that part of your body
upon which my eyes may not rest, are as black pearls
of the rarest. Your lips are redder than rubies, and
your fingers are of ivory.

"And one day shall that necklace be placed in my
hands, and not alone the necklace, but the white ala-

[1] Moles are considered a great beauty among the Egyptian
races.

baster pillar of your body, from your feet like lotus flowers, to the golden rain of your hair, shall you be mine.

"And you shall not make me wait too long, for behold, I love you. Allah! how I love you — as only we men of the desert love. Allah help me," and holding the girl in the bend of his left arm, so that she felt the racing of his heart, he raised his eyes and right hand to Heaven. "Allah! God of all, give me this rose soon!"

For one long moment the girl was still, with face as white as death, and great eyes troubled even as the ocean when swept by gusts of wind; for to the very depths of her stirred her heritage of tremendous passions, untouched, unknown, whilst that which is in all women, from queen to coster, coming down from the day when they were slaves, that which urges them to cry aloud, "Master! Master!" upon their bended knees, stirred not at all; so that even as her eyes, so was her soul troubled, knowing that love had not yet laid hand to draw the curtains from about her womanhood.

Freeing herself gently, she moved towards the fire, trailing the golden raiment after her so that it pulled against the beauty of her body. For a moment she stood unconsciously silhouetted against the wall, virginal in her whiteness and her slimness, and yet, in her build alone, giving such promise of greater beauty, in the maturity of love.

Slowly, whilst her mind worked, she traced the blue vein from her wrist up her forearm, up until the finger stopped suddenly, upon a tiny mark tattooed just above the elbow.

A faint shadow of incomprehension swept across the man's face, for from nowhere, in one brief instant, a little wind, laden with straying particles of fear, distrust and memories, swept between the two, as the girl's voice, biting in its coldness, searing great scars upon the Arab's raging, storming, totally hidden pride, let fall slowly, cruelly, light-spoken, mocking words of French.

"Please tell me my woman's name, so that I may call her, for I would disrobe, being overcome by a great desire to — sleep!"

CHAPTER XXV

THE sun in a great red-gold ball was slipping behind
the sharp edge of sand which like a steel wire marked
the far horizon, the sky resembling some gorgeous
Eastern mantle stretched red and orange and purple
from the West, fastened by one enormous scintillating
diamond star to the pink, grey, fawn and faintest heliotrope shroud which the dying day was wrapping around
her in the East.

Terrific had been the heat throughout the month,
wilting the palms, drawing iridescent vapours from the
diminished stream, making the very sand too hot even
for native feet.

The green reed blinds sheltering the great balcony
room, and over which, in the heat of the day, trickled
a continuous stream of water, were drawn up to allow
the sunset breeze to pass right through the long two-
storeyed building which, the essence of coolness, comfort, and beauty, in the past months by the efforts
of countless skilled workmen, hailing from every conceivable corner of Asia and Egypt, and regardless of
expense and labour, had been built for one beautiful
English girl, who, in a moment of ever regretted contrariness, had refused to participate in the planning
and devising of the work, thereby shutting herself off
from that most fascinating pastime, house-building;
leaving everything down to the minutest details to the
imagination, ingenuity, and inventive genius of the

Arab. For months she had listened to the monotonous chant of the men at work, the tap of hammer, swish of saw, and dull thud of machinery, and also to the grunting and grumbling of the camels who, in great caravans from every point of the compass, had complainingly brought their burdens of riches.

The groves of great date palms around her temporary abode had prevented her from seeing the outcome of all the noise, her misplaced pride or temper, or whatever you will, likewise preventing her from inquiring as to the progress made from the Arab, who, at her bidding, would come and sit with her, talking gravely upon absolutely indifferent subjects, neither showing by word or gesture if she were any more to him than the rug beneath his feet.

Just a month ago, when the moon was at the full, Jill had made what she whimsically called the moonlight flitting.

Veiled closely, she had put her hand into that of the man, and confidingly walked with him through the pitch blackness of the palm groves, and out into the moon-filled space beyond the lake, until they reached and stopped before a heavy iron door let into a massive wall, the top of which bore a crown of flashing, razor-edged, needle-pointed steel blades.

"The treasure of the world will be safe behind those walls, for behold, there are but two golden keys with which to open the door, one is yours the other mine. To Mustapha has been confided the safe-keeping of the walls, and with it power to kill whoever should approach within ten yards without your permit."

And the girl turned quickly as the door swung to

softly, with the scarcely perceptible click of a lock, **and**
then moved forward with as much indifference as **she**
could muster on the spur of the moment, feeling **the**
eyes of the Arab upon her.   Gardens stretched before
her with groves, and arbours, and every device conceivable for throwing shade upon her path.   The
stream, bending in an S, rippled and laughed its way
under the little bridges; fountains splashed, seats of
marble, seats of scented wood, little tables, silken awn-
ings and screens, hanging lanterns of many colours,
and swinging hammocks made of the place a fairyland;
until suddenly, as she turned the last curve of the
stream, she saw the marble building, built as it were
by the waving of a magic wand, glistening in the silver
light.

Imagine four buildings about the height of Buck-
ingham Palace, without the attic windows, or whatever
they represent, built to form a square of snow-white
gleaming marble, with verandahs built out and supported by fairy marble pillars, so as to throw the lower
rooms into complete shade; more fairy pillars springing from the upper side of the verandahs to support
the wide edge of the roof, and so make a great covered-
in balcony to the second floor.

The French windows, divided by columns of different coloured marble, terminated in perfect arches,
studded with great lumps of uncut amethyst, turquoise
matrix, and blocks of quartz in which dully gleamed the
yellow of gold, reminding Jill somewhat of the outer
decorations of a shop she had once seen in the Nevski
Prospekt, the owner of which, dealing in *objets d'arts,*

and precious bibelots of jade and sich, had quite successfully thought out the novel and expensive advertis-
ing method of plastering the front of his shop with
chunks of the precious metal with which the bibelots
were made. The drops of a myriad slender fountain
jets, caught in the light of the hanging lanterns, sparkled and flashed like handfuls of precious stones, and an
almost overpowering perfume filled the air from flowers
only half-asleep.

A great gate of silver and bronze opened silently to
admit them to the inner courtyard, only the rolling,
glistening eyeballs of Mustapha, the eunuch, showing
that there was any life whatever in the massive black
hulk standing within the shadow.

Just for a moment the girl stood absolutely motionless, and then turned sharply as a noiseless shape stole
past her, and purring loudly rose on its hind feet and
laid its velvety paws upon the Arab's shoulder, dropping back in a crouching position as Jill, exclaiming
softly, involuntarily stepped forward and laid her hand
protectingly upon the man's arms.

It takes a long time to write, but hardly a second
had passed before the great animal, snarling viciously,
shot out its velvety paw, plus a row of steel-strong
claws, and ripped the girl's cloak open from neck to
knee. And then indeed did black Mustapha rise to
the occasion, and in his master's esteem, as also without a sound he shot out an ebony black arm, gnarled
and knotted like any centuries old bough of oak,
terminating in an ebony black hand, which could have
easily been divided between four normal men, and

still left a bit over, and picking up the fighting, claw-
ing animal by the neck, held it lightly at arm's length,
whilst awaiting dumbly his master's order.

"Kill it," said Hahmed briefly.

And whilst Jill pinched herself to see if she was
really there or no, the eunuch, with joy-filled eye, and
teeth glistening in a smile of utter satisfaction, gently
tightened his grip on the velvety, tawny throat.

There was a stifled growl, a click, and the dead animal was laid at the girl's slender feet.

"My favourite hunting cheetah, O! woman! Behold, Mustapha, shalt thou spread the news of its un-
timely end as a warning to all those who, by sign of
hand or word of mouth or thought of brain, should
desire to do harm to thy mistress. And even shalt
thou tell me how yon dead beast came to be prowling
in the seclusion of thy mistress's abode."

Great beads of perspiration broke out on the face
and neck of the scared man, as he salaamed deeply
before his master, and knelt to beat his forehead upon
the ground before the woman.

"Behold, O! master! And may Allah grant me
years of life within the blessing of thy shadow. A
slave returning from the exercising and feeding of
four, O! master, of thy hunting cheetahs, came to me
this noon full of idle curiosity. Behold, I spoke with
him outside the open gate, and perchance yon dead
brute crept in unnoticed, whilst I pointed out the evil
of his ways and those of his ancestors; also, perchance
fatigued and full of meat, the animal lay down and
slept until she heard the tread of thy honoured footsteps; perchance also thy slave, fatigued and also full

of meat, passing the hours in slumber, troubled not to count the animals in his care."

For one moment there was silence as the Arab stood looking at the trembling man, then Jill, laying her little hand gently upon the satin sleeve of him whom she loved, whispered softly:

"A boon, O! Hahmed! I know — I *feel* that you are planning the death of this wretched man. I ask his life!"

By this time Mustapha was prone upon his face, piling imaginary dust from the spotless mosaic pavement upon his woolly pate, scrambling to his shaking knees on a word from his master.

"Get to thy feet and make obeisance to thy mistress, who in her manifold bounty has saved this time thy worthless life. For behold, I had planned to give my people a holiday in which to see thee whipped round the wall of thy mistress's dwelling, until thou had died; then would thy black skin have been ripped from thy worthless carcass, and pinned to the ground before the camel paddock, so that in their goings in and coming out they would have befouled what remained of thee uneaten by the vultures."

And taking Jill's hand he crossed the square, leaving the eunuch absolutely gibbering with relief.

Through a massive iron door they passed into the house, Jill exclaiming softly at the beauty of the place. Room after room they traversed until they came to a standstill before a satin curtain. Hahmed lifted it and Jill entered a great room, the floor of which was of pink marble, covered in Persian rugs, their colouring softened in the passing of many, oh! many moons;

the walls panelled in soft brocade, and great mirrors reflecting the simplicity of the exquisite hangings, the tint of flowers, the statuary gleaming half hidden in the corners, the great chairs, the piles of cushions, and the swinging lamps suspended from the ceiling by silver chains.

"I will explain, O! woman, how this house has been built, though verily would I have had your help in these past months, for how was I to know in what or which your desires lay.

"Behold, the rooms upon the level of the ground are rooms for your repasts, and rooms for receiving your guests; above are the rooms for your slumber, and your toilet, for the bathing of your white body, and for your entertainment. In the latter you will find all that appertains to music, to the dance, to the study of books, to the flash of the needle. Above again are the rooms open to the breezes of the night, screened by light screens to enable you, unveiled, to look out upon the world, and yet keep you hidden from the curious eyes of your many slaves who, under the rule of black Mustapha, live within the walls and near to hand to do your slightest bidding, but hidden until you call so as not to disturb you by their unseemly presence. They may not die within the wall, neither may they give birth therein, still less may they make merry without your permission. The slightest breach of your laws will see them flogged to death and cast out into the desert sand. One suite of rooms is pink, and one white, and one is palest heliotrope, and yet another black, and there are many others. May it find favour in your eyes. If perchance it pleases not, then shall it be razed to the ground, and rebuilt upon your design."

And Jill had walked through a building such as she had not dreamed of in her wildest fantasies, and having very sweetly thanked the Arab, had clapped her hands, and being of perverse mood, had indifferently bidden him good night, and entered the rose pink sleeping-room where the couch had been designed by love, and the colouring reflected by the great mirrors by passion; to slip from out her perfumed raiment, and step down into the pink marble Roman bath and hide beneath the rose-tinted waters, the rose-tinted glory of her perfect body.

CHAPTER XXVI

AND just as the dead cheetah was laid at Jill's feet, a huge bull dog, with a face like a gargoyle to be seen on the Western transept of Notre-Dame, and a chest like a steel safe, supported on legs which had given way under the weight, walked across from Sir John Wetherbourne, Bart., of Bourne Manor, and other delectable mansions, to lay his snuffling, stertorous self at the feet of his mistress, the Honourable Mary Bingham, pronounced Beam, in whose sanctum sat the man on the bleak November evening, and of whom he had just asked advice.

People always asked advice of Mary, she was of that kind. On this occasion she sat looking across at the man she loved, and had always loved, just as he loved and had always lover her, since the days they had more or less successfully followed the hounds on fat ponies. She sat meditatively twisting a heavy signet ring up and down her little finger. *The* finger, the one which advises the world of the fact that some man in it has singled you out of the ruck as being fit for the honour of wifehood, was unadorned, showing neither the jewels which betoken the drawn-up contract, nor the pure gold which denotes the contract fulfilled. Those two had grown up in the knowledge that they would some time marry, though never a word had been uttered, and being sure and certain of each other, they

had never worried, or forced the pace. And then Jill
had disappeared! Gone was their pal, their little sister whom they had petted and spoiled from the day she
too had appeared on a fat pony, gone without a trace,
leaving these two honest souls, in a sudden unnecessary
burst of altruism, to come to a mutual, unspoken understanding that their love must be laid aside in folds
of soft tissue, that they must turn the key upon their
treasure, until such time as definite news of the lost
girl should allow them to bring it out with decency,
and deck it with orange blossom. And worry having
entered upon them, they both suddenly discovered that
uncertainty is a never-failing aperitif, and they both
hungered for a care-free hour like unto those they had
carelessly let slip.

Foolish perhaps, but they loved Jill, making of themselves brother and sister; hurt to the quick when after
the *débâcle* she had sweetly declined all offers of help,
and worried to death when she had started out on the
hare-brained scheme of earning her own living off her
own bat.

Mary Bingham was one of those delightful women
peculiar to England, restful to look at, restful to know.
Her thick, glossy brown hair was coiled neatly in plaits,
no matter what the fashion; her skin, devoid of powder, did not shine, even on the hottest day; her smile
was a benison, and her teeth and horsemanship perfect.

Her clothes? Well, she was tailor-made, which
means that near a horse she beat other women to a
frazzle, but on a parquet floor, covered with dainty,
wispy, fox-trotting damsels, she showed up like a double magenta-coloured dahlia in a bed of anemones.

Jack Wetherbourne was of the same comfortable and honest type, and they loved each other in a tailor-made way; one of those tailor-mades of the best tweed, which, cut without distinctive style, is warranted with an occasioual visit to the cleaners to last out its wearer; a garment you can always reply on, and be sure of finding ready for use, no matter how long you have kept it hidden in your old oak chest, or your three-ply wardrobe, or whatever kind of cupboard you may have managed to make out of your life. Although no word of love had ever passed between them, you would have sworn they had been married for years, as they sat on each side of the fire; Mary in a black demi-toilette, cut low at the neck, which does not mean décolleté by any means, but which *does* invariably spell dowdiness, and Jack Wetherbourne with his chin in his hand, and a distinct frown on his usually undisturbed countenance.

A great fire crackled in the old-fashioned grate, the flames jumping from one bit of wood to another, throwing shadows through the comfortable room, and drawing dull lustre from the highly polished floor and Jacobean furniture. It was an extraordinarily restful room for a woman, for with the exception of a few hunting pictures in heavy frames on the wall, a few hunting trophies on solid tables, some books and a big box of chocolates, there were no feminine fripperies, no photographs, nothing with a ribbon attachment, no bits of silver and egg-shell china.

Oh! But the room was typical of the Honourable Mary Bingham, into whose capable hands had slipped the reins controlling the big estate bounded on **one** side by that of the man opposite her.

"There is only one more thing I can suggest," said the deep, clear voice, "and that is that you go over to Egypt yourself. Who knows if you might not pick up a clue. Detectives have failed, though I think we made a mistake in employing English ones, they hardly seem tactful or subtle enough for the East."

Certainly one would have hardly applied either adjective to Detective John Gibbs, who, bull-necked and blustering, had pushed and bullied his way through Egypt's principal cities in search of Jill.

"How like Jill not to have sent us a line," remarked Jack Wetherbourne for the hundredth time as he lit a cigarette.

"Oh, but as I have said before, she may have had sunstroke, and lost her memory, or have been stolen and put away in a harem. She's not dead, that's certain, because she had her hand told before she left on her last trip, and she's to live to over eighty."

"That's splendid," was Wetherbourne's serious answer to a serious statement, as he rose on the entry of Lady Bingham, who, having at the same moment finished her knitting wool and the short commons of consecutive thought of which she was capable, had meandered in on gossip bent, looking quickly and furtively from one to the other for signs of an understanding which would join the estates in matrimony, a pact upon which her heart was set. And seeing none, she sat down with an irritated rustle, which gathered in intensity until it developed into a storm of expostulating petulance when she heard of the proposed programme.

On the stroke of eleven Mary got up and walked

down the broad staircase, and through the great hall, and out on to the steps beside the very splendid man beside her, and they stood under the moon, whilst a nightingale bubbled for a moment, and *yet* they were silent.

"Dear old girl," said Jack Wetherbourne, as he pushed open the little gate in the wall which divided their lands, and waved his hand in the direction of the old Tudor house.

"Dear old Jack," murmured Mary as her capable hand reached for a chocolate as she sat on the window-seat and waited until she heard the faint click of the gate, upon which she waved her handkerchief.

Prosaic sayings, prosaic doings, but those three prosaic words meant as much, and a good deal more to *them,* than the most exquisite poetical outburst, written or uttered, since the world began, might mean to *us.*

CHAPTER XXVII

By degrees Jill had become accustomed to the habits of the East, sleeping peacefully upon the cushion-laden perfumed divan, sitting upon cushions beside the snow-white napery spread upon the floor for meals, eating the curiously attractive Eastern dishes without a single pang for eggs and bacon and golden marmalade, revelling in her Eastern garments, from the ethereal under raiment to the soft loose trousers clasped above her slender ankles by jewel-studded anklets, delighting in the flowing cloaks and veils and over-robes and short jackets of every conceivable texture, shape, and colour, passing hours in designing wondrous garments, which in an incredibly short time she would find in the scented cupboards of her dressing-rooms.

Then would she attire herself therein, and stand before her mirror laughing in genuine amusement at the perfect Eastern picture reflected, and drawing the veil over her sunny head, and the yashmak to beneath her eyes, and a cloak about her body, would summon the Arab to her presence.

Which shows that knowing nothing whatever about the Eastern character, she merely added a hundredfold to her attractions, for if there is one thing a man of the East has brought to perfection, it is his enjoyment of procrastinating in his love-making, passing hours and days and weeks, even months in touching the edge of the cup, until the moment comes when raising it to his lips, he drains it to the last drop.

To keep herself physically fit she had found strenuous recreation in two ways. Firstly, she had made known that her wish was to learn something of the dancing of the East, whereupon for a sum which would have made Pavlova's slender feet tingle in astonishment, the finest dancer in all Egypt and Asia had, for many months, taken up her abode in the beautiful house especially built for honoured guests just without the wall.

The supple, passionate Eastern woman found it in her soul to love the slender white girl who laughed aloud in glee, and showed such amazing aptitude in learning the A.B.C. of this language, especially reserved in the East for the portrayal of the history of love and all its kin. Presents were showered upon the teacher who, with the craft of the Oriental mind, in some cases forbore to fully explain the meaning of certain gestures, so that unintentionally a veritable lightning flash of passion blazed about Jill's head one night, when with the innocent desire of showing the Arab how well she was progressing in the art, she suddenly stood up before him and made a slight movement of her body, holding the slender white arms rigidly to her side, whilst her small, rose-tinted right foot tapped the ground impatiently.

"Allah!" had suddenly exclaimed the Arab, as he had seized her arms and pulled her towards him. "You would mock me, make fun of me, you woman of ice!

"How dare you make me see a picture of you in —

ah! but I cannot speak of it in words, suffice that one day I will — Allah! you — you dare to mock me with a picture of that which you refuse me ——! "

" I haven't the faintest idea of what you are talking about," had replied a very ruffled Jill, as with golden anklets softly clinking she withdrew to a distance. " If that is the effect of my dancing I will never dance for you, *never!* "

"But, woman, do you mean to tell me that you have no idea of the translation put upon your movements? "

" Evidently not," haughtily replied the inwardly laughing girl.

" That you do not know the movement you made just now meant that in the dimness of the night I — oh! I cannot tell you, but I swear before Allah that *I — I,* Hahmed, who have known no woman, will teach you the translation of every movement of all that you have learned."

Whereupon Jill, having seated herself upon the stuffed head of an enormous lion skin, murmured " *soit,*" and proceeded to light a cigarette.

Her second and favourite pastime was riding, and in as few words as possible, so that my book shall not ramble to unseemly length, I will tell you how the fame of her horsemanship had come to be spoken of, even in the almost untrodden corners of Asia and Egypt.

The whim seizing her, she would bid the Arab to her presence, sometimes to her evening repast, sometimes to sweet coffee and still sweeter music, sometimes to wander on foot or on camel-back through the oasis, to the desert stretching like a great sea beyond, and still beyond.

Everything, as you will note if you have the patience to get through to the end of this book, happened to Jill in the light of the full moon. On this night in question, clad all in black, with the moonbeams striking rays from the silver embroidered on her veil, and the anklets above her little feet, she seemed small and fragile, altogether desirable, and infinitely to be protected to the man beside her on the edge of the sand. Still more so when she waxed ecstatic with delight on the approach of two horses, one bay ridden by a man clothed from head to foot in white burnous, and a led mare as white as the man's raiment.

"Hahmed! O! Hahmed! Stop them!" had she cried, forgetting the ice out of which she had elected to hack herself a pedestal. "Oh, you beauty, you priceless thing!" she continued, when the mare, whinnying gently, rubbed its muzzle on her shoulder; whereupon she took the rein from the servant who had dismounted, and led the beast up and down.

Perfect she stood, the Breeze of the Desert, with her flowing tail high set, her streaming mane, the little ears so close together as to almost touch, her great chest, and dainty hoofs which scarcely deigned to touch the sand.

Bit and bridle she had none, her sole harness consisting of a halter with a leather rein on the right side, and a rug upon her back hardly kept in place by a loose girth. It seemed that she was of the Al Hamsa, which, being translated, means being a direct descendant of one of the five great mares of the time of Mohammed; also she was a two-year-old and playful but not over friendly, therefore was it astounding to see her as she listened to the girl's musical voice, and showed no fretfulness at the touch of a strange hand.

And then there was a quick run, a cry, and a rush of tearing hoofs! For Jill, in the twinkling of a star, had let fall the enveloping cloak, standing for one second like some exotic bit of statuary in her black billowing satin trousers and infinitesimal coatee over a silver-spangled frothy vest, her great eyes dancing with glee over the face veil. She had swiftly backed a few yards, and before either man or horse had guessed her intention, with a quick run and a full grasp of the great mane had swung herself into the native saddle, and was away over the desert to wherever the horse listed. Neither was there a second lost before the bay was racing after the mare; and Jill, riding with the loose seat of the native, turned and waved hilariously to Hahmed as he tore like the wind beside her, shouting something she could not distinguish in the rush of the air past her face.

Half-frightened, half-maddened by her own tremendous pace, the Breeze of the Desert laid herself out to beat all speed records.

Mile after mile flew under her dainty feet, whilst Jill by little cries urged her still faster yet, the all-enduring bay keeping alongside without any apparent effort, until at last the Arab, leaning forward, struck the mare lightly upon the left side of the neck, whereupon without slackening speed she turned instinctively in that direction, turning a little each time she felt the light touch, until Jill at last perceived the outline of the oasis and the figure of the Arab servant standing with folded arms awaiting the return of his beloved horses or not, as should be the will of Allah; being, however, shaken from his native calm when this woman when some hundreds of yards from him in a straight line, without stopping the speed of the racing horse, suddenly slipped from the saddle, remaining upon her feet without a tremor, whilst the "Breeze" stopped of her own free-will within a few feet of her attendant.

"And our master whom Allah protect," as recounted the native afterwards to an astonished, almost unbelieving bevy of listeners, "bringing his horse in a circle, suddenly picked up that woman rider. Yea! I tell thee, thou disbelieving son of a different coloured horse, a woman-rider, even she for whom the palace has been built; and swinging her across the saddle so that her feet, as small as thine are big, thou grandchild of a reptile with poisonous tongue, as I say her little feet hung down on one side, and her head, and may Allah protect me from the wrath of my master if I say that it was as the sun in all its glory, hanging down on the other, dashed into the night with her, but *where* it is not meet for me to know."

The "where," as it happened, being Jill's palace, in which, lying full length upon a white divan, with a small brazier of sweet smelling incense sending up spirals of blue haze around her dishevelled head, and an ivory tray laden with coffee and sweetmeats at her side, she promised never to run the risk of getting lost in the desert again, on condition that the Breeze of the Desert became her own property, and that she could ride untroubled whenever and wherever she liked; cheerfully promising also to have made a habit, or rather riding-dress, which would combine the utility of the West with the protective covering properties of the East. After which she got to her feet, standing the very essence of youth and strength in the soft glow of the lamps, smiled into the Arab's stern face with a look in the great eyes which caused his mouth to tighten like a steel trap, clapped her hands and disappeared through a curtain-shrouded door without even looking back.

CHAPTER XXVIII

THE recounting of which true episode has taken me from the evening when the sun had just slipped behind the edge of sand.

Jill sat motionless in a corner of her beautiful room, with a pucker of dissatisfaction on her forehead.

Jill, the girl who only a few moons back had taken the reins of her life into her own hands, and had tangled them into a knot which her henna-tipped fingers seemed unable to unravel. English books, magazines, papers lay on tables, the latest music was stacked on a grand piano, great flowering plants filling the air with heavy scent stood in every corner, the pearls around her neck were worth a king's ransom, the sweetmeats on a filigree stand looked like uncut jewels; in fact everything a woman could want was there, and yet not enough to erase the tiny pucker.

Months ago she had played for her freedom and lost.

This exquisite building had been built for her, horses were hers, and camels; jewels were literally flung at her feet.

She clapped her hands and soft-footed natives ran to do her bidding. Flowers and fruit came daily from the oasis, sweetmeats and books each day from the nearest city. Her smallest whim, even to the mere passing of a shadow of a wish, was fulfilled, and yet ——

A few months ago her mocking words had swung to the silken curtains of her chamber, and since then she had been alone.

Verily, there were no restrictions and no barriers, but the yellow sand stretched away to the East and away to the West, and obedience in the oasis was bred from love and her twin sister fear.

True, the girl had but to bid the Arab to her presence and the curtain would swing back.

But upon the threshold he would stand, or upon the floor he would seat himself, motionless, with a face as expressionless as stone.

By no movement, word or sign, could she find out if she was any more to him than the wooden beads which ceaselessly passed between his fingers.

Nothing showed her if he remembered the first night, when for a moment the man had broken through the inherited reserve of centuries. Had it been merely the East clamouring for the out-of-reach, longed-for West? Perhaps! Just a passing moment, as quickly forgotten, and against which forgetfulness the woman in her rebelled.

It had even come to her to lie awake during the night following the days in which the man had been away from his beloved oasis. The swift rush of naked feet, taking her as swiftly to the roof, where peeping between the carved marble she would look upon a distant scene, which could well have illustrated some Eastern fable.

Either the great camel would stalk slowly, solemnly out of the night, kneeling at a word; or a pure bred Arabian horse would rush swiftly through the palm belt, its speed unchecked as its master threw himself from the saddle.

She could even distinguish a murmured conversation between the eunuch and his master, guessing that he was inquiring as to her welfare, and issuing orders for her comfort, before passing out of sight to his own dwelling, *she in. jined,* though she would rather have died than have asked one question of those around her.

She craved for the nights when he would send to inquire if she would ride, often from sheer contrariness denying herself the exercise she longed for.

In fact, feeling the mystery of love germinating within her, she showed herself rebellious and contrary, and infinitely sweet, surpassing in all things the ways of women, who, since the beginning of all time, have plagued the man into whose keeping their heart is slowly but surely slipping.

And as the shadows fell, so did the pucker of discontent deepen, and a tiny blue-grey marmoset sprang to the top of the piano, chattering shrilly, when a book swished viciously across the floor, and a diminutive gazelle, standing on reed-pipe legs, blinked its soft eyes, and whisked its apology of a tail when a henna-tipped finger tapped its soft nose over sharply, before the girl clapped her hands to summon her body-woman, who, as silently as a wraith, slipped into the room.

"Light all the lamps and come and tell me the news."

The little woman obeyed, and came to kneel beside the girl, gazing up at the fair white face with positive worship in her eyes.

"Great is the news, O! mistress."

" Tell it."

The words were sharp, and the faintest shadow of a smile glinted for a moment in the native's eyes.

"Behold, O! beautiful flower! Unto us, the slaves of our great master, under whose feet we are but as dust, it has been told that he upon whom may Allah's greatest blessings fall, is about to take unto himself a wife."

Silence! Save for a little breath indrawn too quickly.

"Well, proceed with the wonderful news!" The words were icy, but a smile flickered for a moment across the native's face, and was gone.

"Behold has he, the greatest man in Egypt and Arabia, before whom all are but shadows, and unto whom is offered the love and respect of all those who live within the bounty of his great heart, yea! behold has he deigned to look upon Amanreh, the thirteen year old daughter of Sheikh el Hoatassin, second only in wealth and prowess to our own master. Fair is she and young, in very truth meet to wed with him who rules us with a hand of iron, bound in thongs of softest velvet.

"Beautiful, yes! beautiful as the day at dawn, and straight as yon marble pillar, and as delicately tinted, rounded as the bursting lotus bud, and fit to carry the honour of bearing her master's children! In a few moons it ——! "

" Begone! "

The word cracked like a whip through the scented

room, but as the little hunchback crept swiftly t
the curtains, the smile passed from the eyes
mouth, as softly she whispered to herself:

" It is well done! "

CHAPTER XXIX

Out on to the balcony and back, this way, that way, to and fro, paced Jill in her black room. Black skins lay upon the black marble floor, black satin cushions upon the skins. Curtains of scented leather, as soft and supple as satin, hung before the doors let into the walls of black carved wood.

A long couch of ebony, untouched by silver or by gold, stood under one of the gigantic black marble statues, which represented an Ethiopian slave or some wild beast, holding in hand or mouth a lamp with shade of flaming orange, the one touch of colour in the whole room.

There was no sound save for the occasional crackle of resinous log burning in a brazier placed in a far corner, before which Jill suddenly crouched, shivering, though the night was warm. Weary was she from want of sleep, weary was her heart from loneliness, weary her mouth, laden with unuttered words of the great love, which, day by day, hour by hour, yea! even from the moment she had turned to find her fate behind her, had been growing and expanding until naught was left of her but love and fear. For fear had been her companion in the hours of the night, which she had passed in restless pacing upon the balcony.

For two of these restless hours she had put on and discarded the garments within her cupboards, until she had found that which she desired. And an hour she had spent likewise in the adorning of her beauty, before

she stood satisfied in front of her mirror.   The voluminous trousers of softest black fabric, hardly revealing
the exquisite whiteness of her perfect limbs, were
caught by heavy golden anklets above the little feet,
with henna-tipped toes and reddened heel.

Her bare waist shone like a strip of creamy satin
above the belt and stomacher of black leather encrusted
in black pearls, her arms were bare, also the supple
back and glistening shoulders, but the rounded glory of
her breasts was hidden by a covering of soft inter-
laced ribbon, sewn with pearls.   Her hair wound round
and round her head, and, fastened by great combs,
shone like a golden globe, and over it she had thrown
a flimsy veil, and around her a swinging cloak.

There was no touch of paint upon her face, nor did
she, with the exception of her anklets, wear loose jewels, or the ornaments which cause that nerve-break-
ing clatter so beloved by the Eastern woman, and so
superlatively irritating to the Western ear.   In fact
she was the most ravishing picture of delight imagin-
able, her first shyness and awkwardness of her unaccustomed attire having long since vanished, though, be
it confessed, that until this night she had never intended
that human eye should rest upon her loveliness.

But the earth of discontent and the waters of loneliness make fertile soil for the seeds of fear, even if
those seeds be planted by the hand of a misshapen
slave; but a little smile and a sigh of satisfaction had
been the outcome of a prolonged scrutiny in a mirror,
before which she had stood whilst quoting certain words
which ran thusly:

"Beautiful as the dawn, rounded as the bursting

lotus 'bud." And then she had shrugged her glistening shoulders and frowned, and smiled again, before stretching her long arms towards the silken curtains which, though she knew it not, gently blew against the figure of a man, who, prone upon his face, clenched his fingers in the soft stuff, striving to quieten the mad beating of his heart at the sound of the footsteps or the rustle of the raiment of the woman he loved, yea, and desired.

"Hahmed! Oh, Hahmed!"

As faint as the rose of the breaking dawn, as tender as the notes of a cooing dove calling gently to its mate, as soft as the touch of a flower-petal the words drifted through the curtain. With a whispered cry to Allah, his God, the man was upon his feet. With the strength of the oriental, which has its root in patience and its flower in achievement in all that appertains to love, he had uncomplainingly waited through month succeeding month, making no effort to further his cause by either word or movement, content to leave the outcome to the Fate which had inscribed upon the unending, non-beginning rolls of eternity the moment when that voice should break across the desert place in which lay his seed of love.

A rustle of the curtain, and he stood before the woman who loved and desired him, until her soul waxed faint within her.

For a space they stood, the light from one great lamp striking down upon the little veil-wrapped figure and the man in flaming orange cloak over soft satin trousers and vest of black, one huge diamond blazing in the turban upon his dark head.

Silently Jill pointed to a chair carved out of ebony, the ends of the arms representing the snarling face of some wild beast, with great fangs of ivory, and staring ruby eyes flashing in the lamplight.

As silently Hahmed sat down, never once removing his eyes from the girl who stood motionless upon a black panther skin, looking back over her half-turned shoulder at him for whom she was bidding against the unknown. Have you ever watched a rosebud unfold in the warmth of the sun, each petal quivering, widening, until the intoxicating scent of the flower goes to your head like wine as you faintly perceive the rose heart within?

In just such a way did Jill unfold her treasures to the Arab, sitting as some carven image in the shadow. The veil from her head slipped to the ground, leaving exposed her white face with its crimson mouth and shadow-laden eyes; slowly the cloak dropped from her shoulders, so that the whiteness of her skin blazed suddenly in the black marble room. For one long moment she stood before her master in the strength of her virginal beauty, and even as a faint sigh broke the stillness, she moved.

Do not imagine for one moment that she copied the strenuous movements of Salome as understood at the Palace Theatre, London, or the disgusting contortions of certain orientals born in Montmartre, and favoured by the denizens of Paris.

Of very truth she moved not her lower limbs at all, though her exquisite body swayed as if by a passing breeze, her little hands elaborating that which the body originated, the tiny feet punctuating the love story of both.

By one slight movement of her right arm she had told the man she loved him, by half-arrested gestures, a little shrug, an infinitesimal undulation of her body, a faint tapping of the left foot or the right, she described the delights of love, she who knew *nothing,* to him who knowing *all,* had denied himself all.

Heaven alone knows if she really understood that which she described; be that as it may, the man rose to his feet as she turned with outstretched arms towards him, moving almost imperceptibly from the waist, telling him that which her lips would not utter, until suddenly with a great cry he sprang towards her, and sweeping her into his arms, tore the coverings from her breasts, until indeed like a lotus-bud she lay silent upon his heart. For one second he stood, and then he raised her above his head upon his outstretched hands, so that the great pins fell from her head and the perfumed hair like golden rain about his shoulders, then he flung her upon the bed of cushions and stood above her with blazing eyes and dilated, quivering nostrils.

And then he knelt beside her, covering her gleaming nakedness with the cloak, and spoke softly in the Eastern tongue.

" I leave you, woman, to go and give orders for your journey to Cairo. There shall you become my wife, my woman, for behold, I will no longer wait.

" Let not your thoughts dwell upon caprice or tricks of woman, for if you say me nay, *yet* will I make you my wife, and force you unto me. But you will not

gainsay me, for behold you love me, so rest upon your
bed for the three weeks which must pass before the
caravan is ready for the journey, so that in health and
strength and surpassing loveliness you will come to
me."

And having knelt to kiss the rosy feet, he withdrew
from the presence of his beloved, and the English girl
turned on her face and sobbed, and then, gathering her
cloak around her so as to hide the dishevelment of her
raiment, passed to the roof above to hold conclave
with the stars.

CHAPTER XXX

IT seems wellnigh impossible that an English maid *could* look with such equanimity upon the prospect of marriage with a man, an Eastern, of whom she knew nothing outside the tales and anecdotes recounted to her of his exploits and prowess, the which stood good to rival even the adventures of Haroun al Raschid.

As if an English girl, you will say, could ever *dream* of such a thing — a girl brought up in England's best society!

True! brought up within a wall of convention, with her ears for ever filled with the everlasting tag, " It's not done, you know," that shibboleth which for stultifying all original effort surpasses even the mythical but revered sway of Mrs. Grundy. A girl whose brain, and originality, and deep passions, must under the said circumstances and environment inevitably culminate in the same silver-haired, pink-cheeked, grandchildren-adoring old lady, who sees the regulation ending in England of the *brilliant* girl, just as she sees the end of the girl whose brain registers the fact that the sea side is a place to be visited only in August; whose originality finds vent in the different coloured ribbons with which she adorns her dogs and her lingerie; whose passions — oh well! who bothers about the little placid stream flowing without a ripple between the mud flats of that drear country habit?

189

No doubt about it, if money troubles had not given her the opportunity for which she had always craved, Jill *would* have finally metamorphosed her brilliant self into that dear old dame who is as beloved and ubiquitous and uniform as the penny bun.   But seeing her chance she had clutched at it with eager outstretched hands, and in all these months she had not had one single regret, or one moment of longing for peaceful, grey-tinted England, or the friends with whom she had visited and hunted and done the hundred and one trivial things wealthy beautiful girls are accustomed to do in England, and who in her case had continned their social career without breaking their hearts or engagements on account of the monetary *débâcle* of their one time companion.   Her instinct had not failed her in regard to the man who, without consulting her in any way, was even at that hour starting forth to arrange their marriage, and she troubled not her head with the thought of what *might* have happened to her *if* her instinct had failed her, though the chances are that rather than have even the outer petals of her womanhood bruised by the closing of a trap into which she might have placed her feet, she would have sent the vessel of her soul afloat down the great wide river ending in the ocean of eternity.

She was that most interesting and most rare cross-bred result of the elusive something, be it soul, imagination, or ecstasy which had turned a woman ancestress, created for the great honour of bearing children, into the nun, whose maternal instincts had feigned find solace in the marble or plaster child-image, and even that out of reach of those hands which should have

trembled over swaddling clothes; and that passion for
love and light which had driven the dancing wayward
feet of a Belle Marquise ancestress from love to love,
until they had come to a standstill before Madame la
Guillotine, who bothered not herself with those two
minute extremities.

So that on waking after sweet slumber, Jill kissed
the misshapen slave upon the cheek and told her the
news, whereupon the dusky little woman raised her
eyes and hands heavenwards, gibbering like a monkey,
albeit she had just left an excited côterie of serving
folk who, in the mysterious native way, had become
acquainted with the news of the impending function
without the uttering of one word from those most in-
terested in an event which would mean fulfilment of
dreams to more than one of those who had, for months
past, pondered and commented on the strangeness of
their master's love-affair.

And Jill in the softest pink raiment sat like the
perfect heart of a perfect rose in the scented coolness
of the pink chamber, and passed the days designing
garments of which it is useless to give a description,
seeing, that the womenfolk in Northern climes have
only two notes on which to ring the changes of their
wardrobe; the long, shroud-looking thing in silk or
crêpe de Chine or good honest nainsook, picked out in
different coloured ribbons, or the romance killing, stove-
pipe giving effect of the masculine pyjama.

From camel back Jill had watched the departure of
the first caravan of swiftest camels, laden with gifts
on their way to Cairo. The jangling of bells, the
musical cries of the drivers, and the roaring and grum-

bling of the beasts, causing her to laugh aloud from
sheer happiness; whilst the natives, many of whom had
not seen the mystery woman their master was about to
take to wife, fumbled with the packs so as to get a good
look at the little figure, who, Allah! had intercourse
with the man *before* the wedding.

"And may the blessings of Allah fall upon her, for
it is not for us to inquire into the strange ways of our
master upon whom may the sun shine, and beside
whose path may a stream of purest water for ever run
For long years has he lived alone, knowing no woman;
may she whom he hath chosen be fruitful, bearing
many sons, so that our children may live in the blessed
shadow of our master's children for generation after
generation."

That was the outlook of the happy oasis upon the
most untoward proceedings, for in the East the betrothed child passes her life in the seclusion of her
family until the very moment of the wedding, the man
depending absolutely upon the words of his mother or
female relatives as to the appearance and character of
his future partner.

On the second day started another caravan of camels, laden with the household goods with which the
wealthy Eastern always travels, yet more caravans
following, carrying the wherewithal of the enormous
retinue with which Hahmed the Arab saw fit to sur-
round his bride; the ensuing days passing in the prepa-
ration of the greatest caravan of all, that which was
to take Jill to the place where, steam up, the great white
yacht at the water's edge was waiting.

Hahmed and Jill were on the broad balcony the night before the start, the Arab lying at the feet of the woman sitting in an ebony chair covered with cushions of every shade of purple, with the faint haze of incense about her little head, and the light of a great love in the softness of her eyes.

Holding the hem of her cloak in his hands he made love to her by words alone, for in all the time since their first meeting, his hands had not held hers, neither had their lips met; but the music of his words served to send the blood surging to her face, then to draw it back to her heart, leaving her as white as the crescent moon above her.

"Tell me, O! Hahmed," she suddenly exclaimed softly, after a long silence, "will not your people think it strange that I, a bride, should have lived these many months with you? Will they *believe* that I am pure, will they not think harm of me, throwing your good name in shadow?"

The man raised himself so that his face was on a level with hers as he laid one hand upon her chair.

"Woman, I speak not in pride when I say that I, Hahmed the Arabian, have never sought and never desired the opinion of those about me. I do as my heart inclineth, let that suffice. Were I a poorer man these things could not be, but with my wealth I have bought my freedom, loosening the iron shackles of convention from about my feet with a key of gold. Wealth can accomplish all things.

"This oasis is mine because I was the only bidder with wealth enough to pay the exorbitant prices demanded, other oases are mine, and villages and tracts of rich lands. Also the respect of my neighbours, also are their tongues tied on account of my riches.

" I live for years without wife, or woman or child, they say no word.

" I marry a Christian and a white woman, and they will say no word; that she is *my wife* will suffice them, though doubtless whispers in the harems will not be all sweet, seeing that for years the quarry has eluded the traps laid by the henna-tipped fingers of relentless hunters and huntresses. Wealth! It buys peace and freedom, O! woman, so let not your thoughts disturb you. You will be the greatest woman in all Egypt and Arabia — but listen, some one sings the bridal song, which has come down to us unchanged from the time of the great Sesostris."

CHAPTER XXXI

THE love-song broke the stillness of the desert night with the suddenness and sweetness of the nightingale's call in the depths of an English garden, laden with the perfume of June roses.

So softly as to be hardly distinguished from a whisper, the wonderful voice called — called again and stopped, whilst the stars seemed to gather closer until the sky hung as a canopy of softest purple velvet picked out in silver lightings over the heads of those who listened to the call of love, and from very ecstasy were still.

Again, and yet again, the voice cried aloud to its heart's desire, rising like incense from some hidden spot in the village, twining among the feathery leaves of the palms to drop like golden rain upon the heart of some maiden, who doubtless sat upon her roof-top, modestly veiled if in company of friends or relations, but otherwise, I am positively certain, might be found peeking over the top of the balustrade as have peeked the hearts' desires from the beginning of all time.

Jill's face was white as death, as she too sat motionless, listening to the love-song, whilst her great eyes blazing like the stars above watched the man at her feet.

Closely veiled was she, for this was the eve of her wedding journey to Cairo, also had the spirit of perversity prevailed within her for the last month, causing her to resemble the coldness, warmth, eastiness, sweetness, and general warpiness of the English climate, sparkling one day with the dew-drop-on-the-grass-freshness of an early summer morning, to hang the next as passing heavy on the hand as the November fog upon the new hat brim; veering within twelve hours to the sharpness of the East wind, which braces skin and temper to cracking point, and to make up for it all, for one whole hour in the twenty-four, resembling the exquisite moment of the June morning, in which you find the first half-open rose upon the bush just outside your breakfast-room.

She was consumed with love of the man who lay at her feet, with the hem of her rose-satin veil against his lips, and her heart had melted within her as the love-song thrilled, and sobbed, and cried its love through the night; melted until she suddenly leant forward and stretching out her hand laid it for one moment on the man's dark head, whereupon he rose to his knees so that the dark beauty of his face was on a level with hers, the tale in his eyes causing her heavy white lids to close, whilst speechless she lay back among her satin cushions.

"Woman! O! woman! The touch of your hand is like the first breeze after the scorching heat of the day, and yet must I await your word before the love that consumes me may throw aside its coverings to stand in the perfumed freshness of the wind which maketh the delight of the desert dawn.

"Together we have watched the goings out of the caravans on their way to Cairo, laden with gifts and

all that is necessary for the feasting of those who are
invited to attend the marriage of one who, by the wonder of Allah's bounty, has been allowed to gather the
glory of his harvest. In your graciousness you have
troubled your heart with misgivings as to the outcome
of a marriage between a Mohammedan and a Christian,
and I have answered you that there are many such mar-
riages in the East, of which great happiness has been
the outcome, though not such happiness as shall well
forth from the union of our love."

And the man rose to his feet, standing straight as a
pine against the fretted wood-work of the balcony, and
the girl watching him from under the half-closed lids,
suddenly tearing the veil from before her face, sprang
also to her feet, and stood against him with her face
upraised, so that the glory of her red mouth came to
the level of his shoulder, and the thudding of her heart
caused the diamonds on the embroidery of her vest to
flash in the starlight, and the perfume of her skin to
scent the night air.

And the man bent down until it seemed that their
lips must meet in this their first kiss, but instead he
withdrew one pace, though the agony of love drew
all blood from his face, until it shone palely in the
gloom.

" Yea, woman, you love me, else would not your
eyes be suffused with the pain of unsatisfied longing!
Yet have I not said that until you come to me, and
whisper, 'Hahmed, I love you!' until that moment
I will not in love touch even the fairness of your hand,
though as Allah is above us it taxes my strength to
the uttermost shred.

"Perchance I am foolish, missing the untold and unknown delights of wooing the woman of my heart, but in such wise am I built. I will have all the fruit at the plucking or none, for where is the delight of the sweetest peach if the stem, the leaves, the bloom have been bruised by much handling.

"One day, nay in the stillness of one night shall I hear you call me — *then,* ah! Allah!"

The voice stopped suddenly, though the man made no other sign, when the girl before him, beside herself with anger which springs from love denied, suddenly struck him full upon the mouth, and then shaking from head to foot, with rage, and love, and fear, broke the deadly silence.

"Nay, man! In that you are mistaken, for you shall never hear my voice calling you in love. That may become the woman of your land, but not the woman from the West. I will marry you, for I will not bring derision upon a man who has treated me with such courtesy and gentleness. But love! Nay! better far buy some beautiful Circassian upon our wedding trip, for surely you shall never hear my voice upraised in love!"

And gathering her swirling draperies about her, she made to depart, knowing that she had spoken hastily, making vows she could not keep for the very love she denied. Her hand was upon the silken hangings of her door when she was swung round by the shoulder to face the very essence of cold rage.

"So, woman, you are one of those who have ever hidden an inner chamber of perversity, for surely had I thought to have come to the end of your store of moods and whims.   Listen!   By striking me across the face you have but made my love the greater, but as Allah is above me, I will make you pay, as you say in your far cold country.   You will come to me one day, because such love as ours is not to be denied, and when you come, for that blow I will bruise your lips until the red blood starts from them, and I will bruise your body until marks of black show upon its startling fairness, but above all will I bruise your soul with unsatisfied longings, and unrequited desires, until you lie half dead at my feet; then only will I take you in my arms and carry you to the secret chamber, which Fate has prepared somewhere for the fulfilment of my love."

And as the love-song died on the night, Jill passed slowly into the inner chamber, failing to see the man kneel to kiss the rug impressed by the passage of her little feet.

PART II

THE FLOWER

CHAPTER XXXII

THE Rolls Royce containing representatives of the Savoy and Shepherds in the shapes of beautifully gowned, handsome, placid, somewhat dull, the Honourable Mary Bingham, pronounced Beam, her friend Diana Lytham, and the rotund personalities of Sir Timothy and Lady Sarah Ann Gruntham, drew up behind the menacing hand of a policeman alongside a limousine containing representatives of Shepherds and the Savoy in the shapes of two rotund-to-be daughters and one thin son of the race of Gruntham, and the Honourable Mary's faded mother, who were all racing home in the search of cool baths, or cooler drinks, or a few moments' repose in a darkened room in which to forget the stifling half hours of a series of social functions, given in honour of Cairo's most festive week of the season, before starting on a dressing campaign against the depredations made upon the skin by flies, heat, sand, wind, and cosmetics.

The past middle-aged Sir Timothy of the latest birthday honours, partner in life of Lady Gruntham, and therefore part possessor of the Gruntham family, was whole owner of an army of chimney stacks which, morning, noon, and night, belched thick oily smoke across one of England's Northern counties in the process of manufacturing a substitute for something; also he owned a banking account almost as big as his honest old heart.

La famille Gruntham were breaking their first wide-eyed, open-mouthed *tour de monde* in Cairo, having selected their hotel from an advertisement in the **A.B.C.**

The Honourable Mary's nondescript mother sat patiently waiting the decisive moment which would see her *en route* once more to tea in her bedroom and the last chapter of a Hichens novel, as she had patiently awaited decisive moments for years, having uncomplainingly allowed the reins which controlled the large estate, and large fortune, to slip into the large, capable hands of her daughter, just as she had also either as uncomplainingly criss-crossed the world in the wake of her daughter's unaristocratically large footsteps, or submissively remained at home for the hunting, in which field the Honourable Mary excelled.

Diana Lytham, spinster, through no want of trying to remedy the defect, expert at bridge, razor-edged of tongue, but still youthful enough to allow the lid of Pandora's casket to lift on occasions, also to be described by those who feared the razor-edge as petulant instead of peevish, and cendrée instead of sandy, passed the tedious moments of waiting in a running commentary upon the idiosyncrasies and oddities of the people and refreshments of the past hours, with a verve which she fondly believed to be a combination of sarcasm and cynicism, but which, in reality, was the kernel of the nut of spitefulness, hanging from the withering bough of the tree of passing youth.

She, having an atrocious seat and knowing it, with the excuse of England's winter dampness had fled the hunting. The Gruntham's younger generation, knowing not the difference between a hunter and a carriage-horse, had not given the subject a thought, but Mary Bingham had made a whole-hearted sacrifice of the

month she loved best because, although loving her horses
with a love of understanding, she knew that the love in
her heart for just the one man, was a love passing all
understanding whatsoever; feeling, therefore, that the
sacrifice brought its own reward in the qualified bliss of
being near the one man of her heart, whilst he passed
weeks and months in the vain endeavour to find their
friend, who had been lost to them in the land of the
long-dead Pharaohs.

"Most annoying indeed — great negligence on the
part of the city police to allow a hold-up like this at
this hour of the afternoon. No wonder Egypt's in the
mess of ruins it is if this is the way traffic has always
been regulated," fumed and fretted Sir Timothy, whilst
Mary Bingham twirled her sunshade over her hat and
gazed unseeingly at the domes, cupolas, and minarets
of the distant mosque of the Mohamet Ali; and the
thin heir of the race of Gruntham pondered upon the
allurements of the yashmak, which hid all but the eyes
of the few Eastern women who glanced timidly in passing at the occupants of the motor-cars.

"Now then, dearies," smiled the irate old knight's
comfortable wife, "don't you take on so, though I do
allow it's a nuisance, considering I have to get into
my apricot satin to-night, with all those hooks. Pity
Sir John Wetherbourne ain't — isn't here, it u'd never
have happened I'm sure if he had been, seeing the
way he has with him, though I can't say as 'ow I
approve of him so young and good-looking — and all
these Eastern hussies around — wandering about so
much by himself. I do wonder what 'appened — all
right, lad, there's many a slip between the aitch and the

noovoh rich lip, *h'appened* to the girl he's looking **for.**
Over a year ago you say, Mary, my dear, since **she**
disappeared at Ishmael, and not heard of since, **and**
Sir John scouring Egypt with all the energy I used **to**
use to the kitchen floor, and not half the result to show
for it, eh, Timothy lad? Do you think he was in love
with her, or *is* it a case of — oh, what's them **two**
words which mean that you can't think of anything **but**
one thing."

" *Idé fixe,*" enlightened Diana Lytham.

" Eyedyfix! Sounds like one of those cocktails that
heathen feller-me-lad's always trying to poison me with,
eh, Miss Diana," chuckled the old manufacturer, who
worshipped the cloth of aristocracy, and even rever-
enced the fringe.

" Oh, you bet he was in love all right, don't you.
think so, Mary dearest," and the small grey eyes
snapped spitefully across at the good-natured, healthy
girl, who had raised a weak resemblance of hate in
her whilom school friend's breast, more by the matter-
of-course, jolly way she had helped lame dogs over
stiles than the fact that such obstructions had never
lain in her path.

" Are you talking about Jack and Jill? Everybody
loved her, and she was made to be loved, was beautiful,
wilful Jillikins. I wish he could find her, or a trace,
or some news of her! Oh, but surely we are intruding
upon his own affairs too much, and I *wonder* what
has —— Oh, but listen — do listen, did you ever hear
such a noise, and just *look* at the crowds! Why, **the**
whole of old Cairo is coming this way."

Even as she spoke, two Arabs, mounted **on superb**

horses, and brandishing spears, dashed past the cars, shouting continuously what would be the equivalent of " clear the way " in English, just as to the sound of shouting and singing, the beating of drums, and clashing of cymbals, a stream of natives, dancing and waving their arms, poured into the square.

Round and round they spun about six great camels, which, hung with bells and decked from head to stubbly tail with glistening harness and embroidered saddle cloths, stalked ahead, unheeding of the tumult; whilst riders of restless horses did their best to regulate the action and pace of the nervous animals.

Behind them walked scores of young men in snow-white galabeah, their impassive, delicately curved faces surmounted by the scarlet tarboosh, chanting that old Egyptian marriage song of which the music score was lost some few thousand years ago, lying perhaps securely hidden in a secret chamber, undiscovered in the ruins of Karnak, but which song, without a single alteration of note or word, has descended from Rameses the Second down through the history-laden centuries to *us,* the discoverers and worshippers of ragtime.

But the greatest crush surged round two camels which walked disdainfully through the throng, seemingly as oblivious of the excited multitude as the one made herself out to be of the man who walked beside her with a fantastic whip, and the other of the golden chains which fastened her to the blackest eunuch of all Africa.

Upon the one of the golden chains, rested a golden palanquin, closed with curtains of softest white satin, a-glitter with precious stones.

Around the brute's neck hung great garlands of flowers, from its harness chimed golden bells of softest tone, whilst tassels of silver swung from the jewel encrusted net covering her shining coat.

What or who was inside, no one seemed to be able to coherently explain, though the setting alone told of some priceless treasure.

There was no doubt as to the rider of the other camel!

"Hahmed! Hahmed! Hahmed!" rose the unceasing cry from old and young, whilst blessings ranging from the continued comfortable shape of his shadow, to the welfare of his progeny unto the most far-reaching generation, through a life perpetual of sun, sweetmeats, and shady streams, rose and fell from the pavements, roofs, and balconies crowded with the curious, upon the impassive man who held his camel harnessed with native simplicity, just one pace behind its companion.

The crowning touch was added to this delirious moment of festival by the simply scandalous distribution of golden coin, *golden* mind you, which attendants clothed in every colour of an Egyptian sunset, and mounted upon diminutive, but pure bred donkeys, threw right and left with no stinting hand, to the distribution of which largesse responded shrill laughter, and still shriller cries, and thwack of stick on dark brown pate and cries of pain upon the meeting of youthful ivories in the aged ankle or wrist.

No doubt about it, Cairo, *real* Cairo I mean, had been in an uproar from the moment two special trains had chugged into the Central Station a few hours back.

CHAPTER XXXIII

CROWNED and uncrowned queens travel in comfort all the world over, a comfort of over-heated special trains, the most stable part of the boat, the most skilful chauffeur, allied to the most speedy car, an elaboration of the luncheon basket, and the heartening effect of strips of red baize; but the comfort of a church pew compared to the downy recesses of a Chesterfield, against the comfort and regal luxury of Jill's mode of travelling.

Surrounded by an armed guard under the absolute control of black Mustapha, armed to the teeth, chaperoned by Mrs. Grundy in the shape or, as I should say, represented in the shapeless person of a dusky duenna of many moons, a good heart and a vitriolic tongue, who coyly peeped from behind the sombre curtains of her middle-aged palanquin, Jill started on her wedding journey. Over a carpet of flowers, through a long lane of palm leaves, held by veiled maidens, so as to form an arch, she passed, whilst the sweetness of the girls' voices rose to the tops of the acacia and mimosa trees, and gigantic date palms, in the Egyptian bridal song.

In no way did Jill's return journey across the desert and through the mountains to the canal's edge resemble the out going.

She did it with leisure and comfort this time, to find the Arab's great white steam yacht waiting to race her to Ismailiah.

209

She had looked round for the man she loved, but had seen him only when, with great pomp and circumstance, she landed on the other side.

The whole of the town had turned out, so that the white car in which she made the short trajet between the landing-place and the station passed between a lane lined with male faces, dusky, dark brown, and light tan, thousands of soft eyes sparkling over the all-hiding, all-attractive yashmak, and a dotted line, well in the forefront of the leather-brown, European physiognomies, of those who nudged and pointed, exclaiming aloud, so that their words carried even into the interior of the closed car, upon their luck of seeing a *real native show.*

With grave obeisance to the woman, Hahmed the Arab had entered his special train, which preceded Jill's by ten minutes, so that when she arrived at Cairo Central Station, surrounded by her armed guard, and with her duenna rocking painfully by her side in a pair of over small shoes, a little scared at the sea of faces, and the echo of the voices of those who stood outside, kept in order by the swash-buckling native police of fez ornamented heads, she had stood transfixed, wondering what on earth she should do next.

Verily, the Eastern can carry off a situation which would undoubtedly fill the Western with consternation.

Perhaps the clothing has as much to do with it as any national traits, for surely no man in stove-pipe trousers, and all that goes to the well-looking of these garments, could have so composedly traversed the broad flower-strewn carpet, laid with the consent of the authorities and no little distribution of backsheesh upon the dusty station, and making deep obeisance, have so serenely led the little cloaked and veiled figure to the gorgeously caparisoned (if one may apply that term to the ship of the desert's rigging) camel, which sprawled its neck upon the ground for the benefit of the motley crowd without.

Anyway, it was an unbelievable thing to happen in Egypt, the land of veiled and secluded women. It was wonderful enough to know that the great Hahmed was taking unto himself a wife, but that that wife should suddenly appear from out of the desert unknown, unseen — well, it took one's breath away, indeed it did, but well again — seeing the wealth and power of the man, it was wiser to rejoice than to quibble and gossip upon such doings.

So all along the Sharia Clot Bey, which is the electrically lit, motor filled, modern shop-lined road leading from the station, Jill peeped between the curtains at the throngs of jubilant natives, and the surrounding Western looking buildings.

She felt hurt to the soul by the modernity of the latter, just as she had been hurt on arriving in Rome and Venice, until later on she had found balm in the old stones and streets and buildings of both places hidden behind the twentieth century.

Jill knew that she was being taken to the palace of the old Sheikh, uncle of the man she was about to wed, but where it was she had no idea, nor of the names of the streets, the mosques or the palaces and the mansions she could spy upon, from between her satin curtains, on her way to the Bab-es-Shweyla gate. The route they had taken in the glow of the setting sun, once they had

DESERT LOVE

left European Cairo behind, lay through the El Katai quarter, having chosen the road leading from the mosque of Sultan Hassan, through the Bazaar of the Amourers to reach the great gate, the very heart of old Cairo.

And the girl's whole being seemed inundated with the light of the gorgeous heavens above her as she passed down the Sukkariya, the broad and pleasant path running under the gate, and her eyes shone as they rested on the huge and ancient El-Azhar, the university of all Islam.

Past mosque and tomb in the El-Nahassin, whilst minarets turned from gold to rose, and rose to crimson in the dying sun, up through the Gamahyia, danced and sang the ever increasing multitude, until the armed guard suddenly came to a standstill, forming a circle round the two camels, who had haughtily condescended to kneel, as Jill with her hand in that of her chaperon, passing between rows of salaaming servants, wondering what had become of Hahmed, and where she was going, and if tea could possibly be forthcoming instead of coffee, entered a courtyard, beautiful beyond words, and passing through the gates leading to the harem, heard them shut behind her; whilst with little cries of greeting, the four wives and many inhabitants of this secluded spot swept down upon her, their dainty, henna-tipped fingers quickly removing her cloak and veil, their little exclamations of astonishment testifying to their appreciation of the radiant little vision who smiled so sweetly upon them, and returned their greetings in such prettily broken Arabic.

Only one contretemps had marred the perfect organisation of the proceedings, and that happened when the advance guard, turning a corner at full speed, regardless of the life and limbs of the seething mass of adults, babies, and dogs, had found themselves forced to edify the spectators with an exhibition of *haute école,* as their terrified horses, suddenly rearing, pawed the quivering air above a brace of camels, who had lawlessly and obstinately stretched themselves forth upon the soft bed of mud and house garbage spread liberally throughout one of the narrowest streets in El-Katia.

Proddings of spears, and kickings of tender anatomical portions availing nothing, the last means for the hasty moving of obstreperous camels had been resorted to with success.

The following is the recipe:

Take two or more camels, fully laden for choice, stretched at length across a narrow street. For removal of same, apply a vigorous drubbing by means of a stick or sticks. If no result, apply foot with yet more vigour. If this fails, gather an armful of good dry straw, fix it cunningly under the animal's belly, apply match, and fly for your life to the nearest sanctuary.

CHAPTER XXXIV

Jill had been married a fortnight. Everything down to the minutest detail had passed off perfectly, everything had been duly signed and sealed and conducted in the most orthodox and binding manner, leaving the witnesses breathless at the thought of the land, jewels, houses, and cattle with which Hahmed the Arab endowed this woman who brought him nothing excepting beauty, which was not exactly beauty, but rather colouring, plus brain and charm.

Not even love had she brought it seemed, or obedience, for had not her lord and master uncomplainingly allowed her to keep the door of her apartments closed, neither had he insisted on the dyeing of her golden hair to that henna shade, of which so much is thought in the land of black hirsute coverings.

The feasting and rejoicings of the past ten days had surpassed anything ever dreamt of on the banks of the Nile.

There had been tournaments and exhibitions of strength and agility and horsemanship in the day, and dancing by the most famous dancers in the land by night — dances, let me tell you, in spite of what you gather by hearsay or ocular proof in such cesspools as Port Said and kindred towns, which were lessons in modesty compared to that blush-producing exercise called the Tango and its descendants.

The harem was a cage of excited love-birds to whom
were duly brought detailed accounts of the nightly and
daily doings. Never had there been such a commotion
within the somewhat over-decorated walls, nor had the
great mirrors reflected such sheen of wondrous silks,
and satins, and flashing jewels; whilst sweetmeats,
coffee, and cool drinks were the order of the day for
the sustenance and refreshment of the never-ending
stream of high-born ladies, who from far and near and
in all kinds of covered vehicles hastened with the excuse
of greeting the wife of the great Arab, to gather first
hand delectable morsels of gossip anent her strange
methods of procedure, and her master's still stranger
leniency towards her.

" Truly," remarked Fatima (which is not her real
name), the thirteen-year-old and latest addition to the
harem, and therefore favourite of the old Sheikh, as for
the eighth time she changed her costume, and with the
tip of her henna pink finger skilfully removed a too
liberal application of kohl from about her right and
lustrous eye, whilst chatting with her maid. " Truly,
I say, the man is either besotted with love, or suffering
from some strange malady. Nigh upon the passage of
ten days and nights, and yet he bends not the woman
to his will, and she more luscious than a peach from
the southern wall. Thinkest thou it's love, oh Fuddja?
And thinkest thou the whiteness of my bosom shows to
advantage against the gold of my neckband? "

And Fuddja, dutifully likening the beauties of her
mistress to those of the white doe, whereas in verity
they favoured the contour of the plump poussin, with
promise of distinct obesity within the passage of a

very few years, proceeded to recount the latest
which was none other than the fact that within the
few days Hahmed would remove his wife unto hi
habitation on the other side of the city.

CHAPTER XXXV

HAVING just wrested a promise from Hahmed that he would take her one moonlight night to the summit of the Great Pyramid, in spite of the strict rules against such nightly excursions, Jill sat very still and quite content upon her camel gazing at the Sphinx. She turned and looked in the direction where the great eyes were staring, and then turning once more towards the mystery of all ages, she urged her camel on until it stood close to the base, and then, dissatisfied, she urged it back until she could look once more from a distance, and shaking her head with a little sigh, spoke in a whisper to the man at her side.

" I wonder, Hahmed," she said, holding out her hand as was her habit when perplexed or distressed, " I wonder who conceived the idea. No! I mean something quite different — it is — how shall I say — I wonder who it was who, having the *meaning* of that face in his mind, had the power and the will to hold it there while he carved or chipped it — oh! so slowly into stone. It is easy enough to paint from a model, or hew blocks of marble in the shape of a man or a woman or animal, isn't it — when you have them in front with their expressions and their forms? But how did the man who did this with only a picture in his *mind* to rely on *dare* to use a chisel? Because you can't rub out mistakes in stone, and sketches wouldn't have helped him, would they, because even photographs give one no real idea of all the Sphinx means? And I wonder where the look lies — in the eyes or the whole face, or the set of the head, or what? The eyes are rather like a dog's, aren't they — a sort of wistfulness and steadfastness."

"Many have asked, O! woman, though not many who have looked upon the Sphinx have, I think, thought upon just your first point. What do we know about this living stone before which the mightiest, and most wonderful, and most beautiful works of even the greatest masters seem as nothing? Who was he? Whose brain conceived, and hands gave birth to this mystery? Why is his name not engraved somewhere for us pigmies to read? Though doubtless it *is* in the depths of the hidden chambers in the base which up to now have only been superficially examined."

"Yes!" broke in Jill, "but whoever he was, slave or prince, captive or free, *who* taught him what eternity *looks like;* for that surely is is what the Sphinx sees, the circle with no join, the world — not this one — not Egypt — without end. We all say for ever and ever, but *our* brains reel when we *think* for one minute on eternity. Do you think his brain snapped when he put the last stroke? Do you think he was buried with decency with his chisels beside him?"

"No! surely not! Otherwise, Moonflower, somebody would have dug him out along with the Pharaohs, and priests, and courtesans, so that we should have learned something about him by turning his mummified body inside out, and unwinding the burial cloth from about those fingers which have given us the Sphinx. Strange! that a woman's whim, born of vanity, should

be spoken of with bated breath, even to this day! A
woman melts a pearl and the world continues to cry Ah!
through all time; a man creates this, and no record is
left of him. Verily Allah has blessed me in giving you
into my hands, for behold your thoughts are as sweet
to me as the wind that blows through the mimosa trees
at dawn."

The girl turned a serious face towards Hahmed and
smiled sweetly.

" How small and futile we are, Hahmed, in front of
this great thing. See how it, I say *it* because surely
there is no sex in any one part of it, brushes us aside,
not in indifference, but just because to it we simply do
not exist any more than the sand, even less so, because
the sand in time would even blind those eyes. How I
wish I could see it lying uncovered on its base. And I
somehow can't imagine that Mary laid the Infant Christ
to rest between its paws! How did they cross the desert
on one poor ass? How would they, so humble and so
poor, be able to approach the Sphinx with its guards
about it? And I wonder if they will ever open up the
shaft and search until they find the history on the walls
of the base which, I am sure, buries somebody down in
its depths.

" Eternity! and yet I fret and worry, get cross —
cross, Hahmed, which is so much more little than angry
— and love to tease and give pain. Forgive me!"

And something had crept into the girl's voice which
caused the man to lean forward, and very gently to tilt
Jill's face upward so that the moon struck down full
upon it.

But the heavy lids veiled the eyes, so that nothing

could be seen of the wonder of all-time reflected therein. A wonder of the birth of which there is no record; a mystery which has a million times million shapes, each shape fashioned afresh, yet always the same; a mystery besides which the Sphinx is as a grain of sand. The mystery of Love.

And Hahmed the Arab, who had waited since all eternity for this moment of time, raised one hand to heaven and praised his God, and then leant forward to readjust the veil before the woman's face.

"The Sphinx shall not see your face, neither shall the stars, nor shall the wind touch your mouth, O! my beloved! For I would take you to the ruins of the Temple of Khafra, where the rose colour of the stone shall tint your face and your hands, where eyes shall not see nor hear the story of the love I have to tell you."

And leaning across he put his arm about Jill and lifted her from her saddle, and laid her across his knees with her head in the hollow of his shoulder.

"I am of the desert, O! my woman, of the sandstorm and the winds, the rocks, and the heat — I have no desire this night for soft cushions, nor for the fragrance of the hanging curtains of your chamber. I love you, Allah, and this time I will not wait. You have played with me for many moons! Not even once have I laid my lips upon even the whiteness of your hand since Allah in His greatness made you my wife in the name before the law. At your wish I have denied myself all, until I have longed to bring you to my feet with the lash of the whip — yet have I waited, knowing that the moment of your surrender would be the sweeter for it.

"And the spirits of the past shall be your hand-maidens, and the moon shall be your lamp, and the sand shall be your marriage-couch this night — and I, O! woman — I shall be your master."

And who knows if it was not love who wrought upon the granite until the Sphinx was born? For after all Love is eternal, and eternity is Love.

CHAPTER XXXVI

THE silver shafts of the full moon struck down into the ruined outer courts of the Temple of Khafra, turning the rose-colour of the granite to a dull terra-cotta, and picking out the pavement with weird designs of gigantic beasts and flowers, the which, when Jill put her foot upon them, proved to be nothing more harmful than the shadows thrown by the walls and huge blocks of fallen masonry.

Slowly she crossed the court and as slowly climbed the incline leading to the chambers of long dead priests and priestesses, pausing at the opening with a little catch of the breath and a quick glance at the man she loved beside her.

The darkness of Egypt is a common enough expression on the lips of those who know nothing of what they are talking about, and Jill, who had often used the words, stood transfixed at the abysmal blackness in front of her.

Outside it was as clear as day, inside it was darker than any night, and like a flash the girl compared it with her life at that very moment.

Up to now she had been her own mistress, in that she had deliberately and of her own free will done the things she ought and ought not to have done, and had been content with the result.

True, she was married to the man beside her, bound to him by law, his in the eyes of the world, and of Allah

Who is God, but she knew full well that until she called
to him and surrendered herself in love, that she was as
free as any maiden could be in that land, and, she
thought, that doubtless in time he would tire of her
caprice and let her go, taking unto himself another as
wife. In which surmise she was utterly mistaken!

Should she move forward into the darkness? Should
she turn back into the light?

If she crossed the threshold she knew she would seek
the protection of his arms against the threatenings of
the shadows which surely held the spirits of the past;
and in his arms, why! even at the thought her heart
leapt and her face burned beneath the veil.

If she turned back she would return to her position
of honoured guest in the man's house, a barren, unsatis-
fying position for one in whom youth cried for love and
mastery.

If only Hahmed would make a sign, a movement; if
only he would say one word. But he stood motionless
just behind her, waiting himself, with the oriental's
implicit belief for some deciding sign from Fate.

There was no sound, no sign of life as they stood
waiting, and then the night breeze, gently lifting a
corner of the Arab's full white cloak, wrapped it like
some great wing about the girl.

A thrill swept her from head to foot as she pressed
her hands above her heart, and then with eyes wide
open and alight with love stepped across the threshold
into the shadows, unknowingly turning the corner of
that block of granite which hides the opening, leaving
one in complete and utter darkness.

She flung out her hands and felt nothing, turned

swiftly and flung them out again, vainly searching **for** the Arab's cloak, and finding nothing let them fall to her side.

"My God!" she whispered, and moved a step forward, stopped and listened and moved back. "Hahmed! Hahmed!"

She called aloud in fear, she who had never known what it was to be afraid, and she gave a little sob of pure relief when the Arab answered from the distance of a few feet.

"Wherefore are you afraid, O! woman? Behold I am near you, watching you, for my eyes are trained for the night as well as for the day, even though your eyes, which are as the turquoise set in a crown of glory, may not pierce the darkness, being unaccustomed to the violent contrasts and colourings of the East."

Then fell a silence.

And then the perfume of the night, and the scent of the sand and the spirit of the dead women who had lived and loved even in that temple chamber, assailed the nostrils of the girl, entering in unto her and causing a wave of longing and unutterable love to rise and flood her whole being, so that she smiled sweetly to herself and held out her arms, and trembled not at the thought of the moment awaiting her.

"Hahmed! Hahmed!" she called softly from love, and hearing no sound called again and yet more softly. "Come to me, Hahmed! come to me — because — I love you!"

And her master held her in one arm whilst he gently removed the veil from before her face, which she turned and laid against his heart as he poured forth his soul in an ecstasy of love.

"Behold!" he cried, as he removed the outer cloak from about her. "Behold is my beloved like unto a citadel which has fallen before my might, and the gates thereof are unbarred before the conqueror!

"Behold," and Jill's head veil fell to her feet, "is the citadel fair to look upon, from the glistening of the golden cupolas to the feet awash in the River of Love.

"Surrounded by the ivory wall of innocence is she, and unto her lord is the glory of measuring the circumference thereof.

"Even as a flowering tree is she, and beneath my hands shall the bloom of love turn even unto the passion flower.

"Like unto a Court of Love is my heart's delight, and many are the chambers therein, in which in the heat of the day and the coolness of the night I shall find repose.

"Her fingers are as the lattice before the windows of her joy, through which she shall peep, looking for the coming of her lord; her lashes are the silken curtains which she will draw before the twin pools of love which are her eyes; her body is as a column of alabaster in the shadow of which I shall find my delight!

"Yea! the citadel has fallen, and the walls about it are riven at my approach. Allah! Allah! Allah!"

And the shadows crept gently about them as once more the silence fell, and gathered again into the corners as Jill sighed softly.

"Tremble not, my beloved! for behold I love thee!

Gentle is love to such as thee, and soft is the sand of Egypt which shall be thy couch. And yet, thou child of love, even at this moment when my heart waxeth faint within me from love of thee, yet will I listen, and take thee back unto thy dwelling and thy fragrant chamber if so thou desireth!"

But Jill, lifting her arms, laid her hands in utter submission upon the man's breast, and sighed again in perfect content beneath the kisses which covered them, and her arms and her breasts and her beautiful mouth.

"As thou wilt," she whispered softly, " only as thou wilt."

And verily as a young tree she stood in the glory of her youth with her feet upon the sands of Egypt, and verily was her heart glad when she was carried into the inner chamber, and passed into the keeping of her master for ever.

CHAPTER XXXVII

SOME months had gone, and the sun sparkled on the water of the little singing stream, though bitter winds had blown and all-enveloping sand had swirled about the palms which surrounded Jill's beautiful home in the oasis, of which the reins were gradually slipping into fingers skilled in driving anything from a four-in-hand to a donkey in a cart.

Three mornings a week, an hour after dawn, she gave audience to all those who, with grievance or in difficulty, desired her help or advice; for which ceremony, and having the dramatic instinct, she had caused a clearing to be made in the shade of the palms, under the biggest of which she had also had placed a great chair of snow-white marble, in which, clothed always in white, she would seat herself, her passionate mouth smiling happily behind the yashmak whilst over it the great eyes, into which had crept a look of infinite tenderness in the months that had passed, would scrutinise the people standing humbly and astounded before her.

She would look across upon mothers with obstreperous sons who would not work, or would not wed; mothers who beat their breasts in despair at the utter lack of looks or grace in the unfortunately multiplied feminine arrows within the parental quiver; young men who craved a word of recommendation so as to obtain a certain post; older men who craved an overdraft at

the bank of her patience; young mothers whose in-
fants were either too fat or too lean, or with eyes
half-eaten away with disease; all of whom having received a full measure of help, pressed down and running over, and having bestrewn themselves upon the
ground around her chair, would depart in high fettle
to spread the news of this wonder woman, their mistress, in whom they felt such inordinate pride; so that
one, then two, then more, from distances long and short,
would creep into the council with pretexts ranging
from the thin to the absolutely transparent, until one
morning the whole séance ended in an unseemly fracas
between the legitimate and the illegitimate seekers after
help in word or kind, whereupon Hahmed, rising in
his wrath, smote them verbally hip and thigh, and Jill
departed in high dudgeon, leaving the culprits to wilt
in the frost of her keen displeasure.

And from about that date, a month ago, everything
seemed to have gone wrong.

Days of depression would follow days of mad spirits,
hours when she was as the sweetest scented rose within
the hands of the Arab, followed by interminable
stretches of time when the points of the " wait-a-bit "
thorn were blunt compared to the exceeding sharpness
of her temper.

Days when all that was right was wrong, and all
that was wrong *was* wrong, so that her women crept
quietly, and Hahmed wondered sometimes if some
" afreet " [1] haunted the soil and had taken possession
of the soul of his beloved.

Jill swung to and fro in a hammock slung between

[1] Evil Spirit.

two palms at a very early hour indeed of this morning late in December.

She had neither veil before her face nor shoes upon her feet, and the flimsy mauve robe clung to the supple body as she restlessly swung, until she clapped her hands to summon her breakfast, and clapped them again sharply so that a figure came running at high pressure.

"Go, ask thy master if he will break bread with me in the shade of the palms, oh Laleah, and let not the shadows lengthen unduly in thy going for fear that I give thee cause to hasten thy footsteps!"

Which manner of speech shows that Jill had not unduly tarried either in acquiring knowledge of things Eastern. And Hahmed, as he stood before her and greeted her in the beautiful Arabian tongue, wondered if in all the world there could be found such another picture as that of his wife, with the riot of red-gold hair about her little face, which somehow seemed over white in the shade of the palm, and the blueness of her eyes, and the redness of her mouth, which neither the one nor the other smiled at his approach.

"Do sit down and help yourself!" said she indeed, and clapping her hands sharply ordered fresh food and drinks, both hot and cold, to be brought upon the instant.

And her next remark, after the breakfast of tea in a real teapot, a hissing kettle, strange loaves, purest butter, honey, and fruits of every conceivable colour had been laid upon a cloth upon the grass, fell like a bolt from the blue, though the man made no sign of disturbance from the impact.

"I want eggs and bacon, Hahmed!"

For a moment he pondered the remark, whilst he offered Jill a cigarette and lit one for himself.

"The eggs, my woman," and the musical voice made a poem even of the absurd words, "now that thou hast taught thy slaves to poach and scramble and prepare them in divers and pleasant ways, are easy — but bacon — no! that canst thou *not* have amongst these my people!"

And Jill swung ceaselessly to and fro, looking at the man sitting a few yards from her on a rug, before she answered in tersest English:

"Don't be dense, Hahmed! I want eggs and bacon, and a starched finger napkin — toast in a rack — covered dishes — marmalade — I'm — I'm ——"

"Fed up!"

The deep voice filled in the pause also in tersest English.

For one moment Jill sat up as straight as the hammock would allow, and then for the first time in many days broke into a peal of sweetest laughter, and swinging herself clear of the net ran over and laid herself down upon the rug beside the man, with her chin in the palms of her hands, to find herself the next moment in his arms, whilst he looked down into her eyes without speaking. Whereupon she turned her face on to his shoulder and burst into tears.

And Hahmed, being wise, let her cry until there were no more tears, only little sobs which tore at his heart, which lightened considerably when having mopped her eyes with the edge of his cloak, she twisted herself into a sitting position, and smiled as she laid her golden head against his dark one, and entwined her slim fingers in his.

And Hahmed smiled also, knowing that this was the preliminary to some request of which his wife had doubts as to the granting, but never a word did he utter, nor made sign to help, whilst Jill, somewhat at a loss, lit a cigarette, and proceeded to blow rings which on account of the breeze refused to pass one through the other.

"Hahmed!" she managed at last and stopped, and then continued as she got up and moved away: "Hahmed! I'm feeling absolutely *miserable*. I think I want a change — I really do want all I said just now, so — so *can't* we go to Cairo and stay at an English hotel for the New Year? We could *just* do it if we started at once — *couldn't* we? I know you have important business or something next month — *can't* you put it off?"

Hahmed looked at her for a moment, as she stood very fair and straight, with her beautiful feet peeping from under her trailing gown; and frowned a little, noticing the shadows round the big eyes, and the suspicion of a collar-bone showing above the embroidery of her bodice.

"And why didst thou hesitate, little one, to ask — knowing as thou dost that thy wish is law absolute to me? Business affairs, what are they? Let them wait — let the world wait as long as thou art happy. Verily thou art pale and thin ——" Upon which unfortunate remark Jill turned like the spitfire she had lately become.

"Seeing that **you are** allowed four wives, Hahmed,

there is no reason to bemoan your fate; this is not Europe, where once married you are for ever tied to the one girl, who, a bud in her youth, may as time passes turn to one of those dreadful cabbage-roses, which go purple and fat with age. I'm sorry," she continued, as she held out both her hands, " you simply must not notice me these days. I think I am be-witched — I have even sent my darling old Ameena away because her deformity suddenly irritated me, and I told Mustapha I would have him thrown as break-fast to the cheetahs if he dared to make himself seen, and he believed it, and no shampoo will *ever* get the sand out of his hair."

"But he *shall* be thrown to the cheetahs if it would please thee, beloved!"

And the uncalculating cruelty in the man's voice sent the red to the girl's white face, and moving over to him made her lean down and kiss him upon the mouth.

And then she seated herself upon the ground and made tea, laughing like a child when to please her the Arab drank it protestingly.

"By Allah! it is a poison which you drink in Europe, and yet you would go and drink it in a crowded city."

"Are we going, Hahmed, oh Hahmed, *are* we?" whispered Jill, half afraid to break the spell by the raising of her voice.

"But of course, beloved — hast thou not expressed the wish — though surely it were better to go to thine own dwelling, for it will go hard with thee to keep thy face covered and remain undiscovered to thy many friends, who doubtless will be seeking the solace of Egypt's winter sun; for the time is not yet at hand when I will permit thee to make thyself known to them."

But Jill was ready to accept anything as long as her craving could be satisfied, and Hahmed, longing to satisfy her craving, looked with eyes of love upon the sweetness of her face aglow with anticipation, so that both were well content.

And an hour passed in which they ate and drank, and Jill balanced pieces of sweet bread upon the noses of two great hounds, who, scenting their master from afar, had broken bounds and raced to him, leaping the breakfast table to Jill's infinite delight, whilst their groom lay upon the ground out of sight anticipating the thrashing his carelessness merited him, but from which he was spared by reason of his mistress' sweetness.

"And so, Light of Heaven, I must leave thee, for there is much to prepare if we would start at once, for it is difficult to secure the strict privacy due to my wife in these times when the world is overrun by the tourist ants who should by right be underground.

"And my heart inclineth to hours spent with thee, O! Flower of the Desert, hours spent at thy feet in the heat of the day whilst thou slumberest, hours upon the roof of thy dwelling, watching the day prepare herself for the coming of her lover, the night; and yet must I leave thee when my being is overwhelmed with love of thee, thou wind of caprice! Would that I could tell the meaning of my gentleness towards thee, I, Hahmed, who, like a love-sick youth, sleeps the night without the silken curtain of thy door and dare not enter in unto thee."

And his hands suddenly gripped the girl by her shoulders and pulled her towards him, at which roughness she smiled, as women do when so treated, and rested her sweet-scented head above his heart.

"Ah, Hahmed! Who knows if thou are not over timorous even for a love-sick youth," she sighed. "And *must* thou go when my heart inclineth to hours spent with *thee?* And yet at night the stars come out so 'tis said, and can be seen from the roof of my dwelling; and when the wind sweeps over chill across the sands the fire throws shadows in my room of roses, where the love bird with little wings hovers above my couch suspended by a little silken cord."

And the man bent her back towards him so that the ribbon of her bodice snapped and the beauty of her lay under his hands, and she stretched both arms outwards and whispered so that only he could hear, "Kiss me, Hahmed, oh my heart's desire! Kiss me, for I am faint with love of thee."

And even as he bent downwards to her she fell unconscious at his feet, whereupon he raised her in his arms and looked into the white face, speaking so that only she might hear.

"And the love bird shall fly down to thy couch this night, Delight of my Heart, and the shadows upon thy sweet face shall deepen ere the dawn," and he kissed the closed eyes and the red mouth and the white throat and the shadow of a collar-bone which showed above the roundness of her breasts, and then he laid her upon the cushions on the ground, and, clapping his hands, gave her into the care of her handmaidens.

CHAPTER XXXVIII

An hour and more had passed before Jack Wether-bourne suddenly awoke, and stretching his arms above his head apostrophised the full moon shining down upon the Great Pyramid in the shadows of which he was sitting.

"What the dickens Lady Moon brought me to this place of all places to-night," he said lazily, as he struck a match and lit a cigarette. "Let's hope my ship of the desert hasn't upstreamed for Cairo all on her own, else I see myself here until the advent of the next Cook's party. Decent of the camel wallah to let me take the apple of his commercial eye into the desert unaccompanied." He stretched and settled himself more comfortably, continuing to talk aloud. "What a night — what a country — wish I'd brought Mary with me — ideal spot for a heart-to-heart talk. I might have shaken her out of her 'eyedyfix,' as old Gruntham calls it. Silly idea that she won't get married until Jill has been found — why! what! who in heaven's name are coming down the pyramid? Well, I'm blessed! two native wallahs been breaking the rules, and I had no idea they were perched up there above my head."

Safe in the protecting shadows he watched Hahmed and Jill descend.

Little ripples of laughter fell on the night air as Hahmed, letting himself down easily from one gigantic block to another, held out his arms and lifted Jill down, bending his head to kiss her each time he put her on her feet.

They were at the last step but one when, with a little scream, she swayed, and nearly fell to the step beneath.

" Hold me, Hahmed," she cried, " I'm dizzy, everything is going round! "

And Hahmed caught her and lifted her gently down the last steps to the sand, bending to kiss her on the mouth, and shifting her suddenly to his left arm so as to catch Jack Wetherbourne by the throat as he dashed shouting from the shadows upon them.

" Jill! Jill! It's I — Jack! don't let ——"

Until the grip tightening choked back his words, when with a surprising swiftness the Arab let go his hold, and getting one in on the point, sent the Englishman reeling backwards to fall in a heap against the base of the pyramid, and then to scramble to his feet, too dizzy to stop his adversary, who, flinging the veil over the woman's face, passed swiftly to the place where awaited the camels.

And too slow was Jack Wetherbourne to gain the spot in time to stop the flight of the camel which with its double burden was already racing straight ahead into the desert; and too bemused by the blow to recognise the fact when he did get there that the hired brute he was staggering too was built for speed in the image of the tortoise compared to the hare-like-for-swiftness contour of the abandoned beauty who had strolled to the spot from the other side of the pyramid, and quite undisturbed was watching her sister's hurried departure into the unknown.

CHAPTER XXXIX

ALL our lives we all chase wraiths in the moonshine! Be the wraiths the outcome of proximity in the garden under the silvery moon rays, which so often snap the trap about our unwary feet by rounding off the physical angles of our momentary heart's desires, or lending point to the stub ends of their undeveloped mentality; or the wraiths of the midnight soul, otherwise disarranged nervous or digested system, which float invitingly, distractingly, tantalisingly in front of our clogged-by-sleep vision at night; turning out, however, in the early light heralding the early cup of tea, to be nothing more soul distracting than the good old brass knob adorning the end of the bedstead.

But Jack Wetherbourne's wraiths, which he was chasing in the moonlight, were good honest humans with the requisite number of legs and arms wrapped in good white raiment; one of which humans with the other in his arms sat astride a camel, who made up by her muscular development whatever she might lack in goodness of heart and honesty of purpose; she too being wrapped in the silvery drapery which the moon throws pell-mell around pyramid and mud hut, humble fellah, descendant maybe of some long dead Pharaoh, and the jocular, jubilant millionaire, who with luck can trace a grandfather.

But chase he ever so eagerly, Jack Wetherbourne

could barely keep his quarry in sight as on and **on sped**
the racing camel with that curious slithering gait which
denotes great speed, whilst the wind caught at Jill's
veil, blowing it this way and that until she impatiently
tore it from before her face, and struggling against **the**
arm which held her like a vice, managed to screw her
self round to look behind, whereupon the Arab jerked
her suddenly back, looking down into her white face
with eyes ablaze with jealousy.

"Hast thou no circumspection, O! wife of mine?"
he cried, the wind carrying the words from his lips
almost before they were uttered. "Mine, *all* mine
thou art, and yet thou strivest to look upon the countenance of that madman who would have outraged my
honour by looking upon thy face!"

"Oh, but Hahmed! you don't understand — that **was**
Jack Wetherbourne, my neighbour and brother and
friend, and do for pity's sake make the camel go slower,
I am being bumped to bits!"

Which of all foolish utterances was the most foolish
she could have uttered, fanning the man's jealousy **to**
a pitch where it burned right through the barrier of
self-restraint, making him desire to stop her foolish
words with kisses, and long to strangle her as she lay
in his arms, and cast her on to the sands for the vultures to pick at.

"Thy friend and brother! How could any man un-
born of thy parents be anything but the would-be lover
and husband of thy beautiful self! Verily, woman,
could I beat thee for such words until thy shoulders
ran blood. I know of him and his foolish futile search-
ings for thee, yet it is *I* who hold thee, and in **very**

truth can call thee wife; nor will I stay this my camel so that thou mayest have speech with him; this pale faced yearling, who dared to look upon thy shadow; but by the grace of Allah, I will so bewilder him who blundereth after thee astride the product of the bazaar, that his sightless skull shall stare blindly at the moon to-morrow night, whilst I shall feast my eyes upon the whiteness of thy satin skin."

And Jill lay still, knowing that she was up against something with which she could not cope, noticing not at all that the camel began a wide circle to the left, therefore being excessively surprised when an hour before the dawn, upon the very outskirts of Cairo itself, the man caused his camel to kneel, and placing the girl like a bundle of hay upon the ground, turned towards Mecca; and the time of prayer being passed, came to her suddenly and held her to him, raining kisses upon the fairness of her face, shining pale and shadowed in the light of the coming day.

CHAPTER XL

You have only to stare long enough at it to get the image of some distinct object imprinted upon your retina, then you need but stare again at some space of indistinct colouring and you will see the impression of your distinct object reprinted a hundred times upside down.

Who has not tried the experiment in their youth with the aid of the ceiling and red-lettered advertisement of chocolate or soap, and later in years upbraided the reflected blobs of sun which usually choose a critical moment in which to obscure your vision when you have turned your back upon the sunset.

Jack Wetherbourne distinctly saw the fleeing camel in front of him, when he at last got his own to its feet, and being eager to keep his quarry well within his vision, continued to stare and strain his eyes, whilst he raced for hour after hour over mile after mile of sand, until in the end he saw the fleeing camel ahead of him when in reality it was well on its way back to Cairo; and continued, with eyes staring out of a white, dust-covered face, to pursue the phantom until the first ray of the sun hitting him fiercely, caused him to cover his eyes a while, and after, to look about him with refreshed sight, which showed him in the midst of the desert, alone, with a cloud of sand rising before the wind some miles behind him — an infant sandstorm, but strong enough to hide the distant peaks of the pyra-

mids from him, and to send his terrified, idiotic camel
fleeing straight ahead through hours of increasing heat,
without a drop of water upon its foolish back or in its
master's pocket flask, until with a sudden silly chuckle
the man jerked the reins and tumbled headlong from
the saddle, laughing stupidly with sudden sunstroke.

CHAPTER XLI

THE midday sun of the same day blazed down upon a picture which for ghastliness surpassed even the horrors painted by the madman Werth, which, if your mind is steeped in morbidness, you can see for a franc, or for nothing, I really forget which, when next you visit Brussels.

Upon a hillock of sand, the summit of which continually trickled to the base in fine golden streams, a little mound built with the aid of a pair of pumps, sat Jack Wetherbourne, laughing sickeningly, just as he had sat since the moment he had waved a delirious adieu to the quickly disappearing camel. His dress coat, trousers, white waistcoat, shirt, undergarments, socks and shoes, lay upon the sand arranged by the disordered mind in the fantastic design of a scarecrow.

As I have said, the man himself, naked save for a vest twisted round his waist, sat upon the mound gesticulating violently, whilst keeping up a one-sided, unanswered conversation with the figure on the sand. His bronzed face, burnt almost black even in the few hours of sun beating down upon his unshaded head, turned restlessly to the right and left; his long fingers plucked without ceasing at the great blisters which the heat drew up upon his body, bursting them, so that the fluid mingled with the sand blown upon him by the

242

light wind, and upon which flies, thousands of them, settled, to buzz away when he rose to run this way and that in an effort to stay the awful irritation.

Two o'clock by the clocks in Cairo, the hour when workers and idlers, rich and poor, seek the coolest spot in their vicinity in which to lay them down and sleep a while — the hour when Mary Bingham drove up to Shepherds, having raced here, there, and everywhere during the morning in a vain endeavour to awaken a little interest in the minds of those who listened, and shrugged, and looked at each other significantly, at the tale of a man who had got lost in Cairo for a night and a morning — a tale told agitatedly by a charming woman who could give no reason for her agitation.

Also she had tried desperately hard, with the aid of the hotel porter, to make head or tail out of the narrative as recounted by the hirer of camels — a woebegone tale in which the undercurrent was a dismal foreboding as to the fate of the priceless quadruped; the fate of an Englishman seemingly being of small account when compared to that of the snarling, unpleasant brute who represented the native's entire fortune — at least so he said. "Yes, the nobleman had hired the camel as he so often did, and being acquainted with the ways of the animal had gone alone as he always did. No! upon the beard of his grandfather he had no idea in which direction he had gone, though verily upon the outskirts of Cairo there had been a festival in which La Belle, the well-known dancer, was to dance — who knows ——" And the Hon. Mary had flung out of the place in disgust, knowing with a woman's intuition.

sharpened love, in comparison with which a *kukri* is blunt, that no such place hid the man she had been searching for so desperately ever since she had suddenly wakened and sprung out of her bed the night before, for no reason whatever, and, having rung up Shepherds and ascertained the fact that Sir John Wetherbourne was not in the hotel, had paced her room until she could with reason arouse her maid, and, having bathed and breakfasted, had started out on the seemingly mad pursuit of someone who had failed to return to his habitat during the night — and in *Cairo* too!

Is it surprising that men winked secretly at one another, and that their wives, sharers of their joys and sorrows, scandal and gossip inclusive, jingled their bracelets and pursed their lips, and did all those things which jealous women — not necessarily love jealous — are feign to do when the object responsible for the conception of the green-eyed monster within their being is bent on making a fool of herself?

" Come now, dearie," mumbled Lady Sarah Gruntham, who insisted on keeping Lancashire meal hours to the consternation of the hotel staff, native and otherwise, as she mopped her heated brow with her handkerchief and with the other hand patted the dark head leaning wearily upon the row of scarab buttons adorning her tussore front, from which she had forgotten to remove her finger napkin when the girl had entered. " Come now — come now. Don't 'ee take on an' fret so. The lad'll coom back to ye, never ye fear now. Well I remember when yon Tim of mine was down t' mine in t' big explosion — I took on just as ye are takin' on, love, but down in me heart, lass, I never really feared me, because I knew that me love for me lad was that great, lass, that I'd pull him out of danger —.and sure and I did, lass, black as a sweep and with a broken arm, but alive, and a champion tea of shrimps and cress we had, jest as ye'll have with yer lad when he comes back, lass! "

Which motherly comfort served to lighten the heavy heart, but brought not the faintest shadow of a smile to the steadfast eyes. For even the vision of watercress, shrimps and tea on the verandah at Shepherds will not force a light to the windows of the soul when they are blinded with anxiety.

So Mary Bingham, in her cool white dress, lay back in the long chair, with a glass of iced lemonade on a table by her side in a room darkened so as to induce slumber, whilst out in the desert with choked cries of " Good dog! At it! Good dog! " a man began scratching the sand as a ratting terrier does the earth, until he had excavated a hole big enough in which to curl himself, where he lay until desert things that creep and crawl drove him out again, shrieking for water.

CHAPTER XLII

AND the full force of the storm crashed about Jill's defenceless head at the midday hour also of the same day, when she ought to have been searching the coolness of her midday sleeping chamber, and forgetfulness of the last few hours in sleep.

Not quite defenceless was she, however, as she sat back in the chair, her eyes ablaze and her veil torn to shreds at her feet, ripping the moral atmosphere with words which seemed to have been dipped in some corrosive verbal fluid. She was angry, hurt, and deathly tired, and was doing her best to pass some of her mental suffering anyway on to the man who leant with folded arms against the cedar wall.

The inevitable crisis had come!

The independence of Western womanhood had clashed with the Eastern ideas on the privacy and seclusion of the gentler sex. Jill simply could *not* understand that there was any cause for the terrible jealousy which had suddenly blazed up in the Arab when she had innocently repeated her request to be allowed to see her old friend; Hahmed was as incapable of understanding the request, having failed in his sojourn in the West to fully realise the everyday kind of jolly, good, frank camaraderie which can exist between certain types of English man and woman.

Half a word of tenderness, half a gesture of love,

and she would have been sobbing or laughing happily in his arms, but like a prairie fire before the wind, the terrible Eastern rage was blazing through the man, too fierce, too terrific to allow him to analyse the situation, or remember that the upbringing of his girl-wife had been totally different to that of the women of his country.

Jill suddenly sat forward, clasping one slim ankle across her knee in a slim hand, a position she knew perfectly well would rouse Hahmed to a frenzy, and spoke slowly and mockingly in English instead of the pretty lisping Arabic which always entranced him.

"You may lecture, and remonstrate, and admonish, which all comes to the same thing, until night falls, but you will never make me see eye to eye with you in *this*. It is simply *absurd* to threaten that you will shut me in my apartments until I learn reason. If you lock me in, or place guards about me, I will jump from the roof and gain my freedom by breaking my neck. Why Jack Wetherbourne — oh ——"

Hahmed had leant forward, and gripping her by the shoulders had very suddenly, and not over gently, jerked her to her feet, holding her by the strength of his hands alone, as she desperately tried to liberate herself.

"Let me go, Hahmed! let me go! You are hurting me dreadfully. You must *not* hurt me — you must *not* bruise me. Oh! you don't understand!"

She struggled furiously and unavailingly, resorting at last to cruelty to gain her end.

"Let me go, Hahmed! Take your hands away — I — I *hate to feel them upon me!*"

He let her go, pushing her away from him ever so slightly, so that she stumbled against the chair, cracking her ankle-bone, that tenderest bit of anatomical scaffolding, against a projecting piece of ornamental wood.

It was a case of injury added to insult, and she crouched back furious in her physical hurt as she tore the silken covering from her arms, where already showed faint bruises above the little tattoo mark showing itself so black against the white skin, and upon which she put her finger.

"Oh! who would have thought when you tattooed that, Jack ——!"

But she stood her ground and shrugged her naked shoulders irritatingly when Hahmed crossed the dividing space in a bound with his hand upon the hilt of his dagger.

"Bi — smi — llah! what sayest thou? This mark upon the fairness of thy arm which I have thought a blemish, and therefore have not questioned thee thereon — sayest thou it is a *dakkh,* what thou callest a tattoo mark? And if so what has it to do with the man whose name is unceasingly upon thy lips?"

Jill stood like a statue of disdain.

"What *is* the matter now, Hahmed? Please understand that I will not tolerate such continual fault-finding any longer! That is a tattoo mark of a pail of water — you may not know that we have a rhyme in England which begins like this:

"Jack and Jill went up a hill
To fetch a pail of water!"

Oh! shades of ancient Egypt, did you ever hear or

see anything so pathetically absurd as Jill as she solemnly repeated the old doggerel.

"That makes no difference — a pail of water or the
outline of a flower — did this man — this — this *Jack*
make the mark upon thee?"

Jill hesitated for a second and then answered with
a glint in ber eye.

"Yes! he did — and he did Mary too — put the
dinkiest little heart on her arm — we were under the
cherry tree in the vegetable ——!"

"Go!" suddenly thundered the Arab.

And Jill, gathering her raiment about her for departure, turned to look straight into the man's eyes,
whilst her heart, in spite of the little scornful smile
which twisted the corner of her mouth, leapt with the
love which had blossomed a hundredfold under the torrent of jealousy, wrath, and mastery which he had
poured forth upon her during the last hour.

"Behold! art thou weak," she said sweetly in his
own tongue, "having not the strength to kill that which
offends thee. 'Thou shalt not know this man, or any
other man,'" she mocked, quoting his words, "and yet
canst thou not break me to thy will! Of a truth, I
have no further use for thee in thy weakness!"

But Hahmed's control had only been slightly cracked,
so that he merely pointed to the curtain which divided
Jill's quarters from the rest of the house.

"Go!" he said simply, "go to thy apartment,
wherein thou shalt stay until thou seest good to come
to me in obedience and love. Thou shalt *not* go forth
except to the gardens; neither shall thy friends visit
thee, neither shalt thou climb to the roof; and thou

shalt obey me — many, aye, many a woman were dead for far less than this thy disobedience — but thou — thou art too beautiful to kill, except with love — go!"

And Jill went, with beautiful head held high, heart throbbing from love, and blood pounding in her ears from downright rage.

"I will not obey you! I shall do exactly as I wish!" she proclaimed, with the curtain in her hand. In which she was mistaken, for the simple fact that love held her fast.

And the curtain swinging to hide her from the Arab, as she stood for one moment holding out her arms toward him; and for the same reason she did not see him pick up her torn, scented veil, to thrust it between his inner silken vest and his sorely perturbed heart.

CHAPTER XLIII

NIGHT with her blessed wind had come at last, which means coolness for a space beneath the stars, and oblivion for a while in sleep for those who have untroubled heart and good digestion. There was just one black patch in all that silvery stretch of sand, upon which the moon shone, a patch that came neither from rock or tree or cloud, and which moved occasionally in fitful jerks, until it raised itself and collapsed again, and spread itself in a still stranger shape as from underneath garments which had the form of arms and legs and disjointed feet which fell apart, there crawled a man.

A man, though the face was cracked in great seams from brow to chin, whilst the black tongue protruded from the split mouth drawn back from the even teeth until the great bloated face seemed to laugh in derision at the moon's softness.

The body, covered in a mass of sores coated with sand, raised itself to the knees, whilst the hands tried painfully to scoop up the silver moonbeams and raise them to the mouth. There was no sound in all that deathly plain, which Allah knows is accustomed to such scenes, and when the body had fallen forward once more upon the sand, so that the open mouth was filled with grit, neither was there movement, until upon the pale light of dawn a silent shape, and yet another, and

still another one, sailed serenely across the sky, and
with a faint rustle of folding wings settled down around
the heap; to soar noiselessly skyward when it suddenly
twitched convulsively; to settle again with faint rustling
when all once more was still..

"Verily, O! brother, I am led towards that spot
upon which the birds of death have come together."

So said the Egyptian who was partner in the small
caravan proceeding leisurely towards Cairo, as he
shaded his eyes and pointed first up to the ever lighten-
ing sky, across which from all parts floated small black
dots, and then to a distant place upon the sand, where
the black spots seemed to mingle until they formed a
blot of shade.

"Nay! Raise not thy voice in dissent, O! my
brother, for behold we have made good time, and water
faileth us not."

And well was it that they turned aside, and shouted
as they approached so that only one beak had time to
tear a strip of flesh from beneath the naked shoulder,
ere the flock of vultures rose, hovered a second, and
were gone. The two men drew near, and having dismounted, turned the poor thing over, and feeling the
faint beating of the heart, with no more ado than if
they were setting down to food, undid one of the
goatskins from the nearest camel, and soaking the
flowing bernous until it dripped with the precious
water, wrapped the body in its folds; and collecting
the gold watch, money and card-case strewn upon the
sands, slipped everything back into a waistcoat pocket
with the exception of a three day old programme announcing a cotillion at Shepherd's Hotel, a sketch of

which hideous building was elaborately and menda-
ciously reproduced on the cover, so that to the mind
of uneducated Yussuf, unversed in the English tongue,
there was but one thing to do, and that to go straight
to the well-known caravanserai with his burden, and
deliver it safely into the proprietor's hands.

So Yussuf, euphoniously termed a benighted heathen
by some enlightened Christians, seated himself upon
the fastest camel in the caravan, receiving into his arms
the thing that was still a man by their good efforts,
from the hands of the other heathen, who, with hands
raised to heaven, called down the blessing of Allah upon
men and beast as the latter departed at her swiftest
for the great city, leaving him to follow in more leisurely manner.

So that consternation and excitement were great
among those who sat upon the verandah after dinner,
partaking of coffee and cigarettes before undertaking
the more strenuous task of entertaining themselves,
when in the glare of the electric light a great camel
suddenly appeared out of the night, and totally dis-
regarding the upraised voice of the enormous hotel
porter, subsided in the gutter, thereby causing a block
in the street; whilst a man clumsily dismounted and
staggered up the shallow steps, tenderly holding some
covered burden the while in his arms that were breaking with fatigue, and who, speaking with authority,
demanded speech of the proprietor, who, furious at
being disturbed, came forth as furiously to annihilate
the disturber, but instead, at the first word from the
Arab, who clutched a dirty piece of paper in a hand
almost paralysed with cramp, lifted a corner of the

cloth from about that which lay so inertly under **the**
all-hiding cloak, and choked, and stuttered, and the**n**
recovering himself, blandly led the Arab to the lift
which whirled them to the first floor, leaving the **occu-**
pants on the verandah all a-twitter, whilst the **coffee**
grew cold and the cigarettes went **out.**

CHAPTER XLIV

DAYS and nights passed, and still more days and nights, in which the man, bound from head to foot in soft wrappings soaked in unguents, tossed and raved, screaming for water, tearing at the bed-linen which to his distorted mind was alive with every conceivable insect, beating blindly at the faces of the two women who, refusing any help, watched over and tended Jack Wetherbourne through his days of distress.

"Aye, lass! Now don't 'ee lose 'eart," whispered Sarah Ann Gruntham to the girl who, having held consultation with the doctor, was sobbing her heart out on the elder woman's motherly bosom which covered a heart of purest gold. "Don't 'ee listen to such fash, lass, for what's he likely to know outside of Lady Jones's wimble-wambles and me Lor' Fitznoodles' rheumatism. Why 'e couldn't even tell that I 'ad 'ad a touch of my old complaint, and me with an 'andle to me name. Come, lass, oop with ye bonnie head, for I'll tell 'ee the great news — I sees a bead o' perspiration on Sir John's brow — an' so I'm off to take me 'air out of crackers. Though Tim does find it more home-like, 'e says, when I 'ave 'em h'in — oh, dearie! dearie! I often wish I was plain Mrs. Gruntham again with no aitches to mind. I'll be with you in ten minutes, and then, lass, ye'll just run away and have a bath — I managed the aitch that time — and come back as fresh

as a daisy, if there were such a innocent thing in this
land of sphinxes and minxes — and ye'll see ten beads
then, which sounds as tho' I be a Roman instead of a
strict Baptist. I'll run along, love, and don't let 'im
see tears in them bonny eyes of yours when he comes
to know ye, lass."

And the dearest old soul in the world waddled away
to take her hair out of the crackers which had made a
steel halo round her silvery hair for many a night, and
waddled back again to see Mary with a great glow in
her eyes, and her hand clasping the skeleton fingers of
Jack Wetherbourne, who had known her at last, and
was gazing blissfully at his beloved.

His lips moved, though so weak was he that no
sound came from them, so that Mary had to bend to
catch the whisper until her ear just touched the lips
still distorted from the effects of the desert sun.

She sat up, blushing from chin to brow, and smil-
ingly shook her head.

"I will marry you, Jack dear, as soon as we find
Jill!"

Wetherbourne made a feeble and unsuccessful at-
tempt to frown, and then turned his eyes as Mary
turned her head on the opening of the door between
the bedroom and the sitting-room.

In the doorway stood the bewildering picture of an
Eastern woman.

Wrapped round in the voluminous cloak of the East,
with the face and head veils hiding all but her eyes,
she stood quite still as Lady Sarah bustled across the
room towards her, and Mary held up a warning hand.

A twitching of the man's fingers drew Mary's attention, and once more she leant down to him.

" We're engaged," came the faint whisper, " *it's Jill!* "

CHAPTER XLV

DECKED out in Mary's trappings Jill lay on the couch, her pale face shining like an evening flower, whilst she passed the brush over and over again through the burnished strands of her wonderful hair.

Mary had sat spellbound, almost open-mouthed, at the Arabian Nights tale Jill had poured into her astounded ears.

"Hahmed!" she had exclaimed when Jill had told her of her marriage; and be it confessed that Jill had tautened to meet the coming attack, and relaxed when Mary, clasping her capable hands, had suddenly and whole-heartedly beamed upon her. "Why, I've heard the most wonderful things about him since I have been out here, in fact I've been almost wearied to death listening to the accounts of his Haroun al Raschid methods and qualities. His wedding put Cairo in an uproar — I saw the pro —— But *Jill,* darling, is it possible it was you inside the palanquin on the wonderful camel?"

Jill nodded as she busied herself in plaiting her hair into great ropes.

"And you've run away — escaped, you say?"

Jill nodded again.

"Yes!" she said, with three big tortoiseshell combs between her teeth. "We had a *frightful* flare-up — all the fault of my tearing temper. You see I've been absolutely spoilt these last months, and I simply behaved anyhow the first time I got scolded. But I didn't deserve it all the same!" she added as an after-thought, as she wound the plaits round her head. "And," she went on, "I should never have got away if Mustapha had been with us."

"Who's Mustapha?"

"My own special bodyguard! But as he *wasn't* there I managed to thoroughly examine the high wall round the grounds, and found just one spot to give me a foothold. I scrambled up in the heat of the day when everyone was asleep, and had a terrible time with my garments."

She pointed as she spoke to a scented heap of silk and satin thrown on a chair.

"I had to partly disrobe whilst sitting on the top of the wall, and was terrified in case some pedlar might chance along. I tied my face and head veil round my waist, but the *habarah,* that big black cloak — by the way it belongs to one of my women, and I borrowed it with the excuse that I wanted it copied, mine you see are rather ornamental, as, of course, I never walk in the streets — well, I threw that on to the ground, tucked up my *sebleh,* that dressing-gown sort of thing, and scrambled down the other side, as I did not want to jump, ripping the knees of my *shintiyan* — the wide trouser kind of things we wear ——"

Mary's face was a study.

"Thanks to my borrowed cloak I was able to walk through the streets in comfort — drawing my *burko,* face veil, dear, across my face so that only one eye should be seen,[1] and a blue one at that. When I got

---

1 A custom.

to Cairo I hired a car — speaking in Arabic to the astounded and fluttering Englishman — drove to the Savoy, where I guessed you'd be — found you'd moved here — came here — and being mistaken for what I am by marriage, namely, a high-born lady of the land, was conducted straightway to you in spite of the invalid — *et voilà!* "

Mary got up, and crossing to Jill sat down beside her on the couch.

" And what now, Jill? Hahmed will come and fetch you."

" Not Hahmed," said Jill, with a shadow in her eyes as she remembered his parting words after what she had tersely called the flare-up. " Besides, he trusts me *really!* " she added as an afterthought, and continued with a note of feverish excitement in her voice : " No! I'm going to stay with you, Mary, if you'll let me, until something or another happens to help me make up my mind. I want to do a lot of sight-seeing, and wear white skirts and a silk jersey and blouse. I'll find a maid somewhere, I expect."

" Oh! " broke in practical Mary, " don't worry about that — servants are such a nuisance. Do you remember Higgins? Well! she came out with me, and gave me notice the second week —' couldn't abide the 'eathen ways '— and wanted to get back to her home in Vauxhall. But the proprietor found me a native woman, a perfect treasure, whose one complaint is that she hasn't enough work to do! "

Silence fell for a time whilst Mary studied the face of her friend, suddenly leaning forward to stroke the pale cheek and pat the little hand.

"You don't look well, Jillikins! Are you *sure* you are happy?"

"Perfectly," said Jill, turning her face to the cushions and bursting into uncontrollable weeping.

CHAPTER XLVI

WITH short steps the native woman shuffled quickly along the outside of the wall surrounding the house of Hahmed the Arab, stopping in front of the great gates, which were closed at sunset, to peer between the wrought bronze work, standing her ground unconcernedly when a Nubian of gigantic proportions suddenly appeared on the other side.

Terrifying he looked as he towered in the dusk, his huge eyes rolling, and his hand on the hilt of a scimitar, which looked as though it had been tempered more for use than for ornament.

"What wouldst thou?" he demanded in dog Arabic of the woman whose eyes flashed disdainfully over the veil which hid her pock-marked face.

"Speech with they master, who has bidden me to his presence, and move quickly, thou black dog of ill repute; tarry not in saying that his servant from the big house in the city has news for his most august ears."

The son of ill repute stared inquisitively for a moment, and then moved off slowly with the inimitable gait of these ebon specimens of mankind, increasing his pace almost to a run once out of the female's range of vision.

Like a shadow she followed the different people, who, passing her from one to another, led her through rooms and halls into an open court, at the far end of

262

which sat the man she sought, watching two jaguars being led up and down before him.

"Peace unto thee, O! my daughter, and fear not to approach," Hahmed said gently as the woman made deep obeisance, and shrank from the animals who snarled at her viciously. "And thou, my son, take these products of the bazaar hence, for surely hast thou been fooled by him who brought them from distant climes. Verily, the sire may have been a jaguar, but his mate, judging from the shape of the offspring, must most surely have been a jackal. Bring not such trash to me, if thou wouldst not incur my wrath!"

The snarling products of the bazaar were hurriedly jerked out of the court as Hahmed turned to the woman.

"Is all well, O! faithful one?"

"All is well, O! Most High," answered the Honourable Mary's perfect treasure of a maid. "Behold the gracious flower, upon whom it is my joy and honour to wait, changeth her mood one hundred times in the passing hour. She laughs at noon, and her pillow is wet with salt tears at night; her feet, like lotus-buds, carry her hither and thither in the day, the dimness of her room sees her face downwards upon her couch.

"As unto a sweet rose she clings to her friend, the great lady, who forsooth is as pleasing as a well-cooked dish of the flesh of kid mingled with tamarind and rice; but the rose mixeth not with other flowers, and about her heart rests thy most honourable picture."

For some long time Hahmed stared unseeingly in front and then he spoke.

"Thou hast worked well, my daughter, even from the

moment when thou didst take the place of the great lady's white servant, to report to me upon the doings of the white man who strove to find my wife.

"Ask what reward thou will'st, it shall be granted unto thee!"

And the man, knowing the cupidity of his race, was somewhat astounded when, casting herself at his feet, the woman craved to be taken into his household so that, as she put it, "I may dwell in content in thy shadow, and the shadow of the snow-white dove when she wings her way back to happiness." Just for a moment the Arab looked into the eyes of the woman, as, greatly daring, she lifted her right hand.

"For so it is written, O! my lord! the blessing of Allah is upon thee, and thy heart shall be at rest."

CHAPTER XLVII

THE day following the native woman's surreptitious visit to the great Arab saw Jill and Mary and Jack, followed discreetly by the same native woman, set sail at an early, gay and blithesome hour for Denderah, where are to be seen the ruins of the Temple of Hathor, the Venus of Ancient Egypt.

Upon arriving, after much dallying on the way, Jill insisted upon walking along the narrow tracks through the stretches of corn and sweet-smelling flowering bean, among which, to the general horror, cattle ranging from cows to goats were allowed to roam at will.

A temple of love calls up visions of marble halls, marble fretwork, basins with splashing waters and marble doves, pillars crowned with intertwined marble hearts and lovers' knots tied with marble ribbons; therefore Jill stood transfixed as she entered the great hall of columns, with the goddess's somewhat forbidding head carved on each side of each pillar.

She walked across slowly to peer into the inner court, shrouded in deep shadows, shuddered and moved back towards the other two, whose mentality, psychology or temperament responded not in the least to light and shade.

Together they traversed the place, Jill running her hand over the hieroglyphics which cover the pillars to their beautiful capitals, until she stopped before a representation of Hathor the wanton, standing naked **and** verily unashamed before the image of a man whose name I know not, but whose beauty and nudity are **as** great as hers.

Turning sharply she glanced hurriedly at Jack **and** Mary, and slipping a hand through the arm of each, almost pulled them across the floor to a stairway made in the wall and leading to the roof.

For, taken up in their own love story, those two had noticed nothing, not even the uncountable figures of stone in the bas-reliefs which, appearing to turn and whisper to each other, seem in the shadows to take a delight in portraying by pantomimic gestures a love wholly allied to voluptuousness and license.

But Jill had seen, and her ultra fastidiousness had dyed face and neck crimson, and caused her to try and spare her companions similar uncomfortable moments.

For a moment she stood on the roof watching the clouds of twittering birds as they flew in the direction of the Libyan Hills, and then she slipped quietly down the stairway, leaving her friends, supremely oblivious of her presence or absence, weaving their love-tale on the roof of the ruined temple of love.

With nerves a-jangle and heart disturbed Jill longed for shadows and solitude, so that she shrank back, hesitated, and then advanced slowly towards the veiled figure of a woman standing watching her from the shadows of the very heart of the ruins, the holy of holies, the hall of past mysteries and solemn rites.

"What wouldst thou?" Jill asked her in Arabic, which was as wellnigh perfect as any European can make it, and although she could hardly make out one whole sentence of what she took for a dialect spoken by the woman, she grasped enough to understand that the Egyptian, draped in the peasant's cloak, was anxious to read her fortune in the sand she carried in the black handkerchief, and which sand she said she had gathered on the steps of the temple's high altar at the full moon.

Jill sat down on a fallen block of masonry, looking very fragile, very sweet, very fair, with her white throat gleaming above the white silk blouse and jersey, soft blue hat pulled over her sunny head to shade her face, death-white save for the shadows which seemed to make a mask about her eyes, as she drew hieroglyphics on her own account in the sand with the tip of her small white shoe.

She had heard of the extraordinary powers possessed by some of the Egyptian people; Hahmed had told her of their gift of reading the future in the sand; among her own household she had come across authentic cases where the most unlikely things predicted had come to pass.

And the cloud about her was so thick, and weighed so heavily upon her! Of her own free-will she had flung her happiness away, and with her happiness had gone her content and light-heartedness. She laughed with others, and cried softly by herself at night; she shared the amusements with others, and sat up at night, bewildered and afraid, to steal to the mirror and look upon a pinched face with tightened nostrils, and to wipe away the dampness gathered under the golden curls.

Had her marriage been a mistake or not? If not,

why had she fled before the first little sign of storm? If it had been, why was she utterly miserable now that liberty was hers?

Her friends would surely be taking their departure soon. Should she go too, or should she go back in all humbleness to the man she loved? Did he want her, having shown no sign or desire for her return? Did he — did he not? A decision must be made, and soon, but what was it to be? Round and round, like a flock of startled pigeons, went her thoughts, one breaking away to whirr into the back of her mind, another to drift into the shadows, and another, and yet another, whilst the rest flew on, round and round!

And then she shrank back, gripping the stone with two cold little hands as great drops gathered and trickled down her face, her breath coming in silent gasps.

Stricken with terror she threw out her arms passionately.

"Speak, woman, speak! Spread the sand, and read to me what thou seest therein. Thy finger shall point the way, and that way will I follow wherever it may lead."

CHAPTER XLVIII

WHEREUPON the woman of the shadows, turning towards that which had once been an altar, and raising her arms straight above her head with hands out-turned at an acute angle, thrice repeated words that were absolutely unintelligible to Jill.

And then kneeling, she spread the sand upon the ground, dividing it into circles and squares, drawing curious signs with the tip of her hand, which as Jill noticed was passing white and slender for that of a peasant woman, and spoke — in modern tongue.

"Behold, O! woman, who emerged from a grey cloud to enter into the radiance of the sun, thou art beloved by the gods who rule the earth through the countless and eternal ages. Thou dost pause upon the threshold of the temple of love, fearing these shadows which will pass away when thou shalt stand within the great radiance of the goddess. Yea! and fearful art thou of the sand out of which shall spring a tree of many branches, and in the shade of which thou shalt encompass thy life's span. Behold," and the finger drew a line upon the sand, " the grey cloud encloses thee yet once again, and the goddess weeps without! Yet will she rejoice! Before many moons have come and gone, the great god Amen shall tear aside that which blindeth thee, and placing a man son upon thy breast shall lead thee into the innermost temple.

" Six times shall Amen strike thee in love, so that thou bearest sons, and once shall he strike thee upon both breasts so that a woman child shall spring from thy loins.

" Love is thy portion, thy meat, and thy drink, bringing unto thee those who travailing in love shall come for thy wisdom, and those labouring in grief for thy succour.

" And thou shalt not die before thy time, and thou shalt pass to the gods with thy hand in thy master's, for he shall not leave thee through all thy life, nay not even at the last. And thy name shall ring throughout the land of Egypt, and be engraven upon the walls of time.

" Behold Hathor, behold I say! " and three times the unintelligible words rang through the place as Jill sank back staring open-eyed.

The small white hand had pulled the veil aside from about the face, and head, and body of the fortune-teller, so that for a moment she seemed to stand outlined against the pillar, with flashing eyes, scarlet mouth, and brow encircled with a golden band, from which sprang something round with wings set in precious stones; the glory of her gleaming body shone white as ivory in the gloom, her perfect arms stretched straight downwards with hands turned sharply in so that the finger-tips rested on the rounded thighs.

And then Jill rubbed her eyes and stared, and stared again; for the spot was empty, save for a square of sand with strange signs drawn upon it; neither was there sound of retreating footsteps or swish of drapery.

Jill stumbled to her feet, swaying as she caught at a

pillar for support, and then with a violent effort of will walked to a great shaft of sunlight which struck the ground in front of the ruins of the high altar from an opening in the roof.

"Am I mad?" she whispered. "Did I dream that woman — and yet the sand is there!"

A pitiful little smile flickered across the ashen face as she stood motionless and alone in the ruins.

"The temple of love," she cried softly, flinging out her arms, "the temple of love and I am alone. Hahmed beloved, where are you? I feel so — I — I wish you were here to take me in your arms. Hahmed — I want comforting — I do — I'm lonely — I —I'm — oh, oh! God — God have mercy on me — I — we ——"

For a moment the transfigured girl stood upright, her face one blaze of wonder in the light of the sun, her eyes wide open and filled with a great surprise and a greater awe.

And then she slowly sank to her knees and bowed her beautiful head to the sand, whilst the echoes took up her words and carried them to the far corners of the vast ruins.

"I am not worthy, my beloved, for this great honour — I am not worthy in that I am not with thee at this moment when thy child stirs within me. I am covered in shame in that I doubted. I am bowed down with shame and yet lifted up to the heavens with joy."

For long minutes thus knelt she alone with her happiness, and then she raised herself whilst a great sob shook her from head to foot.

"Hahmed," she cried as she flung her arms out wide, "Hahmed, wherever thou art I am calling thee.

Hahmed, Hahmed!" and fell face downward unconscious upon the sand covered floor.

Noiselessly an Arab stepped from behind a pillar,
crossing to the still figure on the ground, and gently
he picked her up in his arms, covering her in the folds
of his great white cloak.

"Little bird! little bird!" he whispered in the beautiful Arabian tongue, "why willst thou beat thy tender
wings against the bars of happiness around thy dwelling? And thou wert frightened — frightened by yon
peasant woman. What said she, my dove, to strike
thee senseless to the ground?

"Thou art pale, O! my heart's delight, and weigh
but as a handful of down upon my arm, and yet must
thou learn thy lesson to the end; and even will I for-
sake thee, leaving thee guided by the star of happiness
to find thy way alone to thy dwelling in the desert.
Yea! there will I await thee, O! my beloved — beloved!"

And Hahmed passed swiftly through the hall of
shadows, and down the fields of waving corn and sweet
scented bean to the banks of the Nile, and there he
placed his sweet burden in the arms of the faithful
native woman, who tenderly wiped the sand from the
golden curls and raised her right hand in fealty to her
master as he turned away, neither did she falter in her
tale to Mary and Jack when, goaded by anxiety and in
spite of the heat, they ran down towards the boat.

"Sunstroke!" said Mary, who had a certificate for
first-aid, and speaking with the certain flat determina-
tion which even her best friends found most trying at
times. "You simply *cannot* go about in Egypt with-

out a green-lined umbrella.   Yes! it's a slight, quite
slight attack of sunstroke," she continued, without noticing the radiance of Jill's eyes, " and I will apply
this damp handkerchief to your medulla oblongata."

CHAPTER XLIX

JILL sat on the edge of her bed in an hotel at Suez.

That she was absolutely alone in Egypt, and ought not to have been alone, never entered her head once, as she gazed through the open window towards the sea.

Her eyes shone like stars, her mouth was a beautiful sign of content, her hands were clasped peacefully on her knee, and she simply radiated happiness.

Mary and Jack, Lady Bingham, Diana Lytham and Sir Timothy and Lady Sarah, had started that morning for England in the great liner which Jill had watched unconcernedly until it disappeared up the canal.

And so for the first time for many weary weeks she was alone, though it must be confessed that the liberty had only been gained by a deliberate perversion of the truth.

Fussed by kind-hearted, though somewhat scanda-lised Lady Gruntham, driven to the point of madness by the never-ending stream of wisdom, advice, and plans which from morning till night flowed unceasingly from the store of Mary's book-gleaned knowledge, Jill had cleared up the situation all round by suddenly announc-ing the imaginative fact that Hahmed was coming to Cairo to fetch her home. Whereupon Mary Bingham had arranged everything to her own entire satisfaction in the twinkling of an eye, told Jack Wetherbourne that she and her mother were leaving for England if he'd like to come too, had worked her maid to death with packing, distributing quite a fair supply of backsheesh, and had bundled her bewildered mother and contented fiancé down to Suez, where Jill had seen them off to the accompaniment of a last final flood of advice which was mercifully lost in the scream of the siren, the rasp of machinery, and the manifold sounds which add hilariously, especially in foreign climes, to the pandemonium that reigns to within a second of the cry which invites some of us to descend to terra firma on the occasion of the sailing of a passenger boat.

Jill suddenly came out of a reverie which had painted her cheeks a most exquisite pink, and caused her teeth to show in the faintest smile.

Then she frowned and shook back her mane of hair, as was her habit when perplexed, and spoke softly to the night wind which was blowing straight in at the window from the other side of the canal.

" The oasis is calling me, night wind, calling, calling, and yet I do not know. You who come from the oasis, tell me, is my beloved there, or shall I find my dwelling empty, and my happiness but as a turned-down cup? "

Who can explain what it is that leads the spirit astraying from its material covering?

Are love and longing its sole companions upon the road of shadows? Surely no! for is not revenge, or jealousy, or the near approach of that which is called death as potent to span the stretches of the world; and will not a vision of stark terror blot out the sun at the commonplace hour of noon, and may not the body, squatting on the market pavement, find it a place of rest, even as unto a seat in paradise through the spirit's communion?

The soul's wireless, mental telepathy, the sympathetic chord, and so on, and so on, good honest words to describe that which no one understands, and which caused the girl sitting on a prosaic bed in a prosaic hotel to smile suddenly as she sat so very still.

For her soul had wandered until she stood with her feet in the sand, looking in at a wide-open door through which a beam of violet-orange light struck across the night.

Two men sat motionless within, until one slowly turned his head and looked through the door straight into her eyes.

For one long moment, with unutterable longing he gazed, and then the vision faded just as Jill, saying softly, "Beloved! I come," stretched out her arms, and with a sudden shiver awoke to her surroundings.

PART III
THE FRUIT

CHAPTER L

"DOUBTLESS my beloved sleeps!" thought Hahmed the Arab, as he looked at the watch on his wrist to find it pointing to midnight, and clapped his hands for fresh coffee, then lit another cigarette whilst his guest who, like himself, sat cross-legged on cushions on the floor, inhaled contentedly from a *shibuk* [1] in a house of rest on the outer edge of a distant oasis.

Weary to death was he of the uninterrupted flow of words which unceasingly streamed from the mouth of the cross-bred man, who was gleefully rubbing the hands of his soul over what he imagined to be the clinching of a remarkable bargain with the Camel King, whereas if he had but known it, his host had merely put a little difficulty in the way so as to lengthen the deal, and thereby kill a few moments of the dreary hours of the dreary time he had passed since had left the woman he loved alone to learn the last words of her lesson.

Turning he called sharply to the servile proprietor of the house, which for the first time was honoured by the presence of its redoubtable landlord.

Salaaming until his tarboosh reached the level of his knees, the inwardly shaking Achmed stood before his two guests.

"Hast thou naught wherewith to entertain thy guests, O! Achmed, or must they perchance pass the hours in counting the flies which flit about the none too clean

[1] Long native pipe.

lamps? Thinkest thou that this house is solely a roof to shade thy head from the sun, or perchance is it a dwelling of comfort for those who pass East and West?"

By this time the oriental's head was bobbing like a mandarin's, whilst in a spasm of terror his mouth opened and shut unceasingly.

"Find thy tongue, O! fool, before I turn thee from the door. Hast thou aught of entertainment, and hast thou other than this mud thou callest coffee? Speak I say!"

With a gulp which served to clench Hahmed's fingers, the wretched Achmed vowed he had music of a kind and dancers of sorts, and that at that moment his first wife was preparing a brew surpassed only by that drunk in the Gardens of Delight by the chosen of Allah, who had passed to their well-earned rest.

"Choose, O! my guest! doubtless they will both be as forlorn as this coffee, for which I crave thy forgiveness — our business is at an end, and some hours stretch unendingly before us."

Ali 'Assan, dying to satisfy his cross-bred inquisitiveness which, with the curiosity of Egypt entire, had been aroused by the strange rumours of some catastrophe happened in his host's household, had not the slightest desire for bed, rather would he have sat up for an entire week of nights, if only he could have got an inkling of the truth; so he plumped for music and dancing whilst his host sat motionless, the light of the hanging lamps throwing strange shadows on the stern, relentless face.

Hahmed the Arab, it is true, sat upon the cushions in the dingy room; you would have certainly touched a human body if you had laid a hand upon his arm, but by an effort of will which left him sitting absolutely motionless with half-closed eyes, he, in spite of the heat, the irritation of his guest's presence, and all that went to make the evening intolerable, had sent his spirit, or soul, or what you will, adrift, searching for his beloved; so unutterable was his longing, so wracked was his heart with love, so utter was his detachment, that neither piping of reed, twanging of stringed instrument or patter of feet could bring him back to his surroundings.

And then under some unexplainable impulse Hahmed turned his head slowly, looking across the shoulder of his guest to the door behind, and his eyes glowed like fires in the darkness of night as in the doorway he saw framed the face of her for whom body and soul craved. The face was pale even unto death, but the red mouth smiled softly, and the golden curls clustered and twisted as they had ever done; the blue eyes were wells of love, in which the Arab's soul sank as he called though his lips moved not, neither was there sound of words in the room.

"Come to me, beloved, beloved! Come to me!"

And the vision faded, and Hahmed's spirit returned to its dwelling as a faint sigh from Ali 'Assan made him remember his duty towards his guest.

The Arab does not indulge in nerves, though Allah only knows how long it will be before he resorts to bromide if he continues to fraternise with the European, but Hahmed, unknown to himself, was suffering from the almost unendurable strain of the past endless empty days.

He was consumed with thirst for his beloved, **agonising** with hunger for his heart's desire, forcing himself to do business in out-of-the-way places in his land so as to keep his thoughts from the exquisite face of his own woman.

True, he could have stayed in Cairo, and waited for further news of her; true, he could have seized her and carried her forcibly back to his own lands, but the pride of centuries raged within him, and until she came back of her own free will he would neither move hand nor foot to compel her.

Anyway, let us put the following episode down to the months of strain culminating in an intense irritation wrought by the babble of Ali 'Assan's meaningless chatter, and the vileness perhaps of the coffee.

He lifted his eyes and looked at the picture before him.

The room was low, and the lighting bad, the air suffocating, whilst a few particles of sand blown in by the hot wind heralded an approaching storm.

Standing before him with a piece of tawdry gauze about her quite unprepossessing form stood the over aged dancer with a set simper upon her silly vacant face.

"Allah!" ejaculated Hahmed, as he lit a cigarette, whilst Achmed, peeping through the door, suddenly smote his forehead.

Now dancing women were no more to the great man than a troupe of performing collies, but his artistic sense demanded the best, and when it was not forthcoming he felt the same annoyance as you or I would feel if arrayed in purple and fine linen we adorned a

box at the opera with our presence, covered with as
many diamonds upon it as possible, to find a street
singer deputising for a Melba or Caruso.

"Thou dog," he said pleasantly to the cringing man,
who tremblingly explained that indeed he had one better — yea, even fair to look upon. "Behold, if thou
offerest yet another insult to this mine guest I will
have thee and thy woman whipped into the desert and
left to die."

Whereupon Achmed fled precipitately in the wake of
her who had annoyed, and snatching a whip beat her
smartly on her plump but ill-formed shoulders, the
while he urged the prima ballerina of the establishment
to anoint herself and depart right quickly to the pacify-
ing of the great Hahmed, which order, alas, put a
totally wrong idea into her Tunisian-Arabian pate.

CHAPTER LI

LA BELLE, a rank cross-breed of Tunisian and French with a dash of Arabian, was the one good part of a bad debt which had overwhelmed Achmed when he had inadvertently over-reached himself.

Her body was passable, lithe, sinewy, with a faint hint of rib and a wonderful bust; her brain was good, intuitive in its non-educated state, and subtle from inheritance; her ambition was superb, it knew no limits, it saw no obstacle.

Born in a kennel in Tunis, she had figuratively and literally fought her way to the upper reaches of the gutter, sleeping in filth, eating it, listening to it, living it; dancing for a meal, selling her strangely seductive body for a piastre or so, settling her quarrels with a knife she carried in her coarse, crisp, henna-dyed hair, with one goal before her slanting orange eyes, that of dancer in chief, prima ballerina, or what you will, in some house of good repute; the explanation of which phrase would overtax my oriental knowldge I fear.

Dance she could, if dancing is the correct term for the subtle portraying of every conceivable vice by every conceivable gesture and posture; and she had felt herself content on the day she had for a good round sum sold herself to take up a dancing position of some importance in the house of him who, unknown to her, had got himself entangled in more than one human money-spider's web.

If her dancing was correct or not, men had begun to foregather in the house, where — if her temper allowed — she would dance o' nights fully clothed or fully unclothed; also her reputation was beginning to be used as a lure to the uninitiated freshly arrived in Cairo, therefore her usually fiendish temper was as hell unloosed when, as part payment of a debt, she found herself willy-nilly strapped to a camel and carted by slow stages to the house of rest whose proprietor was Achmed, and landlord Hahmed, the Camel King.

" Dance I will not, thou descendant of pigs," she stormed at Achmed, who, reducing his fez to a pulp, raved at her as she crouched in a corner with something a-glitter in her hand. " Send in thy wife who ambles like a camel in foal, and whose ankles are thick enough to serve as prop to a falling house."

" Thou fool," hissed the man with sweat pouring down his face, and who through the working of his oriental mind already felt the swish of the whip about his shoulders, and the agony of the desert fly's bite on his flagellated anatomy. " It is *Hahmed* — the great *Hahmed,* who orders thee to his presence. It is thy chance, thou fool — it is ——"

And his dull eyes brightened, and his sensual mouth widened in a grin as the girl sprang to her feet and sped to a mirror on the opposite side of the room.

" Dullard," she cried, as she pulled her clothing furiously from her, and stood with nothing but a plain coloured shawl of gauze covered in tinsel twined about her slim waist, " why hast thou wasted precious moments? Why has thou imperilled my chance by infuriating the great man? Out of my way, thou snail."

And as she fled precipitately from the room she caught the man by the throat and flung him against the wall with the ease of muscle trained to the last point.

"Ow!" exclaimed Ali 'Assan at the apparition in the doorway with the flaming henna head and taut brown body, with long, thin, brown arms stretched down stiff as ramrods to the sides, and "Ow!" he said again, as she suddenly moved and again stood still with the gleaming orange eyes fixed on his host, who looked at her for an instant, and looked away again to the far corner, as he indifferently lit a cigarette.

And then La Belle danced for all she was worth, and for all she knew, whilst the guest watched in sensual enjoyment, and the host took not the slightest notice.

Nearer she came, and nearer still, until the pungent odour of the insufferable Eastern perfume of which the body is musk, suddenly struck the nostrils of the man for whom she danced, bringing a slight frown to his face, and causing him to thoughtlessly raise his right hand, which, as perhaps the reader may not know, is an oriental sign of appreciation.

A flash of triumph swept across the face of the woman, who was absolutely on the wrong tack, as she sidled so near that her bare limbs almost touched the flowing cloak which swept round the man. His mind was full of his exquisite, delicate, tantalising, fastidious wife, his body ached for her, his soul fainted for even a touch of her little hand, so that once again he raised his right hand as though to sweep away some pestilential insect from his path, just one little careless gesture which proved a woman's undoing.

Back bent La Belle, and still farther back until her

evil face was on a level with that of the man she was trying to subjugate, and when for an instant his eyes rested on hers, which peered at him from the strange angle of her upside down position, she whispered one little word.

And then a great fury suddenly blazed in Hahmed's eyes, a sudden storm of hate swept across the stern face, as his hand steel strong closed fiercely about the long thin neck.

"Thou daughter of gutter dogs," he whispered, so low that the words were hardly caught by Ali 'Assan, who with fingers twining uncontrollably in his white garment, sat petrified by the suddenly arisen storm. "Thou essence of evil, go back to the devil who spawned thee."

There was a choked gurgling cry as the hand closed tighter, a little click like the closing of a safe door, and the body of the dead woman was hurled into the middle of the room, whilst Hahmed lit a cigarette and clapped his hands for the presence of Achmed, who, his legs refusing to support his shaking body, crawled in on his hands and knees.

"Carry that carrion out, O! thou trafficker in evil, and throw it to the jackals."

"Master, O! master! May the light of Allah shine upon thee in thy wisdom, may the houris of paradise make thy couch one of delight when thou art gathered to thy forefathers! In all ignorance I sent yon ignoble female to dance before my honoured guest — a great price I paid for her in the market."

"Thou liest," gently replied his master.

Whereupon Achmed gathered good handfuls of dust

from the floor and massaged it into his oily hair, whilst Hahmed, rising to his great height, prayed forgiveness from his guest, who was even then thinking what a waste of good material the dead woman represented.

"Let this serve thee as a lesson, thou perverter of Allah's truth," spake Hahmed, in a voice as caressing as that of a woman, "and teach thee to acquire property which does honour to thy house. Camels, a male and female, shall be sent in payment for that for which thou hast not paid one piastre.

"Breed with them so that the milk refreshes the traveller, and the hair spins soft covering for their bed, and fail me not again, for behold when I strike it is as the lightning which blasts the tree."

And the two men stalked silently from the scene of the tragedy, leaving Achmed rubbing his hands in glee, with intervals of removing particles of dust from his eyes and mouth, whilst his virago of a first wife ambled in to ascertain the proceeds of the evening, an account of which caused her to raise dirty hands to heaven and praise Allah, before she ambled out again, contemptuously kicking the dead body *en passant,* which action nearly upset the equilibrium of her cumbersome body, as she hastened to summon the help necessary to lift and carry to the jackals the body of La Belle who had missed her chance.

CHAPTER LII

THE full moon shone down on the scene, which surely had not changed since the wise men of the East — led by a star — came to find a Babe.

The palms swayed slightly in a faint breeze, the sand stretched a restful grey, and there was no sound whatever save the faint ripple of the life-giving stream singing its way through the oasis. Neither was there sign of human life excepting the figure of an Arab standing as if carved in bronze in the black shadow of the palms. Immobile, with arms folded he stood, eyes intent on the road leading to civilisation, watching and waiting, as he had watched and waited through many a night until dawn.

"Allah!" and the words were indistinguishable from the brook's murmuring. "God of all, send her back to me. Behold! with patience I have waited these last long months — and yet would I wait even until death — for thou, O! Allah, in Thy greatness hast allowed me dimly to understand this woman's mind — *my* woman, my heritage of all time.

"The Eastern night will draw her back, as surely as the moon will make a silvery path for her return; for she has but tried her soft white wings, and I have no fear that she will have sullied them in her flight.

"But this time, this time there shall be no escape."

The long brown hand stretched out as if to seize and

hold, the slender fingers closed gently, but with a grip of steel, as though upon the whiteness of some woman's throat.

"When she comes back my wife," continued the voice, as the moon slowly swung up to her throne, blinding in her power the million twinkling eyes that had watched for her coming. "Yet, when she comes it will be for very love of me, her lover, and for love of the night and the scent of the dawn, for the stillness of the dusk, and the longing to lay her pure whiteness at rest within my arms."

And then he threw his hands heavenwards with a great cry.

"Allah, be praised! Oh Allah, unto thee I give thanks."

And sank upon his knees, touching the sand with his forehead, and rising with hands outstretched strode quickly to the clump of palms near the gate in the wall surrounding Jill's dwelling, to meet three camels stalking upon the road leading from civilisation towards him; one golden-brown with a closed palanquin swaying upon its back, the others dark brown, one laden with great skins, almost empty of water, and bundles of every size and description, the other mounted by the head keeper of camels, who, having brought the animals to their knees, ran to his master and knelt before him with his mouth open as though to speak, and a look of wracking anxiety and indecision upon his usually imperturbable countenance.

But a slight motion of his master's hand sent him hurriedly towards the servants' quarters, where he was received by scores of his own kind simply bursting with

curiosity, whilst Hahmed silently held out his hands
to help Jill from the palanquin.

She stumbled badly as her feet touched the ground,
and bit on a cry as the man's strong hand caught and
steadied her as she stood swaying slightly.

"Remove thy veil for I fain would see what winds
have blown upon thee!"

The little figure, wrapped in countless yards of the
soft purple satin habarah, recoiled a step as the words
fell with the hiss of icy water upon red hot steel; a
little nervous laugh rising like thin vapour on the
strained atmosphere.

"And so the great Hahmed would expose the face of
his wife to the driver of camels! Behold, has his pride
fallen."

And she continued with the sharp edge of an approaching nerve storm in her voice.

"Methinks it would be better for him to send his
fleetest camel to the great city, and bid it wait without
the house of the Blue Door, wherein are to be found
those who, unveiled and unashamed, will come and
dance upon the sand before such men as — yon camel
driver!"

A slight sound of tearing silk and the scented veil
lay in Hahmed's hands, whilst the great moon threw
its rays mercilessly on the little face.

Deep purple rings made the eyes seem twice their
size, the nose looked pinched, the mouth slightly
twisted, whilst great drops from the damp brow fell
upon the silk covering she held heaped up around her.

"Allah!" ejaculated Hahmed, as he looked and
looked again. "Methinks the winds have been ill which

have blown upon thee. Thou lookest stricken unto death — and I know not how, but thou hast changed inconceivably — thou art shorter. No! I know not what it is, but hearken.

"Thou hast filled my cup of endurance, O! woman, to the brim. Yea! until the drops of bitterness have overflowed and fallen upon the sands, but now thou art come back, rather than let thee go I would drive this dagger through thy heart.

"Fear not that I will pass uncalled the silken hangings of thy chamber, or force upon thee the sweet title of wife which against my wish thou hast so long disdained, but thou art my prisoner. If love could not bind thee to me, then shall care be taken that thou strayest not again from thy home.

"Thy body woman has orders to come to thee only when I command her to do so, though such is her love for thee that she beats her shrivelled body in despair at thy absence, and is like to die for weariness of thy empty chamber. So when thou wilt retire, if perchance the silken ribbon of thy raiment has become knotted, there are no hands but these to the unravelling of the mysteries of thy toilet.

"If thou hast need of me, thou needest but call me, and I will speed to thy bidding, for behold! I will lay across thy portal, as I have lain these many moons since thy nest has been without the bird for whom it was my pleasure to build."

For a moment fell a mighty silence between the two, broken only by the stream which hurried past them on its way to the great green Nile.

Not a frond stirred, neither did the breeze even move the multitudinous folds of Jill's raiment.

From the West the sand swept up to her feet, and as far as eye could see to the East it stretched.

Slowly she turned and looked at the motionless figure under the palms, then silently she held out her hands with a little movement of utter submission, as a sound, twixt a sob and a moan, fell gently on the soft air.

For one long moment they looked across the sand at each other, these two who had been tried to their utmost limit, and then the man was at her feet, with flimsy veil held in his hands. Lower he bent and lower, as his white cloak swept out on each side of the girl like great protecting wings, as catching the hem of her dress he raised it to his forehead, and then rising to fasten the veil before her face, led her by the hand to the door of her dwelling, pulling back the white silk curtain for her to pass.

CHAPTER LIII

A very ecstasy of love radiated upon the Arab's face as he stood behind Jill, who in amazement stopped dead on the threshold.

Beautiful her many rooms had been, but none to compare with the snow-white beauty of this. Great white Persian rugs with faint tracings worked in gold and silver lay upon the white marble of the floor; white cushions, with little corner gold and silver tassels, lay piled upon a great divan raised a foot on ivory feet above the floor, and half hidden behind white damask curtains hanging from a finely wrought arch carved out of creamy stretches of ivory held together with gold and silver clasps of rare workmanship.

Stools of ivory, and one great perfect chair, made of innumerable tusks with each tip blunted by a ball of crystal, shone in the dim light cast by the hanging lamps, which drew countless rays from the four fountains playing in the four corners. Bibelots, jewelled boxes, rare books in rare age-dulled covers, things of use and things of luxury lay in every corner, and yet so big was the room that it gave Jill an infinitely refreshing feeling of space as she walked slowly through to another one, leading out from the far side, where crystal and ivory gleamed from low tables, and full length mirrors reflected the water in the Roman bath over which hung flowering plants scenting the air from the great gold and white cups, whilst two snow-white doves cooed to each other in a silver cage at the approach of the coming dawn.

" So would I have it for my — ah ——! " Hahmed stopped suddenly, as with a little cry the girl falling forward clutched frantically at his fine white clothing, tearing it in many places under her weight.

" Woman — wife, art thou stricken with fear of him who loves thee — Allah! That I should have lived to see thy face distorted in anguish in my presence. I spoke in anger, O! my heart, but my wrath waxeth faint within me in thy beloved presence," and speaking soft words of love he raised her in his arms, causing the voluminous mantle which she held so closely about her to slip from her shoulders to the ground.

Speechless she stood before him with her hands before her face, and speechless stood Hahmed, as, holding her at arm's length, he gazed upon his woman, gazed until a great tremor suddenly shook him.

For behold he saw that the glory of womanhood had descended upon her, and that her hour was nigh.

" Allah! " he whispered, as he gently drew her into his arms. " Thou art with child, O! my beloved. Why was I not stricken blind for this my senseless folly? Why was I not stricken dumb for those my words of wrath spoken to *thee,* thou tree bearing the fruit of love? Oh! glory be to Allah in this most wonderful thing."

He picked her up, and carrying her into the first room, laid her upon the divan and knelt beside her with her hand against his mouth whilst she whispered to him the great, the everlastingly wonderful and new tidings of the coming of her babe.

"Oh, dearest of men and most little understanding. Truly it is that within me I hold thy great gift. How was it thou didst not guess when I no longer raced thee across the sands upon my horse, or sprang to the ground to greet thee on my return.

"And even when my moods changed even as changeth the colour of the sands, even then, dear heart, thou didst not guess; and I in my foolish woman's way was contrary, and could not even then be sure that my happiness lay here in the desert. And so I left thee, to try thee and myself, and not until I could no longer see thee, and have speech with thee, did I —— Hahmed! Ah, beloved! Nay, 'tis nothing — it can be nothing — because two moons have yet to rise and wane before — ah, and yet — maybe — maybe the journey, although not tedious, has brought about my happiness before its time. Beloved, I ——"

With eyes alight, with a great pride and face aglow with tenderness, Hahmed bent and kissed the little agonised face.

"I go one instant, Queen of Women, to bid thy body woman come, she, praise be to Allah, being well versed in the mighty miracle of birth.

"She will tend thee with the tenderness of a mother, and the skill of the greatest doctor in the land.

"Fret not, beloved, I am gone but for one moment."

Jill lay silent, and then smiled sweetly as out of the shadows ran a little hunchback figure who stood without word, for a moment gazing with love-laden eyes at the white woman, then kneeling suddenly, kissed the cushion upon which rested the girl's dainty feet.

For half an hour Jill submitted to the adoring little

woman's ministrations, who made water to splash, and scented the air with aromatic perfume, and spread white loose gowns and softest linens before her mistress for her choice.

"Leave me, Ameena, now," whispered Jill, and she was alone with the golden glory of her hair falling about her, as she pressed her hands against her mouth, until uncontrollably and insistently her cry for her master tore the air.

"Hahmed! Ah, Hahmed! Come to me!"

And he was beside her.

The Arab had faced death more than once, had witnessed things unmoved which had served to freeze the very blood of others; but never had he heard such a cry as this which cleft the shadows in the room.

Great drops of sweat shone upon his forehead as he stooped above the couch, his strong white teeth biting into his under lip.

Swiftly he crossed the room, pulling back the silken curtain which served as a door, leaving an opening through which the dying moon struck a mighty silver spear.

And as swiftly he passed out into the gardens scented with sweet flowers, a little gate in the wall swinging back at his touch, through which he sped on and on to the great plains of his beloved desert.

It was the hour before the dawn, and turning in the direction of Mecca he prayed, and the prayer finished, advanced yet another twenty yards and, divesting himself of his cloak, laid it upon the ground, and then turning, sped back to his woman who honoured him before all men.

A little breeze heralding the coming dawn blew the silken curtains gently to and fro as the man knelt beside the low divan.

"Hahmed! the hour strikes — I am afraid — I — oh! Hahmed, I cannot see they face, beloved."

Two little white hands sought and grasped the strong ones held out to help, for through the faint voice had crept a note of fear.

But even though the little teeth had bit until red drops of blood had spilled from her mouth on to the white cushion, the great eyes smiled up into the man's tortured face as he bent closer to the golden head.

"Harken! Woman of women, thou who bringest honour unto me, in this thou shalt please thyself, for art thou not in this moment a very queen, and I but a slave at thy feet.

"Behold is it the custom of my tribe, dwellers of the desert, children of the sand, that the woman give birth to her first-born upon the very sand of this mighty desert.

"Not upon couch and silken cloth does the first-born draw its breath, but upon the sand with the desert wind upon his little head.

"I have no command for thee, beloved, because thou art of the West, where different customs rule, and I — I mind not — for my love for thee is above all custom, and all manner and fashioning of mankind! Choose then and I am satisfied!"

Once again two little hands shone dimly as they were raised, searching blindly.

"Take me into thy arms, beloved, and carry me to the desert sand, for behold, thy will is my will and my ways are henceforth thy ways! But hasten! for the moment is at hand. Hold me in thy strength for I faint!"

Tenderly the great man stooped and gathered the girl to his breast. Swiftly he crossed the threshold, and passing through the gate gently laid her down upon his mantle, stretched upon the ground.

． ． ． ． ． ． ．

The wind of dawn blew the stars out one by one, the great plains of sand changed from purple to steel, to grey, to yellow.

The palms whispered gently together, the water sang on its swift way to the river, a faint movement everywhere heralded the coming of the day.

Motionless, Hahmed knelt beside Jill, whose snow-white face, half-ridden in the folds of cloth, looked like some faint spring flower in a world of shadows.

And then, as the woman whose unbound hair rippled in golden streams about the Arab's feet, put out her hands to grasp her master's robe, a long-drawn cry which spoke of pain and joy, death and ecstasy and Life, crept over the sands, rising, rising to the very heavens, to sink back in faintest moan to her who in that moment had fulfilled the miracle of Love.

A hush fell upon the earth, a mighty stillness upon those two.

And then!

A little sound, soft as a bird's call at dawn, broke the silence of the sands!

And at the little sound the man sprang upright, with hands and blazing eyes upraised to heaven.

And as he stood towering over the motionless woman

at his feet, the sound of rejoicing was great in the
land; for over the yellow sand, tearing apart the last
dim shadows of the night, up struck the sun's first
golden shaft, and as it spread, piling gold upon red, and
red upon gold, across the great plains and up to the
very highest of high heaven thundered the Mohammedan's tumultuous, triumphant hymn of praise.

" *La Allāh illā Allāh! Muhammed rasūl Allāh!* "

THE END

Unveiling the wayward
modern family

Unchastened Youth

by Jean Devanny

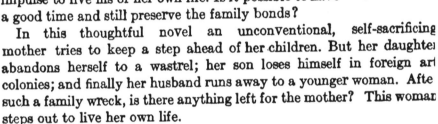

In the intimate life of the modern family there is a clash of feelings and ideas between parents and children, a clash between family life and the individual's impulse to live his or her own life. Is it possible to have a good time and still preserve the family bonds?

In this thoughtful novel an unconventional, self-sacrificing mother tries to keep a step ahead of her children. But her daughter abandons herself to a wastrel; her son loses himself in foreign art colonies; and finally her husband runs away to a younger woman. After such a family wreck, is there anything left for the mother? This woman steps out to live her own life.

Other books by Jean Devanny

BUSHMAN BURKE A fascinating drama of the conflict between the superficial sophistication of a city girl and the clean simplicity of a man from the bush country.

DAWN BELOVED An untamed girl from the New Zealand hills, follows the blind impulse of love that leads to tremendous experiences in a rough and ready mining town.

THE BUTCHER SHOP The strange, compellingly real story of a girl caught in the tempest of modern unrest. She tries to make a sublimated desire the only test of fidelity.

Macaula • **381 Fo rth Av .** • **New York**

Hollywood Gold

by Phyllis Gordon Demarest
Author of Children of Hollywood

YOU who know Hollywood will recognize the realness of this story. And you who do not know it must glimpse the glory — sometimes stained, sometimes fine—that is a very part of the film city. Each character has been drawn with a fine pen, each a representative type true to the Hollywood of today.

This widely-embracing novel is, first of all, the story of Eden. Eden who loved Terry O'Day and helped him to stardom, little dreaming that her unselfishness would only bring tragedy in its wake. But Julian Falcon, greatest of all directors, knew and warned her—too late. It was only after that that he came to play his big part in Eden's life, along with the loveliest star of the screen, Gay Maynard. . . .

"Hollywood Gold." Gold—that is the secret god trailing the destinies of those high and mighty, those insignificant and lowly connected with the film industry. How many lives does the great god ruin? How many does he illumine?

In this the only honest novel of Hollywood ever published, lies the answer.

Macaulay   Publishers   New York

Lightning Source UK Ltd.
Milton Keynes UK
UKHW052125231118
332797UK00034B/2122/P